RANGER

ELEMENTAL PALADINS: BOOK FOUR

MONTANA ASH

This is an IndieMosh book

brought to you by MoshPit Publishing
an imprint of Mosher's Business Support Pty Ltd

PO Box 147
Hazelbrook NSW 2779

indiemosh.com.au

Cataloguing-in-Publication entry is available from the National Library of Australia: http://catalogue.nla.gov.au/

Title:	Ranger: Elemental Paladins: Book Four
Author:	Ash, Montana (1984–)
ISBNs:	978-1-925666-50-2 (paperback)
	978-1-925666-51-9 (ebook – epub)
	978-1-925666-52-6 (ebook – mobi)

Cover design by Montana Ash, author, and Ally Mosher of IndieMosh.

Stock photography from Adobe Stock

RANGER

ELEMENTAL PALADINS: BOOK FOUR

ONE

Screams. Shouts. Grunts. Cries. Lark closed his eyes in order to block out the images but he couldn't block his ears and stop the sounds from penetrating his eardrums. The sounds were familiar to him, having been the soundtrack of his youth and a testament to the cruelty of the man that was his father.

"Yo, Lark! Get your head out of that book and come help us. The women-folk are slaughtering us," Axel's voice penetrated his somewhat maudlin thoughts at the same time a ball landed perilously close to his head, sending sand into his hair – and very annoyingly – into his ear.

Ah, yes. The beach volleyball game. The images he had been attempting to save his retinas from had been those of his fellow male soldiers getting their arses whipped shamefully by the females. The screams? Not screams of helplessness but screams of delight; the shouts weren't shouts of rage, but of teasing and fun; the grunts weren't the result of flesh pounding flesh to illicit pain, but were grunts of satisfaction from a ball making it over a net. And the cries? Not cries of fear, of sorrow, of torment. No, they were cries of laughter, of glee, and of fun.

Oh, how the times change, he thought, letting the satisfaction roll over him.

"Hey, bookworm! Are you listening to me? Put it down and come play. It's not like it's going anywhere."

That part was true at least. The copy of the latest release in his favourite series was all his and had even been signed by the author. *Mine, mine, mine,* he chanted gleefully, running his hands over the brightly illustrated cover. But just because he could pick it up anytime he wanted, didn't mean he wanted to put it down. He still couldn't believe one of his favourite authors was letting him read her newest book a full month before it was even due out. Luna Rose was a graphic novelist, writing and illustrating all of her own work. She wrote all things paranormal and supernatural and her stories had literally saved his life.

For all his father's faults – and they were many and unforgivable – he valued intellectual strength almost as much as physical strength. As such, books had been an integral part of his education. Not that such trivial things as fiction had been a part of his forced curriculum, but Lark had managed very successfully to sneak into the library and read books of his own choosing from the hundreds of shelves, as well as download an extensive collection of e-books. It wasn't the same thing as holding a book in your hands, turning the pages, and smelling the paper but beggars couldn't be choosers. Besides, it was darn convenient.

He still remembered the first time he had lost himself within the magic of the written word. The wonder and the freedom of it. His mind had been taken on a journey to Terabithia and his emotions had run the gauntlet from happiness, to shock, to sorrow and back again. As far as he was concerned, books were transportation devices. His father could mess with his body all he wanted; discipline, training, sparring ... torturing. But he couldn't touch him where it really mattered – his mind. His mind was his own and thanks to that very first magical book and the countless he had read since, he could escape into his own mind and enter fantastical worlds whenever he chose. Books were magic. Full stop.

And this particular author – Luna Rose – had ensnared him with her assassins, her humour, and unexpectedly – her warmth. As one of those quirks of fate would have it, Luna Rose also happened to be the pen name for his very own liege. Despite the fact she was now a recognised goddess for all intents and purposes, Max still insisted on earning an income and contributing to the household expenses – that was her practical excuse for her continued writing anyway. But Lark knew the real reason – she was a storyteller, a tale-spinner, and an artist. She could no more stop writing and drawing than he could stop reading.

So lost in his own thoughts, he didn't see the ball heading his way again until he heard the thunking-splat sound by his knee. Sand sprayed up, covering his precious book and making him gasp in outrage; "Will you barbarians be careful! You're ruining the precious!"

Grumbles, mutters, and snickers answered his cry, "You know Max has a box of those stored in the study, right?" Ryker queried.

"It's not the same thing. Those aren't mine. This one is," Lark assured him, firmly.

Ryker threw his hands up in the air in a classic 'I surrender' gesture. The man may not share his infatuation with the written word but Ry still respected it. Lark really had to give the man credit; he was a fine Captain. He was strict, strong, and disciplined but also compassionate, respectful, and fair. If you did something wrong, the big man would be the first to kick you in the butt – and hard. But he was also the first person to congratulate you or pat you on the back when you did good too. He treated everyone equally – if he liked you, that is. And he was fiercely protective of everyone he considered his responsibility – which was pretty much all of them. But then, that was why he was the Captain and being born a potentate, he was quite literally born for the role. Potentates were basically super paladins. They had a little something extra in their DNA that enabled them to maintain and regulate the link within an Order. They were absolutely integral to it.

Usually, only a warden was able to create the psychic bridge that bonded all the individuals within an Order and allowed them to talk telepathically. It meant that when the link wasn't open they were unable to talk to each other – only to Max because she was their liege. She was, of course, able to talk to any of them at any time. However, paladins who were born potentates were also able to maintain that link. That was why they were highly sought after and inevitably ended up as the commanding officer within an Order. It was one of the reasons why Ryker had been given the position of the head trainer at the training lodge when his first liege had been tragically killed. There was also the fact that Ryker was a paladin associated with the element of life. They were very few and far between these days. So, despite his less than stellar attitude of 'fuck the world' and his lacklustre personality of growls and curse words, the council had ensured the man didn't get lost in the bottom of a bottle. Lark could only be grateful for that, for the man was the sole reason he was even here in the first place.

Dusting off his graphic novel, he made a show of tsking and shaking his head. He knew he was holding up the game but he figured some patience would be good for the bunch of heathens. Picking up the ball, he eyed it thoughtfully, procrastinating a little more, "Who wants it?" he yelled.

"Bring it with you. You can serve," Axel offered.

But Lark merely shook his head, "Reading, Axel!"

"Team sport, Lark!" was the surfer-boy's rebuttal.

"Don't wanna. Besides, you know I'm not the athletic type," he said, tongue in cheek. They were *all* the athletic type. But a flicker in the expressionless face of their newly acquired ranger, made him think she didn't see the joke.

No doubt, he sniped, internally. The truly badass female seemed to have a very low opinion of him, though he had no idea why. It was something she was going to have to get over soon, however. Lark lobbed the ball back, perhaps a little harder than the moment called for given the way Axel grunted when he caught it. Was he really trying to show off in front of the woman? Boy, he hoped not. That would be totally lame ... right?

Other than himself, Ivy was the only other person not joining in the game. Well, there was also Cali but that was due to her newly rounded stomach. She was now fifteen weeks pregnant and there was a subtle bump on her slender frame that hinted at new life. Lark was completely thrilled over the little hitchhiker. Not that he'd had any experience with babies before. In fact, he was pretty sure none of them had. But the thought of being an uncle? It made him practically glow with pride. He had already called dibs on teaching the little guy to read.

And it was because of the little guy she was harbouring so securely, that no-one was allowing her to do much in the game – especially Dex. She had grumbled and complained until they had reached a compromise; Cali was deemed to be solely in charge of the serves. Watching her serve and spike the ball powerfully into the back, left quadrant, scoring another point for the girls, Lark was sure the men were regretting their insistence that she serve. The woman had a frightfully good arm on her.

Casting just his eyes to the left without moving his head, Lark was able to surreptitiously scrutinise the – *ha ha* – lone ranger. Ivy appeared to be watching the game and ignoring it at the same time. As if she felt the recreational activity of hitting a ball over a net in the sand was somehow beneath her. Or maybe he was being unkind because, well, he was wildly attracted to her and had been since he had first laid his eyes on her months ago. The woman was outrageously beautiful with gleaming straight, black hair and almond-shaped brown eyes which were a testament to her Asian heritage. She was short – not as short as Max – but definitely more petite and fragile-looking with her much slender frame and subtle curves. She looked decidedly feminine and almost dainty. But looks could be deceiving, Lark knew. Ivy was nothing of the sort.

Groaning, he threw himself backwards onto the sand, covering his face with his hands. The attraction was stupidly inappropriate on a plethora of levels. For one, she was a Ranger. Rangers were like police, enforcers, and assassins all rolled into one lethal package. They were notorious within their society for their ruthless nature and take no prisoners attitude. They were absolutely terrifying to the general populace – and rightly so. Rangers made a very forbidding image with their long cloaks of dark, forest green with hoods that obscured their features. And then there was their weapon of choice. He and his fellow knights used handheld scythes – the small but lethal blades were portable as well as effective against chades for protecting their lieges. But the rangers? They used the big brothers of the scythes – full-length sickles. He was talking Grim Reaper style sickles. They were wicked and deadly and sexy as hell.

Wait, sexy? Since when was he so kinky? He was seriously losing it. A loud laugh had him refocusing back on the game. Beyden was offering his giant paw to a downed Dex who looked like he had just face-planted into the sand. Lark couldn't contain his wince as he looked at his friend ... and also his second reason why Ivy was off limits; she was Bey's sister.

The beast paladin and he were the closest in age and anywhere from sixty years up to a thousand years younger than their fellow knights. It had given them something in common and they had become incredibly close over the past three years. In fact, Lark considered the beast paladin to be his closest friend. At first, having a friend was a novel experience for him, having never had friends in the past. His father was not supportive of such 'wasted' relationships. The only relationships that mattered were the ones you could use, exploit, or manipulate to profit from. But Beyden – and the rest of the crew – offered him companionship with no strings attached. So, it would be a fine way to repay his selfless friend by panting after his sister, wouldn't it?

And the last reason he shouldn't be picturing the female ranger naked? He was going to be partnered with the woman. Just days prior, Max had asked him if he would go on a reconnaissance mission to identify the chades who had the potential to be healed. Max was set on the course of healing the wretched creatures – well, the ones who still clung to their souls anyway. At first, he and everyone else in the Order had been dead-set against any such endeavour. But after seeing the proof of Max's beliefs it was hard to argue with her now.

Rolling his head to the side, he allowed his gaze to travel over the newest member of their ragtag family. Dex was smiling and laughing as he slapped his brother, Darius, on the back before he tripped Ryker over – even though they were on the same team. Dex was a rangy six-foot-three, his body packed with leanly cut muscles, his face glowing with health. The man in front of him now was the polar opposite of the one he had met mere months ago; thin, pale, lank black hair, hollow cheeks and even hollower eyes. He had been condemned as a chade forty years ago and all but forgotten about. That was despite his impeccable and noble history as one of the most revered wardens in their society. But when one gave up on their domains they were condemned without a trial and wiped from the history books.

So hard, Lark thought, *so hard on the ones left behind.*

As he watched, he saw the would-be chade scold his new fiancé for running after the volleyball before it made its way into the surf. Cali rolled her eyes, serving the ball directly at his head. Dex raised a hand and the ball stopped mere inches before his face, hovering in the air. As a (kind of) warden of the air domain, he could pretty much do anything with the invisible element. Dex sent the ball flying back towards the others so the game could resume but ran for Cali, scooping her up and planting noisy kisses against her neck as one large hand splayed protectively over her lower stomach.

Lark felt himself gulp down the lump in his throat; *This,* he thought, *this is what we could have taken away from the world if it wasn't for Max and her stubbornness.* He didn't want to think about what a waste and tragedy that would have been. So, even though he had been sceptical about saving the chades, he wasn't any longer. Max said she wanted him to search for redeemable chades, so he would do it, no questions asked. He only wished his partner in crime wasn't fated to be one short, exotic, stoic ranger with sultry eyes and a mouth he wished he could make smile.

TWO

She wasn't hiding, Ivy assured herself as she sat in the darkened kitchen at two in the morning. She was merely seeking some privacy – potentially the last moment of privacy she was likely to experience for the foreseeable future. She groaned, twirling the spaghetti onto her fork in a thick swirl of carbohydrate bliss before shovelling the entire thing into her mouth. Her cheeks puffed out as she chewed and she wondered idly if perhaps she had bitten off more than she could chew. She barely restrained the self-deprecating snort; she had well and truly gotten in too deep here and she wasn't talking about the pasta.

She was a ranger, the boogeymen of their society. Rangers were notoriously lone wolves, working within their five-man unit only when absolutely necessary to track, capture, or kill chades – the plague of their society. They were also responsible for policing and punishing the paladins and even wardens when they committed a crime. As such, they were not viewed in a kind light. Not that Ivy cared. She was an anti-social loner who preferred her own company and found the social airs of their society tiresome and distasteful. So, being feared and avoided suited her right down to her very marrow.

The other perk to being a ranger instead of a sworn knight was that she didn't have to share her vitality if she didn't choose to. Vitality was what they called the life-giving energy all wardens required to maintain their elements. Being a paladin, she produced the unique energy in a continuous loop but was unable to harness the power of it. Without wardens, who could not produce it but could utilise it, the precious source of energy would be wasted and nature would be unable to thrive. The world would basically come to one big crashing halt – not ideal, even to a grouch like her.

As a ranger, she was rarely called upon to recharge a warden because rangers never bonded to an Order. The intimacy of such a bond was never something she had been interested in, nor was the permanency of such a relationship. She knew most paladins were born with a deep sense of duty where wardens and nature were concerned but it was not the case for her. It wasn't that she didn't have a sense of responsibility but her calling had led her in a different direction; to the rangers. And although becoming a ranger had essentially made her a social outcast – through fear and superstition – she was more than content with her life.

And yet, here she was, voluntarily providing Dex with vitality. Somehow, she had become the sole source of vitality to a redeemed chade. It was certifiable, considering she literally removed chades' heads for a living. What's more, she had also managed to become Max's personal spy within the International Domain Council. She shook her head, unsure how her world had spiralled so swiftly out of control to a point where she was the trusted operative of a legit goddess. *Life is weird,* she reflected.

A few months ago, her brother had invited her to meet

his new liege. When Beyden had first told her he was now a sworn paladin in an Order with six other knights, she had been thrilled for him. Beyden had been deemed socially unacceptable eight years prior and had been banned from ever completing the Paladin Trials unless he renounced his 'abhorrent ways'. It was a social castration in their society and had meant her very friendly and very honourable brother would never be permitted to fulfil his calling. Beyden had been intensely disappointed and ashamed – but not of himself. No, he had been royally pissed at their society. It had been the first time she had ever seen her kind-hearted brother with bitterness in his beautiful amber eyes.

She had been more than a little concerned about what would happen to her baby brother in such an elitist society but he hadn't been adrift for long, thankfully. Beyden had been offered a roof over his head here with Ryker as well as honest work at the training lodge. As a ranger, she was posted all over the world and, in the past, had preferred to move from one encampment to another. But she had requested a more permanent position at the New South Wales encampment here in Australia the day after Beyden had moved into the huge converted barn. Nikolai had been her commanding officer for years and had been stationed here since the Great Massacre, so it hadn't been difficult to ensure she remained close to her brother. Not that she saw him often, she admitted.

Growing up, they had been extremely close. She had been an only child for one hundred and twenty years – that had suited her personality just fine. So when her mother had announced she was pregnant again – with a warden Ivy had never met – she had been somewhat less than enthusiastic at the prospect of a sibling. But almost nine months later, she had fallen in love for the very first time. Beyden had curled his tiny fingers around her thumb and gazed up at her with his unique golden eyes and she had been a goner. She had loved spending time with him – almost as much as their mother had. Beyden's sperm donor had taken one look at the beautiful, bouncing baby boy, realised he wasn't a warden and had left that very day.

Good riddance. She, Beyden, and their mother had never even noticed his absence and his name had rarely been spoken since. Beyden had grown into a man with the perfect temperament to become a sworn knight within an Order – unlike herself. And although he was somewhat of a pacifist at heart, his deep sense of honour made him a valuable and loyal addition to any liege. That's why when Bey told her he was finally in an Order, she had been so happy for him she had almost cried. But then she had learned he was a part of an Order of outcasts and rejects with some unknown, long lost warden. She had been disappointed because she wanted nothing more for her brother than to thrive in their society. He was the best man she knew and she wanted the rest of the world to have the chance to know him as she did.

She shook her head over her initial assumptions – boy, had she been wrong. The Order was made up of some of the most famous – and infamous – paladins of their history. And, oh yeah – a freaking Custodian! Not that she knew that at the time Beyden had asked her to come and meet his new liege. But because Beyden rarely asked anything of her, she hadn't hesitated to accept his request – even though the situation had the potential to be awkward for her on a few levels.

Just last year, she had gotten horrendously drunk and had made the decision to sleep with Beyden's landlord and boss, Ryker. The man had been a real arsehole – snarling and snapping at everyone all the time. At the time, his rude disposition was reinforced by the large, angry scar running down one side of his face. But for all that, the man was flippin' smoking hot; six-foot-four of solid muscle, ripped abs, thick black hair ... and nipple rings. He was the very epitome of a bad boy and she would challenge any female to say he wasn't sexy as hell. It had been one night of scratching mutual itches and if she was being honest, she only had vague recollections of the evening. She had always thought her fuzzy memories were a shame until she had stepped foot into the kitchen and realised Ryker was now very seriously involved with his new liege. After getting to know Max, she was now very glad she wasn't able to swap stories with the outspoken redhead.

Because she was still alone in the kitchen, she allowed herself to grin when she remembered her very first conversation with Max when they were alone. The woman had wanted to know what Ryker had been like in the sack back when he was a 'major douche'. The woman didn't have an ounce of guile in her and even Ivy had been helpless against the woman's charms. Max had patted her on the back in sympathy, explaining that Ryker was now off the menu but that there were still two eligible, and edible men, available in the house. The notorious flirt, Axel and the fresh-faced, Lark.

She shivered and was promptly annoyed at herself for her girly reaction to a mere name. Despite herself, her eyes seemed to have taken a liking to the earth paladin – *which was pure ridiculousness,* she assured herself. He was only thirty-one and technically was only just old enough to undertake the Trials let alone serve in an Order. But here he was, serving alongside six fellow paladins as well as bound to the daughter of Mother Nature. She wasn't sure how the hell he had managed to achieve all that given there wasn't anything remarkable about him as far as she could tell. And she was a very good judge of character – even if she did say so herself.

Sure, maybe he was okay looking with that lush auburn

hair and the brightest green eyes she had ever seen. His smile wasn't too bad either – and he smiled a damn lot she noticed. And fine – maybe she could admit that his body was pretty much one long, lean line of toned musculature. And he was smart, like genius smart apparently, but none of those things made him special. Nope – there was nothing special about Lark ... at all.

Wanting to bash her head against the table, she contented herself with another overly-full fork of pasta instead – almost choking when a large shadow loomed behind her. Luckily, she recognised that shadow and the moment wasn't going to be as demoralising as it could have been.

"Ivy? What are you – oh," her brother choked off his original question in order to laugh at her expense.

She was sure she in no way resembled the infamous rangers of their world right at this moment. Her cheeks were puffed out like a rabid chipmunk and she was tenderly cradling a bowl of spaghetti like it was a newborn baby. Carbohydrates were her one weakness. She figured that was allowed. Even Superman had his kryptonite.

"Are you okay?" Beyden asked, sitting directly across from her at the large wooden table.

She chewed maniacally for a few seconds, swallowing noisily before replying, "Of course. Why?"

Beyden shrugged, "I dunno. It kind of looks like you're trying to eat your feelings."

She scowled fiercely in his direction and knew he could see her clearly even in the dim light because he swiftly raised his hands in apology;

"Or something ..." he added.

She snorted, "Sarcasm, Bey? From you? I think you've been hanging around these people too much."

The chair creaked as he leaned forward, "These people

are my family – yours too if you let them."

She barely repressed her sigh of impatience. She really hoped he wasn't going to try to get her *involved* or some shit. She was here and she was contributing for a specific purpose. She wasn't there to be adopted by a bunch of ragtag knights and their nutty liege. "I'm good with what I've got, thanks," she informed her brother.

He shook his head, "And what is that, exactly? Your Ranger Unit and that hyperactive hippie Commander of yours?"

She smiled – something she rarely did in public, but could do freely in front of her brother, "You know Nik hates it when people call him a hippie."

Beyden grunted, "Well then, he shouldn't wear that bloody earring, should he?"

Ivy didn't answer, figuring the question was rhetorical. Sure enough, her baby bro had already moved on to more important things – eyeing her bowl of spaghetti napolitana like he hadn't eaten in a week.

"Are you going to finish that?" he nodded to the half-eaten bowl.

She smiled again and pushed the bowl across the table. Beyden was an absolute bottomless pit when it came to food – strictly vegetarian though. He didn't eat meat in any of its forms. He was, as she had thought earlier, a pacifist at his core. She indulged herself by watching him eat for the next few minutes. The silence was a comfortable one and the act of him eating with her watching was familiar and brought back fond memories of his childhood for her. They had both been very lucky to have been raised in a loving home with a wonderful mother who hadn't given two shits if they were paladins or wardens or spotted penguins. She imagined not even half of the population could say the same thing. And wasn't that a wretched testament to their society? But, although Bey had grown up happy and secure, there was a new sense of contentment about him now that she had never seen in him before. She figured she owed that to this house and its occupants.

"You're really happy here, huh?" she asked.

Beyden licked off the last of the rich tomato sauce from the fork as he nodded his head, "Happier than I thought I could be. I had no idea that being in an Order would feel like this. I didn't feel like anything was missing before but now that I have something to compare it with? There was a definite lack. And to think I may never have known if Max hadn't come along ..."

Ivy knew Beyden had resigned himself to being Order-less after the 'incident' had occurred. It was still a touchy subject and she was loathe to upset the easy atmosphere but she couldn't stop herself from asking;

"Why didn't you ever just deny it, Bey?" She didn't say what the *it* was; there was no need.

Beyden sighed, a long-suffering sigh as if he had heard the question numerous times. And indeed, he had. Both herself and her mother had pressed him for answers – not that they cared one way or another what the answer was. But Ivy had been hurt that Beyden hadn't felt he could talk to her. He should have felt safe with her. They were family.

"Because I shouldn't have had to. It shouldn't have mattered," Beyden recited, just as he had done countless times in the past.

"But ..."

"No buts, Ivy. Buts can't change the past. Besides, we're never going to agree on this," he stated.

"But it was so unfair!" she exploded, anger and pain and humiliation on her brother's behalf hitting her full force again. "You took the blame for something you didn't even do and you were ostracised for it."

Bey shrugged massive shoulders, "So what?" he asked, as if the past was no big deal, "Look where I am now. I'm the beast paladin to the only Custodian in existence. I'd say I've ended up right where I was supposed to."

Ivy inhaled through her nose a couple of times and tried to replicate the calm Beyden was projecting. Her outburst and display of emotion were totally out of character for her and if anyone other than Beyden could see her now, they would think she was having a stroke or something. Rangers did not show emotions. Rangers were stoic and didn't give a fuck what anyone thought of them. But this slight against her brother wasn't something she had been able to forgive or forget.

"But your life would have been so much easier if you –" she began, only to be rudely interrupted by her eternally polite brother.

"I don't want my life to be easy, Ivy. I want it to be right."

Stupid, big, noble idiot, she raged internally – but it was with affection … kind of; "And you think this is right? This house full of crazy knights, a mysterious Custodian, a half-chade-half-warden, and a dog called Zombie? In what world is that right?"

Bey laughed out loud and had her lips twitching despite herself; his laugh was contagious.

"In my world," he answered, "It's all perfectly right in my world," he reached across the table and grabbed her hand, "Why don't you see if it can be right for you too?" He patted her hand before taking his empty bowl to the sink and rinsing it out. "Think about it, huh?"

When he left her alone in the early hours of the morning, in the magnificent kitchen of timber and stone, she admitted she could think of little else.

THREE

Lark woke up slick with sweat and his heart pounding a mile a minute. He fumbled with his bedside lamp, cursing his shaking hands when he couldn't find the button to illuminate the dark confines of his room. Finally, he found the switch and released a pent-up breath when soft warm light bathed the room, reaching even the darkest corners. He'd never had a problem with the dark before, despite often being locked in a black room or even being buried under the ground. He'd only had to reach out with his senses to gain comfort from the earth which always surrounded him. But when the nightmares of a deep, endless, black, abyss had begun, he'd had to invest in some heavy-duty lightbulbs.

He flopped onto his back as the light did its job, chasing away the dread and the pain the dark brought with it. Glancing to his right, he saw the plastic bottle held no water to assuage his parched throat and he cursed again. The one litre water bottle had become another new addition to his nightly routine. Forcing his shaky limbs to obey his brain's command, he pushed from the bed and headed to the bathroom attached to his room. He didn't have his own en-suite like a lot of the others. Instead, he shared a Jack and Jill bathroom with Beyden. Not that he minded – the other man was scarily tidy and they kept quite different hours, with Beyden preferring to sleep in and himself being a notorious early bird.

Hoping he wouldn't wake his fellow paladin and be forced to mumble another lame excuse, he splashed cold water on his face and cupped his hands, drinking down the cool liquid. He didn't bother turning on a light, the room was partially illuminated from the bulbs in his bedroom. Besides, he had no desire to see the paleness of his skin or the dark circles under his eyes. He couldn't remember the last time he had slept the whole night through.

Probably since before Max moved in, he admitted. For some inexplicable reason, he often shared nightmares with his liege. He had no idea why, considering he wasn't empathic in any way and he was no more connected to Max than any other member of the Order. He knew the others used to experience the leaking of Max's emotions when she had first joined them. The poor woman had been so open with her powers, her energy had practically flowed from her like water. But that had long since ceased – due in part to her own vigilance with shielding herself but more so because she was now bound to seven paladins in her very own Order.

Running wet fingers through his ever-lengthening hair, he shook his head; he was the earth element in an Order which encompassed every single domain – a-never-before-seen occurrence. But then, Max was a-never-before-seen occurrence as well. She was the daughter of Mother Nature herself, a true Custodian of nature and was the protector of every domain on the planet; life, death, beast, earth, air, fire, and water. As far as anyone was aware, she was the most powerful being on Earth and the fact that these nightmares continued to plague her was a real concern for him. Even though he now had an understanding where the night terrors were stemming from, it didn't relieve his anxiety.

Making his way back to his bed, he sat on the edge and thought back to when he had first met Max. It was a few weeks into their acquaintance when he had witnessed her powerful potential downstairs in the kitchen. She had been quite magnificent in her fury, with her power whipping around her like a living thing and her vitality seeping from her very pores. So much so, that the earth had been shaking and a mini tornado had swept through the room. Animals had lined up outside and the waves had crashed against the shore. Looking back, it should have been obvious that she was attuned to all seven elements – each of them answering the call of their master. But he had been just as ignorant of her true potential, and her true pain, to have noticed. He had even overlooked some of the words she had said, but he recalled them now – verbatim, thanks to his photographic memory;

"You know, I don't sleep? Those nightmares you see me have every night? They're not really nightmares. It's the world. Every time I close my eyes I hear it – pounding out a rhythm of pain and fear and wrongness. Nature screams its agony ... souls beg for mercy ... life cries in pain. The roar of injustice is a perpetual loop in my head. I can't turn it off, I can't turn it down. Life scrapes its tortured nails against my gut, peeling layers and leaving nothing but raw flesh in its wake. It's an acid in my veins, corrosive and scarring. It's all I hear and all I see; every day and every night."

Shaking his head at his own stupidity and ineptitude, he flopped back onto his rumpled sheets. She had described her nightmares as the world's pain and at the time he had let it pass right over his head. No doubt that was exactly what had been keeping her up at night but he knew that wasn't the whole of it. It had taken him far longer than it should have considering his IQ and their shared dreams to puzzle out that the bulk of the pain she was feeling, the injustice she was describing, was in fact the chades. There was no greater offence to nature, after all, than its guardians turning against her. No wonder Max had been such a staunch supporter of those hapless beings. No wonder they were drawn to her like a magnet. No wonder she had been so drawn to Dex during the years she had been lost. She alone seemed to have a direct connection to them and ever since he had been participating in these nightly terrors of hers, he had begun wondering if this was her whole purpose for being; the chades.

Scrubbing a hand over his face, he decided sleep was fruitless. Looking to the crack between his sloppily closed curtains, he noted that the sun's rays would be brightening the pre-dawn sky any minute, so he pushed himself up, threw on some loose track pants and a tee shirt and made his way down the stairs. He didn't bother putting on shoes, preferring to feel the earth beneath his feet as he made his way through the picturesque garden attached to the back of the house. His feet sank just as appreciatively into the cool sand where the beach met the edge of their established yard.

Breathing in deep and scrunching his toes, he felt his shoulders relax and the last vestiges of the nightmare slip away. Even though something about this last dream was niggling at him – it had seemed very centred around one chade in particular – he chose to let it go and enjoy the peace of the –

"Holy shit!" he yelled, clutching at his shirt as his heart beat frantically beneath the ratty fabric. A dark shape had come barrelling in his periphery vision before pouncing on him and taking him down to the sand. A frantic tongue licked enthusiastic kisses over every inch of exposed skin and he soon found himself laughing and patting the playful puppy instead of cursing and pushing him away.

"Zombie! Boy, you almost gave me a heart attack," Zombie's ever-growing paws perched on his shoulders and the dog tilted his head to the side as if he were really listening. If Beyden or Max were here, they would no doubt tell him that the animal could in fact understand him. "What are you doing out here, huh?"

"He's with me."

If anyone were to ask in the future the sound he made in that moment when he experienced his second jolt of the morning, he would forever say it was a manly battle cry and not a high-pitch squeal; "Max!" he reprimanded. "What do the two of you think you're doing?" He knew it was still barely past five in the morning and even now there was only the barest hint of light emerging from the deep blue of the ocean on the horizon. "You're up awfully early."

"I could say the same about you," Max pointed out as she sat down next to him on the sand.

For once, Zombie didn't abandon ship and jump immediately to his master. Instead, he circled around a couple of times before curling up in his lap. It was no small achievement either, given the way the dog seemed to keep growing and growing. The once ankle-height, stripy and spotty, mongrel stray, was now knee-high to Max – calf-height on most of the rest of them. He was still a strange mishmash of colours and patterns and only one ear was standing up straight. His tail had recently started sprouting more fur and constantly waved like a fuzzy, maniacal flag whenever he was awake. Not even Max could tell what mix of breeds he was – not that any of them cared. He had quickly become the official, not-so-little, mascot of the Order of Aurora.

Deep, rumbling sounds had him half turning to identify the source. He wasn't really surprised to see his Captain mumbling to himself as he tried to get comfortable with his coffee mug on the hammock strung between two large trees in the backyard. Lark was unable to discern the exact words but the pitch and the cadence let him know they were very likely curse words. He grinned; Ryker really wasn't a morning person.

"The old man wouldn't let you come out here on your own, huh?" he guessed.

Max sighed, running sand through her fingers, "Well, last time I said I couldn't sleep and wandered downstairs I kind of had the life-force sucked out of me. Ryker's still a little touchy about it."

Lark widened his eyes comically, "That man is so sensitive."

"Right?" Max bumped his shoulder and they shared a laugh. He still found moments like these surreal; sharing jokes and sarcasm with a goddess. But then, Max wasn't just a goddess, was she? She was also family.

"Bad dreams?" Max enquired, presently.

He looked at her from under his lashes. She was facing forward, watching the tentative rays of the new sun breach the horizon. Her face was blank and Lark wondered how he was supposed to answer. He had told Darius and Dex about his perpetual night terrors but he had never volunteered the information to anyone else. He suspected Max knew but she had never said anything about them and he had respected her need for privacy and secrecy. This was the first time she had mentioned them so overtly.

"Yes," he confirmed, "Bad dreams."

Max sighed, a huge sigh that seemed to move her entire frame on the sand. "I'm sorry about that, Lark. No matter how strong my shields are when I'm awake, they weaken when I sleep. It's my subconscious or something. I know some of my feelings trickle through to you. I —"

"Stop, Max. I don't want your apology. I don't mean to make you feel bad. It's why I've never brought it up before. If it eases your burden in any way, then I am grateful for them," he told her. And it was true, no matter how disturbing they were. As a sworn knight, it was his duty and his privilege to ensure his liege was protected, happy, and healthy at all times. That included when she was asleep.

Max let out an aggrieved sigh, "You knights ..."

"We're cool, huh?" he puffed out his chest, which he knew was the smallest amongst all the males in the household. He didn't mind. His dancer's physique more than got the job done.

Max chuckled, "Very cool," she confirmed, humouring him. "But I'm still sorry. It's not fair to you – even though it's going to be an asset when you head off in search of the chades with souls."

He frowned at that, "Is that why you asked me to go and not one of the others? Because I dream about them too?"

"It certainly factored in, of course. You're able to see them in a different light now – with more sympathy, more compassion. But that's not the whole reason. You're also an amazing paladin, Lark. A real asset with your brains as well as brawn. Plus, your background gives you a unique perspective," Max explained.

He couldn't help but jolt at her mention of his past. He hadn't discussed it with her. Hell, he hadn't discussed it with anyone other than Ryker and that had just been superficial stuff because he figured the man should know who he was letting into his house. But he wouldn't be surprised if Max knew every little detail of his life leading up to this moment. And not because she could read his mind either.

"What do you mean by a 'unique perspective'?" he couldn't help asking.

"Well, besides Dex, you're the one who should be able to

relate to pain and helplessness the best. And you haven't
been damaged by the chades the same way most of the others
have. As far as they've come in adjusting their opinions of the
chades, I'm very aware that these things take time. I can't
expect their feelings and attitudes to shift overnight.
Thankfully, Dex has helped immensely. He's walking, talking
proof that some chades can be saved. But I know the rest of
the gang are going to need further time, patience, and proof.
You don't need that time; you're already there," she stated.

He *was* already there, he acknowledged and he supposed
he shouldn't be surprised that she knew it. He nodded his
head once, "Fair enough. Can you tell me something
though?" he asked, running his hand over the warmth of
Zombie's fur.

"Shoot."

"Why am I sharing your dreams? It doesn't make sense
to me. I mean, I'm not psychic in any way or empathic. Our
bond isn't stronger than anyone else in the Order ..." he
trailed off.

Max smiled at him strangely, as if he should have figured
out the why of it by now, "It's because we're connected. We
were connected before we even met."

"What?" That certainly wasn't what he had been
expecting, "I don't know what you mean."

"We're so similar, Lark. That's one of the things that
ensures the connection; like recognises like."

The further explanation still didn't help him and he
shook his head, "Alike? Max, we are nothing alike." She was
the most precious thing on the planet and he was the rejected
son of a violent sociopath.

"Sure we are. Crappy childhoods, bad decisions of other's
thrust upon us, adrift and searching for a family ... But not
arseholes. We didn't let it turn us into arseholes," she
explained, causing him to laugh despite himself.

"And then there's that other cosmic connection linking us together before we met," Max pointed out.

"What do you mean this time?"

Max smiled, "Luna Rose."

"Your pen name?" he questioned in confusion.

Max nodded, "I know you're a fan – a genuine fan. That is totally trippy by the way – having fans. Anyway, you knew me before you even met me. I may use a pseudonym when I write but it's still me. Everything I need to vent, everything I need to escape, everything I need to celebrate, I put into my writing. That's me, right there on those pages. You connected with my books, Lark. You identified with them. Therefore, you connected with me, identified with me. I'd say that's a very intimate connection. Wouldn't you?"

Lark opened and closed his mouth a couple of times, unable to form words. It was a strange kind of logic that made perfect sense to him. Turning to her, he admitted, "I read them when I need to escape. Or when I need to vent. Or when I want to celebrate something."

"See! Connections," Max put her closed fist out and he couldn't help smiling as he fist-bumped her liked she wanted. "Righteous!" she crowed, making a noise like an explosion as she shook her hand out.

The darn woman really is kooky in the best way, he thought.

"Oh, and there is also that other thing. It might also be helping with the whole subconsciousness mind-meld thing we have going on," Max threw out, completely throwing him off guard.

"What thing?" he asked.

"That other thing you were born with that you haven't revealed to your Captain or your fellow knights," she pointed out, knowingly.

He felt himself swallow hard in nervousness and began

tugging on Zombie's ears. *She knows,* his internal voice was almost panicked, *of course she knows. She knows everything!* He scolded himself and wondered if this kind of resigned panic was how other people felt around him when he was popping off facts and information left and right, thanks to his photographic memory. He really hoped not. It was incredibly annoying. He cleared his throat;

"It's not important."

Max snorted, "Uh huh. If it's not important, why haven't you told them?"

Lark gritted his teeth and saw that Zombie had compassionate bi-coloured eyes focused on him as if he understood there was no arguing with Max. Damned if the dog wasn't right, "Max ..." he began.

She held up a hand before using it to push herself up off the ground and dust sand off her rear end. Her timing was perfect because the sun chose that moment to make its full and spectacular appearance beyond the horizon. Her curvy frame became silhouetted against the pink and orange backdrop and the bright rays of light ignited the fire in her hair. He shook his head over the sheer powerful beauty of her. She practically glowed everywhere the light touched and he wondered fancifully if perhaps the sun rose every morning just for her.

She smiled at him, a warm, tender smile and he couldn't help but wonder if she had heard his thoughts ... or had stood up at that particular time on purpose to remind him she was a goddess. *Probably the latter,* he admitted. The woman was darn devious. Her smile grew decidedly more wicked and he knew with certainty that she had heard him that time.

"I won't say anything to Ryker or the others and I won't ask you to either. You have a right to your privacy. But you need to know; it won't change anything for them. You'll still just be you."

He nodded because what else could he do? She was giving him a free pass. But he heard himself seeking further reassurance as he asked; "And you're sure *just me* is enough?"

Max nodded decisively, "I have no doubt you are the correct man for the job."

"And Ivy is the correct woman for the job?" he hazarded, suppressing the warm tingle her name on his lips wrought.

"Oh, yes. Absolutely. Fair warning though," she bent down to pinch his cheek, "she'll end up either killing you or kissing you."

Hearing the words *kissing* in conjunction with Ivy had his mind nose-diving into the gutter for a split second before he gained his wits back. Max was already walking away but he couldn't let her have the last word. Not about this. No matter what she thought she knew. "Maybe I'll be the one doing the killing and kissing. Did you ever think of that?"

Max spun around to face him but kept walking backwards, "Please! Haven't you men realised it yet? It's the women around here who wear the pants."

He heard her chuckle even as she turned back around and he watched as she gave her butt a hearty slap through said pants as she walked away.

The women wore the pants? Well, maybe he would just have to take them off.

FOUR

A couple of hours later, with the last vestiges of the nightmare still clinging stubbornly to his mind, he decided the best way to rid himself of the sticky residue was to work it off. Entering the combined kitchen-dining area, he paused so he could take in the flurry of activity. Axel was tempting fate by drinking his pulp-free orange juice straight from the carton once again. Lark knew he only did it to piss off the rather staid Darius and sure enough, the Order's second in command snatched the juice carton from Axel's hand, pointed his finger at the jokester and began his predictably long-winded lecture. Lark watched as Axel winked one electric blue peeper at Diana – Darius's partner – and she returned the gesture with the addition of a huge grin.

The big table held Max, Dex, Cali and Beyden; Max was sitting cross-legged on her chair, a sketch pad and charcoals in front of her as she scribbled madly on the paper. Dex was unsuccessfully attempting to get Cali to eat the bowl of mixed fruit in front of her. The tall blonde was studiously ignoring the father of her child and instead was leaning against

Beyden, sniffing his coffee like it was her personal crack. Lark knew she could no longer stomach the bitter brew but she still loved the smell. Beyden indulged the mother-to-be by tucking her under his arm and fanning the air over the mug in her direction. Cali planted a noisy kiss on Bey's cheek and Lark saw the instant colour which infused his friend's cheeks.

And what was their hard-boiled, cranky Captain doing throughout it all? He was leaning against the island bench, a cup of steaming coffee in his hand and a very indulgent, very paternal smile on his lips. Lark could hardly believe the change in Ryker's countenance sometimes and he often wondered if this was how the man had been before he'd lost his first liege and Order. Although scenes like this were a common occurrence in his life now, it was times like these when he was grateful for his photographic memory. Because even as his eyes tracked everything, his brain quickly analysed it all in real-time before storing it permanently in his brain, ensuring his synapses would be able to retrieve the data in every minute, chaotic detail whenever he desired.

His eyes finally latched onto the one figure who seemed out of place in such a warm, domesticated scene. He immediately felt a twinge of guilt at the thought because he knew what it was like to be on the outside looking in and wishing for something more. Not that he could say for sure Ivy even wanted something more. Perhaps she truly was the very epitome of a ranger and had no desire to become entrenched in their little family. Perhaps the cold, distant look in her eyes and the disdain that flittered over her features as she took in the happy, boisterous scene really was the true her.

But he didn't think so and it wasn't because he was crushing on the woman either, he assured himself. No, Lark had seen the way her brown eyes smiled whenever she looked at her brother and the way her hands held onto him tightly when they hugged. The woman was definitely capable of warmth. Which meant, there was only other one explanation for her behaviour; *she* believed she wasn't capable. He couldn't help wondering why that bothered him so much.

*****

Ivy retained her aloof and almost bored countenance as the household went through its noisy and slightly insane morning ritual. It was no small feat either, given the ridiculous behaviour of the kitchen's occupants. Ivy could hardly believe they were all mature adults – ones who had overcome many a tragic past too. How the hardened Captain could lean down and nibble casually on his liege's ear, causing her to bat him negligently away as she continued her frenetic drawing, she had no clue. She also couldn't understand why Darius insisted on repeating his germ lecture every day when it was so obvious that Axel thrived on the inane biology lesson. What's more, she knew the man would soon seat himself at the large table, proceed to rock back on the chair legs and receive yet another lecture from the second in command.

Ivy barely refrained from rolling her eyes as she noticed Cali sitting on her brother's lap as he sipped his morning coffee so she could be closer to the fumes. A quick glance at the baby-daddy more than deserved another eye roll, Ivy thought. The former chade was watching his fiancé's antics with an indulgent smile and a sappy, love-struck look in his dark eyes. The man practically had little hearts shining in them. *Sorry excuse for a lethal warrior,* she thought with disdain. *Not with envy,* she assured herself, *definitely disdain.* She had nothing to be envious about.

A feeling of being watched stole over her and she straightened her back against the wall a little where she had begun to slouch. Green eyes were focused on her and she swore she could almost see pity in their depths. She raked her gaze over Lark slowly before shifting her focus even though she wanted to quickly look away from that knowing stare. The man saw too much. *No, not a man,* she corrected. He was a boy, barely legal and she'd do well to remember that. The boy chose that moment to enter the room fully and she knew he had been observing and cataloguing the rambunctious crew just as she had been.

"I'm heading to the beach for a yoga session. Anyone want to join?" Lark asked, slinging a flexible blue mat over his shoulder as he headed to the back door on the opposite side of the room to her. He was wearing plain black pants that rode low on his hips and ended at his calves in a cuff, as well as a loose fitting grey tee with a picture of a rabbit on it. *Really? A rabbit?* It just served to prove how painfully young the earth paladin was.

"Yoga?" Dex asked, seemingly coming out of his love-stupor. "You really do yoga?"

"Lark is our resident yoga guru," Cali announced, proudly. "He's the reason I'm able to do that Sunday Special you enjoy so much," she informed Dex with a saucy wink.

"Cali, please!" Darius reprimanded.

The blonde's face was a mask of innocence, "What?"

"You're pregnant! You shouldn't be talking about things like ..." he trailed off, apparently not able to finish the rest of the sentence and Ivy noted the tips of his ears were turning an interesting shade of red.

Cali was grinning now – as well as most of the occupants in the room, "Things like what?" she prodded.

"And what does being pregnant have to do with anything?" Max quickly followed up.

"Good question, my liege," Cali bowed her head, looking respectful for all intents and purposes but Ivy doubted anyone was fooled by that look. She knew they all gained too much sick pleasure from poking fun at the by-the-rules air paladin.

"Cali ..." Darius sounded even more aggrieved as he turned to his brother, "Can't you control your woman?"

Dex cast a rather salacious look towards his lover, "Now, why would I want to do a thing like that?" he grinned as Darius growled, "Are you going to tell me you have your own woman under control?"

"Of course I do!" Darius's assertion was firm and immediate.

"Oh, really?" Diana asked quietly from behind his left shoulder. Ivy would bet Darius could feel the breath on the back of his neck and had no doubt it felt hot enough to scorch.

"No, not really," Darius's chuckle was forced and fear-filled, "I was just joking."

Dex snorted, "Uh huh, 'cause we all know how much of a comedian you are."

Darius let out an unmanly yelp as Diana tugged on a lock of his hair – hard – and Dex burst out laughing, "Fat lot of help you are," Darius grumbled at his brother.

A sharp whistle had multiple heads whipping toward the back door, "Focus, people. Yoga. Beach. Now. Any takers?"

A series of 'no's' and 'not today's' met Lark's question and he nodded before placing his hand on the doorknob. Ivy wanted to sigh in relief; the sight of the lean paladin was getting to her. How the hell was she supposed to work one-on-one with the man? She ruthlessly shut off her brain as it tried to conjure very detailed ways of how they could quite effectively 'work' together. Unfortunately, he didn't step out immediately, instead turning to face the table once again;

"What about you, Dex? If you like the Sunday Special, wait until you try the Friday Special," Lark ribbed, clearly unable to stop from joining in the teasing.

See; immature, Ivy sternly reminded herself.

Dex laughed, "Although I appreciate the sentiment, I was hoping for a hard workout this morning. You know – get the heart rate up and the sweat pouring."

Lark raised his eyebrows at that, "Well then, you should definitely join me."

"Um ..." Ivy watched as Dex looked around the room, clearly trying to think of a polite way to call bullshit on that statement. Apparently, Dex had never tried yoga before because Ivy knew if he had, he wouldn't be questioning the strenuousness of the workout.

"You have a problem with yoga?" Lark's green eyes narrowed in the reformed chade's direction but Ivy was certain it was in mock insult.

"No. Not at all," he hunched his shoulders a little when he realised he was now the centre of attention, "It just wasn't a big thing back when I was last in society, so I haven't tried it before. But I know it's really good for you for a lot of reasons ..." he spoke quickly, obviously fearing he had caused offence.

"Relax, Dexter." Lark chuckled and walked over, slapping him on the back in a friendly way, "I'll tell you what; you join me this morning for an hour of yoga and if your heart rate doesn't get up as high as it would on the treadmill and you're not as sore as if you've done a bunch of reps on the weight bench, I'll take over all your kitchen duties for a month."

Dex narrowed his dark eyes – eyes that were no longer black, but certainly weren't the light hazel they had been rumoured to have been, "And what do you get out of it?"

"Well ... if it turns out to be one of the hardest workouts you've had, you unstack the dishwasher whenever it's my turn," Lark offered.

Dex raised his eyebrows in surprise, "Unstack the dishwasher?"

Lark nodded, causing his sun-streaked auburn hair to flop into his eyes, "Yep. I hate doing that. I pack the thing and then an hour later I have to unpack it again. It's redundant."

"Redundant?" Dex asked, sounding perplexed.

"Uh huh. So ... what say you?" Lark held out a hand.

Ivy watched as Dex considered the proffered hand for a moment, looking around the room, perhaps for guidance. But eyes and faces were suspiciously diverted and were clearly of no help, "I'll take that bet. One hour" he stated, shaking Lark's hand firmly.

Lark's wicked grin evolved slowly and there was a definite glint of evilness in his eyes if Ivy wasn't mistaken. *Oh dear,* seems Lark was going to put Dex through an advanced class of yoga his first time out. She almost winced in sympathy for how Dex's muscles were going to feel in two days but caught herself in time. She was a Ranger – she didn't sympathise with anyone or anything. Or at least, that was the persona she portrayed to the world. She was pretty sure everyone here thought she was a stone-cold bitch – an image she had taken years to cultivate, it was true. So why was she now wanting these people to see her as something else? She firmed her jaw and gave herself a stern lecture about going soft before catching the end of the discussion.

"Excellent," the earth paladin literally rubbed his hands together in glee. "Go ahead and change into something loose and comfortable."

Dex looked confused again, "Loose? Aren't you supposed to wear tight stuff for yoga?"

Lark shrugged, "I'm sure Ryker will let you borrow his leotard if you ask nicely."

A swift motion from the corner of her eye preceded a small throwing knife thunking into the wood mere inches from Lark's head. The owner of the head didn't seem to have the good sense the Mother had blessed him with, for he merely chuckled and pulled the blade free.

"Ryker!" Max reprimanded. "You'll damage the wood," she said, hurrying over to examine the door frame. "Wait, is that what all these marks are? From you Neanderthals throwing knives at each other?"

The men quickly found various mundane objects exceedingly interesting; Lark and Ryker began examining the door knob, Axel picked at a hole in his shirt, Darius unfolded the newspaper loudly, and Beyden quickly gulped down the contents of his mug. Judging by his suddenly bulging eyes, Ivy figured the coffee was still extremely hot.

Cowards, she thought and was surprised when the one word rebounded in her skull in amusement rather than disgust. She could see Dex grinning openly now and she fought not to move her own lips when he gave her a friendly nod as if including her in the private joke. Just because she was sharing her vitality with the man, didn't mean she needed to become friends with him.

Dex stood up, "Okay, I'll go change. But isn't anyone else going to take that bet?" Dex asked the room at large.

Axel snorted, rocking his chair negligently back on two legs, "Dude, we've all taken that bet."

"And ...?" Dex enquired.

"And have you seen Lark unpack the dishwasher even once since you arrived?" The Captain himself asked.

Dex seemed to think about that for a moment before narrowing his eyes in Lark's direction, "You've snowed me, haven't you?"

"I have no idea what you're talking about," Lark assured him, innocence dripping from his voice.

Axel laughed, "Just go get changed, dish-pig."

"Dish-pig?!" Dex exclaimed.

Axel grinned, "That's what you're gonna be in about one hour. Be prepared to sweat, my friend."

FIVE

Wow ... and I thought I was cold, Ivy thought as she watched the entire household leave a begging Dex on the sand, repeating one word over and over. Watching Lark put Dex through his paces had been as entertaining as it had been stimulating. After everyone had filed out of the house to heckle poor Dex, she had tried hard to remain aloof and uninterested in the kitchen. However, several wolf whistles and bouts of raucous laughter later, she had been helpless to resist peeking out the window. And what she had seen had almost made her swallow her tongue.

It wasn't the once esteemed Charlemagne-come-felon twisted into a strange and painful-looking pretzel that had her eyes bugging out of her head. No, it was the lean, muscular form of Lark with his smooth lines, flexible body, and undeniable skill. One look at him mastering the Firefly pose and she had made her way swiftly from the seclusion of the house and out to the noisy audience lining the sand.

Lark's legs had been raised and stretched out in front of him so they were parallel to the ground as his forearms held his entire body weight. The difficult pose was only for those who practised yoga at an advanced level. She knew because she had been trying to master it herself for over a year. She was strong and disciplined in both mind and body yet she could never balance her centre of gravity properly in order to achieve the tricky position. But Lark had accomplished it so effortlessly. It was obvious the man was truly skilled and was no amateur like she had assumed.

She had figured he practised some stretches and breathing, maybe a little meditation, as a weekend hobby. But as she watched the natural light hit every disciplined line of his body, she had felt a curious flutter in her stomach – like maybe she had been wrong. And if she was wrong about one thing, was it possible she was wrong about others?

One thing she hadn't been wrong about; Lark sure was pretty to look at. The only negative had been that the man hadn't once removed his shirt to show off what she was sure were a bunch of sinewy muscles. Picturing a man's muscles – sinewy or not – on someone who was young enough to be her son was unacceptable. Instead, she forced herself to focus on the object at her feet.

"Water, water, water," came the pathetic whimpers from the heap of sweaty, tired flesh lying on the beach – rather close to the waves now, given the tide was coming in.

Casting her eyes toward the house, she waited hopefully – and fruitlessly – for anyone else to ride to the reformed man's rescue. But after a solid thirty seconds of listening to nothing but whines and ragged breathing, she accepted the fact that no-one was coming. Not even his fiancé. Expelling an annoyed breath, she said;

"Get up."

"Water ..." was the thin reply.

Rolling her eyes, she squatted down in front of him, "If you don't move, you're soon going to have more water than you know what to do with. The tide is coming in," she informed him.

He flung an arm back and began searching blindly, for what – she had no idea. He just kept feeling around with his hand and she couldn't help but think it looked remarkably like Thing from the Addams Family, "What are you doing?" she finally asked.

"I'm seeking aid, woman! You're supposed to help me up," was his muffled reply because his face was still buried in the sand.

"Do I look like a servant to you?" she snapped, almost instantly regretting her tone. There was no point taking out her poor mood on Dex. But she didn't apologise.

"Sheesh, Ivy. Will you loosen up?" Dex reprimanded as he finally rolled to his back. His face and body were completely covered with sand thanks to the sheen of sweat that layered his torso and limbs. But even as she watched, a gust of wind kicked up and the sand disappeared almost instantly.

"Neat trick," she acknowledged.

"Thanks. Cali thinks so too," he flashed a teasing smile up at her.

Although he no longer looked half dead and his breathing no longer resembled a smoking asthmatic, he made no attempt to move even as the waves began to kiss his feet. He seemed to be staring at her, so she did what she did best and completely ignored him.

"You're really not going to give me a hand?" he asked, sounding curious.

"Don't I help you enough?" she returned, unable to help her waspish replies. Old habits die hard.

"Indeed you do. Perhaps I don't thank you enough for that ..." he offered, sounding chastised and genuine.

She sighed, feeling about an inch tall, "There's no need. I

volunteered."

"Doesn't make it any less of a sacrifice or a duty," he assured her.

"Whatever," she muttered, feeling uncomfortable. She hadn't come down here for a deep and meaningful. For some reason, her response made him smile and he held his hand out to her once more. Resigned to the inevitable, she grasped his arms at the wrist and felt him return the gesture as she used her body weight to lever him to his feet. It was no small feat either, given the man was practically dead weight.

He groaned as he straightened, rubbing his lower back, "I am so going to feel this in the morning. That man is a yoga shark."

The comment startled her into a spontaneous reaction and she turned to him quizzically, "A yoga shark?"

"Yeah, you know, like a pool shark except with yoga. I was played," he admitted, looking very sheepish, "I should have known better. Lark is a master of all trades and Jack of none."

Ivy snorted at that. Just because the guy could pull off the Firefly pose didn't mean he was good at everything.

"Problem?" Dex inquired.

Ivy glanced at him before looking quickly away, not liking the curiosity on his face but liking the hint of censure even less. "No problem," she assured him.

Dex rolled his neck on his shoulders, eliciting several loud cracks from the vertebrae, "Really? Because you seem tense."

She threw him a look from the corner of her eye, "I'm always tense."

"No. You're always stiff," he corrected, "not tense. Big difference."

"Whatever," she shrugged. She loved that one word. It covered so many bases and was a far politer way of saying *piss off*.

"You know if you want me to fuck off, you could just say it," Dex pointed out, mildly.

She was completely caught off guard for once, turning to face him and stuttering; "Huh? What?"

"That tone you use – you're saying one thing but you really mean 'fuck off and mind your own business', right?" he laughed, quietly. "Darius is the master of the exact same thing. As a kid, he was always so contained and rational. He kept everything bottled up and smiled for the world when inside he was getting ready to explode. It would take weeks of me poking at him and teasing him to get him to finally open up. He was stubborn, even as a child. But I became a master at dragging the truth from him. It's not a skill that goes away," he informed her. "Now, if we had weeks at our disposal, I could pick at you day in and day out until you erupted but we don't have that kind of time. You'll be heading out soon with Lark and –"

She couldn't contain the grimace that transformed her face at the mention of that name and she knew Dex saw it when he raised his eyebrows;

"Ah, so that's your problem. Lark."

She struggled to maintain her composure and keep her mouth shut. She felt too comfortable with the affable man – that was the problem. She didn't want to admit it but providing vitality to Dex had made her feel closer to him. It was hard to remain aloof when you were sharing life-sustaining energy. He wasn't a friend – she wouldn't call him that – but she could admit he wasn't an enemy or a stranger. Although he was no longer the celebrated man she had studied in her history books, he was still a good man – far more decent than many she knew – and the urge to talk to him was strong.

"Just spit it out. Did you already forget what I said about Darius?" Dex sounded exasperated.

She threw her hands up in the air, "Yes, I have a problem with Lark. Why wouldn't I have a problem walking neck-deep into enemy territory with a kid who's young enough to be my son? A kid who lives to smile and joke and please others. I mean, come on, Dex! He probably doesn't even have callouses!"

Dex had watched her impartially throughout her entire rant but he frowned at her now, "Do you really think Max would have an incompetent knight in her Order, let alone entrust such an important task to one?"

"I don't know, Dex. I barely know the woman. Who knows why she does the things she does."

"Now I know you're lying, Ivy. You must know Max just as well as I do, otherwise you wouldn't be wearing that brand on your upper arm. So, I'll ask you again; if Max didn't trust Lark as a warrior, why is he in her Order?"

"Because she loves him," the answer was obvious to her.

"That she does. She loves everyone in that house and everyone standing out here too. She can't seem to help herself. But that's beside the point. You don't respect him," he stated.

She knew who *him* was, so she answered, "He's a kid."

"He's a man and a paladin," Dex corrected, "Born to protect and serve nature's caretakers. He's a soldier, Ivy. Just like you."

She didn't bother answering because she clearly saw whose side Dex was on. She knew it was a mistake to talk to him in the first place. She should have just kept her mouth shut.

"Tell me; how do you think we become tough?"

"What?" she asked, surprised by the apparent topic change.

"Toughness. It comes from being exposed to adversity, to pain, to coldness," he explained.

She looked at him, blandly, "And you think the kid's tough? That he's been exposed to adversity? Come on – he's the happiest person here."

Dex merely shook his head, looking at her with something akin to pity, "You're misjudging him. I did the same thing. It was a mistake."

"And you're protective of him," she fired back.

"He doesn't need me to protect him, trust me."

Ivy shook her head, turning in the opposite direction of the house. The last thing she wanted was to be surrounded by more meddling people.

"Ivy, wait," Dex called, and it was only her inherent duty to a superior that had her pausing. "Look, I get where you're coming from. You don't know him. But Max thinks you and he are the best ones for the job – a very important job. Like, world-altering important. So I suggest you get your shit together and fix it because you can't fight next to someone you don't trust," he stepped away from her then and began heading to the house.

She was just petty enough to gain satisfaction from the stiffness of his gait before he stopped and faced her once again; "Talk to him, Ivy. Get to know him."

Get to know him? That was exactly what she had been hoping to avoid because she was worried she might just like what she discovered. And that would make him even more dangerous than a boy who couldn't fight – to her, anyway.

SIX

Ivy sat sharpening her sickle in the blessed quiet and coolness of the wine cellar. The sound of scraping metal as she ran the stone over the long, curved edge of her full-length sickle never failed to soothe her nerves. The cellar was a traditional underground storage area, filled to the brim with barrels and bottles of wine as well as other forms of alcohol. If she didn't know any better, she would have thought the occupants of the household had a major alcohol problem given the sheer volume and variety. But she did know better. She knew that each member of the camp had been gifted with their own sanctuary of sorts from Ryker well before he was their Captain. And this square room, accessed from the same building as the gym and the indoor heated swimming pool, was her brother's personal slice of paradise.

Beyden had always been a wine lover, ever since she had snuck him his first sip of merlot when he had been sixteen. He loved examining the textures, flavours, and ingredients of different wines just as much as he enjoyed popping the corks over a cheese board or a slice of pizza. Beyden could match wine to any food, whether humble or extravagant. As far as hobbies went, she supposed it could be worse. Plus, it made birthdays and Christmases very easy.

Given that it was her brother's haven, she also felt safe down here and it had quickly become her little refuge for when she needed some peace and quiet. Like after her conversation with Dex this morning. That frustrating talk had quickly been followed by another, briefer and somewhat more amusing chat from Max. Max had bailed her up before she could seek her solitude in the cellar, asking her a series of questions in her typical blunt fashion. Ivy's responses had been equally as blunt. She had learned very early on in their acquaintance not to let Max get carried away;

"Yo, Ivy. You still cool to do reconnaissance for the chades with souls?"

"Yes."

"Have you talked with Lark yet?"

"No."

"Do it. You guys head out tomorrow."

"Fine."

"Can I play with your sickle?"

"No."

"Can I wear your cloak?"

"No."

"Party pooper."

And then Max had personally held the door open for her so she could enter the stillness of the cellar. Ivy shook her head and couldn't help smiling when she thought of the short woman. Max was refreshing in every way and so far removed from what she envisioned a goddess would be like, it was ridiculous. Max had no clue – or more likely, no interest – in social niceties or politics. She treated everyone the same based on their merits as a human being rather than their perceived standings within society. She was funny, strong, and surprisingly sweet. She asked Ivy almost every day if she could train with the ranger's sacred weapon or wear her dark, forest green cloak. Ivy's response was the same every day; no.

Looking down to where her blade rested on her cargo pants, Ivy couldn't help but feel guilty when she saw the plain black material. Rangers wore their uniforms every day without reprieve. She was both proud and bitter to wear the uniform of her brethren. Proud because she had earned her right to the dark cloak through blood, sweat, and tears. But bitter because they instilled such fear and loathing from paladins and wardens alike. As a ranger, she could never blend in and if the long, hooded cloak wasn't obvious enough then the sickle with the ten-inch curved blade and five-foot metal handle, screamed *killer*. But as her position had become more semi-permanent here, she had ceased wearing her ranger robes around the house. Although the plain black cargo pants and tee shirts were by no means fancy or special, it was still a special kind of freedom to her.

Feet on the stairs had her gripping the handle of her sickle hard before she relaxed ever so slightly. Anyone who had the ability to walk down the stairs was no threat to her. Or so she thought, before a messy head of reddish-brown hair preceded a lean body into the room.

Lark didn't say anything as he entered, just immediately began prowling the racks. The silence stretched out uncomfortably before she finally decided to break the quiet; "Red or white?

The abrupt question gained his attention and he stilled where he was, "I'm sorry, what?"

"Wine," she clarified, "Are you wanting a bottle of red or white? I assume that's why you've come into the cellar."

He looked at her without blinking, "It's ten in the morning."

"And?" When he didn't answer at first, Ivy was hoping he

would get her unspoken message and leave her in peace. He did shift his penetrating green gaze from hers but he made no attempt to leave.

"No. I'm not here to swill the contents of Bey's wine cellar before midday. You know what they say when you assume ..." was all he volunteered as he began wandering around the large underground room once more.

She did know and she wondered if he was deliberately baiting her by calling her an arse. Watching his face in the dull light, all she could see was a mask of indifference ... and some truly superb cheekbones. Annoyed with herself for noticing his face and annoyed with him for putting his face in front of her, she picked up her sharpening stone again and ran it over her blade. The rich sound of metal singing echoed obnoxiously throughout the confined space.

He glanced at her deadly weapon and she saw no signs of awe or trepidation in his gaze, "I actually came down here to sharpen my weapon. This is the best place for it."

Her hand paused ever so slightly; the kid had a smart mouth on him. Just like Axel ... and Max ... and Cali ... and Diana. In fact, damn near everyone in the house had a smart mouth. No wonder her poor, gentle brother was learning the fine art of sarcasm. Too bad for him, she had no patience for smart mouths, "What do you want, Lark?"

"Straight up?" he stopped directly in front of her.

"That'd be nice," she responded.

"I need to know if I can trust you to have my back."

That caused her to stop her rhythmic motions and she felt her eyes go round, unable to believe what she had just heard, "You need to know if *you* can trust *me* in a fight?"

He didn't so much as twitch at her incredulous tone, merely crossed his arms over his chest and widened his stance, "That's right. Let's be realistic, shall we? You've been imprisoning and killing chades since before I was even born.

Max comes along and says she can cure them and you're immediately on board."

Ivy raised her chin, "I didn't hear a question there."

"Okay," he nodded, "can you really go from slaughtering chades to saving them?"

She fought the urge to frown and immediately defend herself against what he said. She didn't think of it as slaughtering chades. She never had. To her, it was saving them from an endless non-life of misery and dishonour. It was no different than putting down an ailing, beloved pet. Yeah, hunting your own kind was a shitty job but as clichéd as it was – somebody had to do it. And there were too many others out there who revelled in the opportunity to cut down the poor beasts. At least she gave them some dignity. Although, she was sure nobody else would see it like that. Clearly, Lark didn't.

"You don't agree with me."

"What?" She asked, refocusing on the paladin in front of her.

"You don't agree with what I just said. Which part? The slaughtering or the saving?" his green eyes narrowed, studying her face for a moment before he nodded; "Slaughtering them. You don't see it that way."

Instead of answering immediately, she took a moment to study him – like, really study him. She knew he wasn't psychic in any way and there was no way his element was talking to him either. As paladins, their connection to their domains didn't work that way. She knew he was supposed to be a genius. She had heard numerous comments and good-natured jibes about it but she hadn't really thought they were being literal. She had just assumed he had earned the moniker because he was such a heavy reader. But perhaps she had been wrong. If he truly was highly intelligent, it was possible he also had an eidetic memory.

"Do you have an eidetic memory?"

He didn't look surprised by the question but he shook his head, "No. Not a true eidetic memory. I don't get the precision recall from sensory input like sounds and smells. It's more visual – images or words on a page. So, it's only a photographic memory."

"But you can read micro-expressions," she prompted. His eyes remained steady on hers as he nodded and she cursed inwardly. She only knew one other person who was skilled enough to read her very expressionless face and the damn man had used it to his advantage to tear down every barrier she had. She didn't need another Nikolai in her life, thank you very much. One was definitely more than enough.

"Perfect," she muttered.

"You have something to hide?" he asked, sounding suspicious.

"Just my own business," she was sorely tempted to snap back but she managed to reign herself in and come across as disinterested instead. Three sentences from the guy and her nerves were already fraying. It didn't bode well for their working relationship.

"And would that be your business of killing chades or the part where you somehow became an informant for Max?" he questioned.

"Take your pick," she told him.

He shook his head, looking irritated, "Why are you even here?"

She studied him openly, a little confused as to why he was being so combative. She had no problem dealing with bad attitudes but she knew Lark wasn't prone to having them. He was always laughing, always happy, always easy-going. She had barely spoken a handful of words to him in the few weeks she had been here, so perhaps he just had an instant dislike of her. Or perhaps, it was that he'd noticed she had barely spoken a handful of words to him and he thought she was a total bitch. If so, it would be an opinion of her own making because she was the one taking pains to ignore him. All because his pretty face made her heart go pitty-pat.

He was still waiting patiently – or stubbornly – for her answer, so she decided to be honest instead of belligerent, "I'm here because Max asked me to be here."

Lark's eyebrows rose, "And you do what Max tells you?"

"That's right."

"Just like that," he snapped his fingers.

"Just like that," she responded, without explaining further. Her reasons for trusting Max were her own and she wasn't about to be drawn into a debate with anyone about how that implicit trust had come about. But she was going to speak to the woman about assigning someone else for her little errand. Lark and she were clearly incompatible; "Look, if you have a problem with Max's choices then go talk to her about it. Better yet, I'll do it for you."

He watched her in silence as she packed up her things and put the leather cover over the blade of her sickle. Just as she was about to stand, she heard him mumble something unintelligible under his breath before he raked his fingers through his hair. He took a couple of steps forward, eating up the distance between them before he spoke;

"I'm sorry, I owe you an apology. I came down here on the defensive because I figured you have a problem working with me – my age, my status ... my hair colour," he threw her a smile before adopting his serious face once more, "I'm good at reading people, as we've already established, so I know you're not happy with the arrangement. That pissed me off and bruised my ego and so, I acted like a Ryker. I'm sorry."

His young face was earnest and his green eyes were lit with sincerity and although she appreciated the olive branch, her mind became stuck on one thing; "A Ryker?" she questioned.

"Yeah, you know – like an arsehole," he explained, helpfully.

She didn't laugh like she wanted to but she did finally relax her own shoulders and allow her lips to quirk a little at the corners, "You did do a fairly good job of acting like a Ryker."

He laughed and she felt the happy sound skitter over her skin, "Thanks," he said, "Why don't we start again? Hi, I'm Lark. I'm the earth paladin in the Order of Aurora under my liege, Max, daughter of the Great Mother."

Ivy was glad he made no attempt to offer his hand. She had no desire to touch his skin and gain confirmation that it was just as pleasant as his laughter, so she just nodded, "Ivy, Ranger."

He waited a beat, obviously thinking she was going to add something else but when she didn't his smile grew, dimpling his cheeks; "Well, Ivy, Ranger, it's nice to officially meet you. Once again, I apologise for my earlier antics. I made my own assumptions and it was unfair of me."

"It's fine," she said. What else could she say? His assumptions had been correct; she didn't want to work with him. And although his age and therefore lack of field experience was a big issue for her, the main issue was her wayward imagination and traitorous body.

"Okay, great. Well, Max wants us to get started and I have to admit, I'm curious to see if Max's little idea for widespread chade redemption is plausible," he offered, crossing his ankles and leaning against a particularly large barrel.

She was too. In fact, she was pinning her reputation, her career, and even her life on the hopes that it would work. Because the main reason she became a ranger in the first place was for the seemingly impossible dream of helping the fallen wardens – not hurting them. It was a silly dream and one seemingly at odds with her job description but it was true nonetheless. Not that she volunteered that information to Lark. She didn't want to open herself up to disbelief and ridicule.

"I'm ready when you are," was all she said.

He didn't appear bothered by her short responses. He nodded, "Dex is going to be joining us. I've already spoken to him and he's fine to head off at first light."

"That works for me too," she assured him. "I can call Nikolai and ask where the latest chade sightings were."

Lark straightened up, "Oh, that's a good idea, thanks. But I actually know a place we can start."

Now that piqued her interest, "Oh? And where is that?"

"There's a small rest stop off the highway between here and the city. It backs onto the state forest. There's at least one chade there who has a soul. Or at least there was a few months ago," he told her.

"How do you know that?" she asked.

"A few months ago, Max was attacked by a pack of chades at that reserve," Lark explained, "There were five of them. We were able to kill four of them before Max took exception to Darius killing the last one. She used her power to spank him. He landed straight on his arse."

She ignored the humour in his voice at his comrade's expense, "And she took exception because she believed the last chade had a soul?" She queried.

"Yep," he nodded. "It's what prompted us to call you that first time."

It certainly would simplify things if Max had already determined the chade still had an intact soul. It would surely increase the odds of their little experiment working. The easiest and quickest option would probably be to just escort Max to the local chade encampment. But that was something Ivy never wanted to do and she prayed Max never asked her to either because it was one order she would have to say no to. She looked in Lark's direction, glad they were at least on speaking terms even though most of her worries where he was concerned weren't resolved;

"Tomorrow then?"

Lark nodded once, "Tomorrow."

SEVEN

The next morning, bright and early, Lark drove to the rest stop with Dex riding shotgun and Ivy in the back seat. The drive was quiet but Lark didn't mind the quiet. All the best ideas sprang from the quiet – at least he thought so. Max, on the other hand, couldn't write or draw a single thing unless she had music blaring or a movie on in the background. He smiled at the thought – he didn't know how she did it but if it kept him in graphic novels, he'd buy her a lifetime supply of music.

As for the quiet in the car today, he knew Dex's thoughts centred on Cali and his unborn son back at the camp. They weren't even an hour away by car but he was sure the distance felt like days to the expectant father. Lark had no idea how Dex would manage when Max decided they needed to venture further away to find more chades. Ivy's silence, on the other hand, was pretty much par for the course, despite their amicable parting the day before.

Over the past few weeks, he had watched as Ivy had warmed perceptibly to a couple of members of the household, including Max, Dex, and surprisingly, Axel. He had seen her engage in a handful of conversations which didn't revolve around her duties as a ranger – practically a miracle. Unfortunately, her opinion of him hadn't changed much and she was typically stoic and non-verbal in his presence; her face an emotionless mask – which he despised.

In those precious few times he had caught her face full of animation, he thought she was the most incredibly beautiful woman he had ever seen. He really hoped she was able to get over whatever her hang-up with him was. However, after his initial poor behaviour during their meeting the day before, he was sure Ivy's already less than stellar impression of him had only gotten worse. It was his own fault. He had gone down prepared to do battle. He should have known he couldn't pull off hard-arse-Lark and all he'd succeeded at was looking like a moron. He really hoped Max hadn't been wrong to pair them up for such an important task.

Speaking of Max, she had been in one of her more mystical moods as she had hugged him goodbye that morning, he recalled;

"Lark."

"Hmm ...?" he halted with his hand on the door handle of the car and turned back to his liege. Darn – her eyes are doing that swirly thing, he thought. His coat of arms writhed, responding directly to the power his sworn liege was projecting.

"Names are powerful things. Not only do they make up our identity, but they give us purpose and they keep us grounded. The chade ... his name is Knox. He's forgotten it, along with his humanity. Remind him of one and he may remember the other," she intoned.

"Ookaay," he responded slowly, unsure what one could say to that but curious to know if Max's intuition would prove correct.

He shivered as he thought about it now. Max's 'feelings' were proving correct at an alarming rate and they had no doubt she wasn't just empathic and in tune with the world around her, but was precognitive. It didn't surprise him as much as it did the others; the woman was a goddess, she was bound to have astounding gifts. But he could admit that it alarmed him a little. Especially when she went around talking about squirrel armies filled with reformed chades.

And I'm the one doing the recruiting? He shook his head, realising they had already arrived at their destination, so he turned off the ignition and grabbed his scythe before opening the car door.

As if by silent agreement, the other two also stepped out of the car and stood wordlessly looking at the tree line that edged the open parkland of the reserve. Given it was kind of in the middle of nowhere and off a main highway, he would have expected it to be ugly but it was surprisingly clean and well-kept. A couple of tables with attached bench seats dotted the open area and a simple swing set sat looking rather lonely to his right. Those swings had been the motivation for them stopping here in the first place all those months ago and when he thought about it, had been the catalyst for Dex being cured and the possible shift of society's beliefs. If Max hadn't have wanted to play on the swings, they never would have been attacked by the chades. The hate Darius had had festering bone-deep for the chades would never have been exorcised and they would never have given Max the opportunity to reveal her 'pet' chade to them – Dex.

Life sure was a weird tangle of connections, he thought.

"What if it – he," he quickly corrected himself, "isn't here anymore?" he asked, presently.

"He's here," Dex assured him, his dark eyes focused on the dense trees to their left.

"Definitely here," Ivy confirmed, looking in the same

direction as Dex.

"You can feel him?" Dex asked Ivy, clearly curious.

She nodded her head, sending her long pony tail swinging madly, before shaking her head and sending the same hair swishing from side to side. Both Lark and Dex waited for the female ranger to clear up that mixed answer but Lark figured he really should have known better; even a warmed-up Ivy wasn't the talkative sort.

"Well, which is it?" Dex asked, "You can either feel him or you can't."

Ivy sighed, "*I* can't feel him. But the earth can and I can feel the earth," she explained.

Lark found that very interesting. As paladins – for even though Ivy was a ranger by occupation, she was still a paladin by birth – they were connected to their domains but not on the same intimate level as the wardens. They couldn't manifest, manipulate, or control their elements but they could feel them and communicate with them to a certain degree. What Ivy had just said, inferred her connection with the earth was unusually strong for a paladin.

"Huh," Dex stroked his chin in thought, "When you and your team were hunting the chades that were amassing near the Lodge a couple of months ago, you knew I was up in that tree, didn't you?" Dex asked.

Ivy shrugged like it was no big deal, never taking her eyes from the shadowy tree line in the distance, "I felt a vibration under my feet but when I looked up, I couldn't see anything. I knew something was there though."

"The others couldn't sense anything, including the two wardens who were with you," Dex pointed out.

Ivy finally turned her dark eyes toward Dex, "The wardens were Silas and Jasper – they're brothers and only about forty years old, practically babies. Plus, they're water wardens and there was no water nearby for them to communicate with. They were really only there as bait – to draw out the chades so we could deal with them."

She thought forty was a baby? What must she think of me then? Lark wondered. He was only thirty-one.

"The other guys in my team aren't as in tune with their elements as I am and Nik wasn't there. I assure you, if he had been you probably wouldn't be standing here with a head on your shoulders right now. He would have sensed you far more clearly than me," she asserted.

"He always was good," Dex acknowledged.

"Still is," Ivy confirmed, a mysterious tiny smile playing at her lips.

And just what the hell did that mean? Lark turned his face to hide his immediate scowl. Was Ivy insinuating she and her Commander were more than friends? The flare of anger and jealousy took him by surprise. Sure, he was attracted to the woman but feelings of possessiveness were something new. Swallowing down his somewhat irrational feelings, he gestured toward the trees, "Shall we ..."

EIGHT

"I don't think we're going to have to do much. I'm sure I've already gained his attention," Dex said.

"Oh?" Lark queried, eyeing Darius's brother carefully. He still got a kick out of the fact that Dex was once the famous warden known as Charlemagne. Historically, he had been one of the most respected knights, not only in their society but the human one too. He had been one of the few wardens who had immersed themselves in human affairs – defending humans, wardens and paladins alike in countless battles over the centuries. When he had gone off the reservation, it had been a terrible blow – not just to Darius as his brother – but also to their society. They had lost one of their most noble and powerful protectors of Air.

Dex shrugged his shoulders, now broad and firm with muscles, "Chades usually react to me in one of two ways; either they embrace me as one of their own or they hate me on sight. My differences either comfort them or piss them off."

"Really?" Ivy asked, saving Lark from doing the same.

Dex nodded and began walking in the direction of the tree-line, "They can feel me just like I can feel them. In the past, I was regarded as similar enough to be accepted or different enough to be shunned. Assuming Max hasn't gone overboard with her healing mojo, I figure the chade will recognise me on some level."

Even as he spoke, Lark felt a small shudder beneath his feet. It may have been a subtle disturbance physically but the feeling of wrongness that accompanied it was intense. It was always this way, he acknowledged. Wardens were supposed to be the guardians of nature; protectors, cultivators, nurturers. When one converted to a chade, nature reeled in fear and pain. Even as a paladin he could feel the injustice in his element. A warden felt it on a much grander and much more intense level. And Max being a Custodian? It was an intimate horror to her, Lark knew.

The feeling of unease increased as the shadows near the trees lengthened and the sunlight seemed to sputter and die as gloomy darkness replaced the sunny, light-filled day. The air began to chill and wind whipped up the stray leaves and dirt, creating menacing tiny tornadoes. A dark form began to take shape from the ground up as it made its way steadily closer to him and his two companions. Mere moments later, a very pale, very thin male with black straw-like hair and hollow eyes stood before them. The chade raised his head and sniffed even as the wind continued to kick up angrily around them. He glared in their direction, looking almost disgruntled to Lark, probably because there was no warden with them.

Chades always focused on the largest power source and that was wardens. It wasn't unheard of for chades to target paladins as well and although they could drain their energy to a certain extent, it never resulted in the complete draining of their life-force as it did with the wardens. Wardens who had their vitality completely drained, withered in on themselves; muscles, skin, and even bones wilting and collapsing like dried-out husks. It was the singularly most disturbing thing he had ever had the displeasure of witnessing. He couldn't even imagine the horror of witnessing it on a mass scale like many of his fellow knights. And for Ryker and Diana to have lost their lieges to these creatures in battle? It was no wonder Ryker had been such a miserable, mean bastard for so many years.

The chade, having determined no living battery pack was with them, had apparently decided it was pissed enough to take out its frustrations on them, for he began his forward momentum once again. And this time it was swift, gliding – chades never appeared to walk or run – in their direction at a rapid pace, his mouth elongating obscenely.

Hoping they would be able to incapacitate the fallen warden and not have to take its head, Lark readied himself for a fight. He was completely shocked though when Dex stepped up beside him and appeared to become as insubstantial as air for a few seconds. His feet hovered off the ground, his form wavered in and out, and his eyes turned black as night. His shadow also lengthened in a way which was very reminiscent of the chades.

The one thing wardens could not do was literally become their element. That strange ability was reserved solely for chades once they had turned to the dark side. He had no idea what it meant that Dex was still able to perform the action now but it sure gained the attention of the advancing chade, who had stopped in its tracks and was staring hollowly at Dex.

The chade was only metres from them now and it took everything in him not to retrieve his scythe from its leather harness strapped across his back. They were hoping to bring the chade in peacefully. A fact Ivy seemed to have forgotten if the sickle gripped tightly in her hand was any indication.

He wagged his finger at her, "Uh uh uh," he tsked, "no killy of the creepy – but hopefully redeemable – stick-man."

Her stance relaxed minutely and she lowered her weapon a few stingy inches, "Sorry. Force of habit."

He snorted, about to reply when abrupt movement from the chade recaptured his attention. He needn't have concerned himself. Dex made a few controlled hand gestures and had two of his very own mini tornadoes swirling to life in front of them. Lark watched as they quickly crossed the distance to the chade and seemed to wrap around his ankles. The chade's mouth opened wider and Lark swore he saw anger in those dark orbs as it struggled futilely against the makeshift bonds. Anger was good, Lark assured himself. Anger meant the chade still had some emotions and was perhaps redeemable as Max hoped.

Lark eyed the chade for another moment before turning to Dex, "You can still transform into a pure element like the chades? How?"

Dex sighed, shoving fingers through the dark locks of his hair, "I'm not a warden, Lark. Despite Max's magic and the change in my appearance. I'm not a chade either, but something in between. I have abilities from both my lives. And yes – that includes being able to make myself as insubstantial as the wind."

"Max knows you can still do that?" he asked.

Dex raised an eyebrow at him, "Of course. It's one of the reasons she sent me with you. Darn woman seems to know every bloody thing," he muttered, as if in afterthought and sounding much like Ryker did when he was both disgruntled and awed by the little custodian.

Despite the seriousness of the situation, Lark laughed, slapping Dex on the back, "It's one of her charms. You'll grow to love it – and her," he assured him.

Dex smiled a little, "Seems I already do. Hard not to."

Indeed it was, Lark confirmed, silently. Max was so naturally appealing that just about everyone ended up loving her. Either that, or it was the opposite end of the spectrum; they hated her. There weren't too many people who remained on the fence and were ambivalent. He supposed the curse of being so open and alluring was that she elicited only intense emotions in those people around her; love or hate. The only problem with such extreme feelings? They created extremists – those that blindly followed or those that wanted to destroy.

He was torn between wanting her plan of curing the chades to work and praying there was no need for them to garner more loyal followers. Because that is what Max was aiming for; her squirrel army of redeemed monsters.

He shook himself from his thoughts, glancing from the eerily silent chade to his two companions, "Well, looks like we've caught ourselves a chade."

Ivy huffed, "Now what do we do with him?"

Dex shrugged, "Take him back to Max, I guess."

"This was just supposed to be a scouting expedition," Lark reminded them.

"Well, we've successfully scouted and identified a chade. No point wasting him. I say we take him with us. Ivy, you have those fancy chade cuffs?" Dex turned to ask the ranger.

She nodded, "Of course. But I'm not sure if they will work on him. He looks too far gone."

Along with the sickle being the unique weapon of the rangers, they also had specially made shackles that have the ability to bind soon-to-be chades. But once the chades were able to dissolve into an element, Lark knew the cuffs were essentially useless.

"We should at least try," was Dex's response. "If not, I can probably maintain my little whirlwinds long enough to get us back to the house. I'll need to recharge as soon as we get there though," he informed Ivy. "I can already feel the drain on my powers."

Ivy shrugged negligently as if that were no big deal when Lark knew that it was. Ranger's never bonded themselves with wardens. And although they produced the life-giving energy just like he and his fellow paladins, they volunteered that energy sparingly. It was one of the reasons why he had been so shocked when Ivy had offered to be Dex's semi-permanent keeper – watching him for signs of diminishing faculties as well as providing vitality on a regular basis. That was, until two weeks ago when Max had asked Ivy to reveal her left bicep and the brand of seven symbols etched on it. Then it had begun to make sense. Still, it couldn't be an entirely comfortable situation for the woman. He wondered why he cared so much – she had made it abundantly clear she wanted nothing to do with him. He should stop worrying about her thoughts and feelings. Too bad his fickle heart wouldn't listen to his head.

"Well?" Dex questioned, awaiting his answer.

Despite the huge age gap, power disparity, and standing within society between them, Lark was technically in charge of this little operation; he was the sworn knight of a Custodian and Dex was a reformed chade; "I don't know," he admitted, "Ryker won't like us bringing him back."

Sure enough, seconds later his Captain's booming voice resonated within his skull;

'No, I sure as hell do not!'

'Babe, will you chill? Of course he needs to come here. How else am I going to heal him?' Max asked, sounding reasonable to herself, Lark was sure. But to Ryker – and the rest of her paladins, including himself – having an unknown chade at their home was anything but.

'Max, you can't bring an unidentified chade into the

house. Especially not one that is so feral,' the voice belonged to Darius.

'Fine then. You don't want him here? I'll go to him.'

Lark winced, hearing the stubbornness in his liege's voice. She was going to get her way sooner or later and he wished Ryker would just give in before they got too pissy with each other.

'I do not *get pissy!'*

Lark rolled his eyes – Ryker was right; of course he didn't get pissy. A more even-tempered man he'd never met.

'I can hear you, Lark,' he was promptly informed by the man himself.

'Yes sir, sorry sir.'

An ill-tempered snort was Ryker's only response.

"Lark!"

He jumped at Dex's loud voice, "Huh?"

"You're spacing," the ex-chade pointed out.

"I'm not spacing. The Order is *discussing* the best way to deal with the chade."

Dex frowned, "The best way to deal with him? I thought we all agreed to help cure the poor souls."

Lark knew Dex had become a little protective of the chades. The situation was very close to home for him. "And that's what we're going to do. I'm just not sure taking this one home to the Max-buffet is the wisest choice."

"You were the first person to talk to me other than Max, the first person to treat me like a human being instead of an animal," Dex reminded him.

Lark nodded, "I know. And I truly want to help this chade, just like I want to help all the others. But this situation is different. For one, none of us have the history with this chade as we did with you. He's not a long-lost brother, an old friend, or a new lover. He's a complete unknown. What's more, his degeneration is far worse than yours ever was.

Look at him," he demanded, eying the lank hair, pallid skin, and thin frame of the chade, "He's so white he looks like an albino, his hair is like limp black straw, and his mouth does that creepy unhinging thing."

The chade appeared to take exception to his words if the long hiss was anything to go by. So, he wasn't beyond comprehending them – or personal vanity – it would seem.

"I think you hurt his feelings," Ivy smiled a little as she cracked the first joke he had ever heard her utter.

Typical, he thought, *her sense of humour would have to be twisted just like the other females in his life.* Seems he and his fellow soldiers were doomed to be surrounded by warped, independent women who were as mouthy as they were beautiful. He tried for all of a second to be disappointed by that fact but all he could feel was happiness. He loved the whole kooky bunch of them.

Lark rubbed absently at his coat of arms as the thick vines squirmed and wriggled across his forearm. The Order was still 'discussing' the situation – *probably something that would have been helpful to do prior to coming here,* Lark thought with humour.

It was becoming more and more heated and more power was surging through the bond, hence why his brand was practically jumping off his skin. It hadn't taken them long to figure out that Max's unique Heraldry was like a conduit for her power. The sheer size of the brand – a full sleeve from shoulder to wrist – and the odd fact that it moved were all testaments to her Custodian status and incredible abilities. He believed it was one of the reasons why the Order link was so strong and they could communicate across such large distances. It was also why Max could now recharge her vitality without actually having to touch them. In fact, Lark bet she could even syphon his endless supply of the power-giving energy from here. She ... that's it! He had an idea!

NINE

'Guys, that's it! The brand! We use the brand!'

Familiar voices, both male and female, continued to swirl inside his cranium, heedless to his words. Max was now accusing Ryker of being a closet Dom and wanting her to be his Sub because he had repressed control issues; Diana was purring at Darius that she'd be his Sub anytime; Axel was volunteering for *both* roles; and Cali and Beyden were alternating between eye rolls and laughter.

This, Lark thought, *this was the strongest Order in their history. Just shoot me now.*

'Aw, Lark, don't be that way. You know you love us,' he could practically see the smile on Cali's lips.

He sighed, *'Maybe I do. But I need you to listen. I have an idea.'*

'Another one?' Cali asked.

Now it was his turn to roll his eyes, *'Yes. Another one.'*

'Beyden ...' was Cali's swift response.

Lark heard Beyden sigh but his sharp whistle followed quickly, *'Enough!'* Beyden yelled, *'Have you all forgotten*

71

that Lark, Ivy, and Dex are alone out there with a chade? Focus team.'

Silence immediately reigned and Lark could feel the chagrin spread throughout the link. Beyden rarely raised his voice but when he did, everyone listened.

'Dammit! Sorry, Lark. Are you guys okay?' Ryker quickly asked.

'We're fine. The chade is behaving himself, thanks to Dex and the very sinister looking Ivy.' He heard a few chuckles over that, *'I think I have a way to make our boy here a little more tame before we attempt to move him. That way, Max doesn't have to be exposed out in the open and it will be less risky when we bring him back.'*

'What are you thinking?' Ryker enquired, warming Lark with his immediate support and trust.

'Our coats of arms. We know they are a direct link to Max's power; she can draw on our vitality through them, keep the Order link open ... What if she can also make it work in the opposite direction?' He could hear the excitement in his own voice as he warmed to the idea more and more. The confusion in the minds of the others was almost tangible in its intensity – but so was the curiosity.

'You think I can use you as a conduit, that I can manifest my powers through you, even from here?'

He could almost see Max's head cocked to the side as she questioned him and contemplated his idea. He shrugged, *'I'm not sure. But it's worth a try, right?'*

'It's a good idea,' his Captain agreed; Axel, Darius, Cali, and Diana also murmuring their agreement.

'I don't know, guys. We've never tried anything like it ...' Max sounded hesitant but Lark was sure this would work. He decided to push his case;

'Just try. If it doesn't work, we're no worse off than we were and the whole team can load up and bring you here.

But it's going to be hard completing your secret squirrel mission if all I can do is recon. What are we going to do? Drag you to every chade we find with a soul so you can give it some happy juice before transporting it? That's not practical, Max. Nor is securing a rabid chade to drag it back to you.'

'He's right, Max,' Darius agreed.

'Maybe,' Max was wavering but he could still feel her reluctance.

'It's a really good plan, Max. Why do you feel so reluctant?' his Captain asked, gently.

Lark could see them in his mind's eye; Max biting her bottom lip and Ryker running comforting hands over the dense mass of her rich hair.

Max sighed, *'If this works, I'm going to have to keep the link wide open. I'm going to have to draw on all of you and you're all going to feel what I feel. Lark is going to cop the worst of it.'*

'Max,' Darius drew her attention, *'that's what an Order is for. You really should be leaving the link open every time you do stuff like this anyway. We all know you like your privacy and that you respect ours. But we're here to serve you, sweetie. We're your team.'*

'I know. It's just ...'

'Just what?' Diana asked and Max hesitated again, *'It's that it's painful, right? And you don't want us to know, let alone feel it. Well, we all know already. We're not stupid, Max. Darius is right, it's time you let us fulfil our duties.'*

Diana's voice was firm and Lark could have kissed her. He'd lost count of the number of times they had tried to make Max understand the sense of duty they shared because they were paladins. It wasn't a job to them, nor an obligation. It was a bone-deep purpose they had all been born with.

'Fine,' Max sounded pouty but also resolved, *'we'll try.*

But I have no idea what I'm doing. This could hurt you, Lark.'

He shrugged, barely refraining from rolling his eyes. His pain threshold was extremely high and he was a damn knight for crying out loud.

'Okay, okay, sheesh. There's no need for the testosterone rush. I get enough of that from Ryker, Darius, and Axel always wanting to be he-men all the time. I count on you and Beyden to be the balanced ones.'

The three paladins in question grumbled, making Lark grin. They *were* fairly obvious in their masculinity, *'How do you want to do this?'* he asked, refocusing the team on the matter at hand.

'I think if I focus on following your thread, maybe pushing my powers directly through that, you might be able to manifest the vitality like I do instead of just making it,' Max suggested.

Lark nodded. Not only could Max see souls but she could also see the threads that connected people to everyone and everything. Every thread was unique because their relationships with people and places were all unique. She had once told him that Diana and Darius were connected by a solid golden thread even before they were together. It was evidence of their feelings and their bond, even if it had been subconscious on their parts.

'Can you feel this?' Max's voice brought him back to the present a moment before a tugging sensation inside his chest hit him.

'Yes,' he responded, slowly, *'it kinda tickles.'* It was also rather disconcerting but he didn't mention that.

Max snorted, *'Trust me, it won't tickle for long.'*

He took a deep breath, this was his idea after all, *'Let me update Ivy and Dex and see if I can communicate what we're attempting to do to the chade as well. You've always said the subject of your healing powers needs to be receptive, otherwise it won't work,'* he pointed out.

He could feel the warmth as Max smiled at him, *'You're correct. Plus, it's polite. Thank you, Lark.'*

Turning to Ivy and Dex, he saw that they were splitting their time between watching him and watching the chade, "Lucky we're here. You're totally useless when you're talking to your Order. You should be more aware of your surroundings."

Lark knew a reprimand when he heard one. Instead of assuring Ivy he could have jumped into a fight within seconds if the situation called for it, he merely said; "Well, it's lucky I have two warriors with me whom I trust to watch my back, isn't it?"

Ivy narrowed her eyes, not responding but Dex threw him a quick grin and a wink, "What's the verdict?" he asked.

"Max is going to try to do a quick healing remotely – through me."

Dex's black eyebrows winged up. Lark knew they used to be several shades lighter but after years of sickness, his physical appearance retained many features of the chades, including darker hair and darker irises; "She can do that?"

"We're about to find out," he answered Dex, before focusing on the chade in front of him.

Midnight-black eyes stared back, devoid of any emotion and he struggled not to shiver. These sick wardens really were creepy. But his new friend standing beside him was proof enough that they weren't beyond redemption. If Max hadn't have been so stubborn and convinced them of the chades' plight, Lark wouldn't be getting a little nephew, Cali wouldn't have the love of her life, and Darius wouldn't have his brother back. That was one hell of a ripple effect. Who knew what this ex-warden's future would hold? What his destiny was. *Max did, no doubt,* he answered himself, shaking his head a little.

Taking a couple of steps forward, he approached the chade slowly only to stop warily when the chade hissed and took a swipe at him with his poisoned claws. Where once normal fingernails would reside, the chade now had extendable, sharp, lethal claws. And he meant *lethal* quite literally. Once a chade's fingernails began to lengthen they also started to secrete a poisonous substance from the ends. Lark assumed it was their adaptation to fight paladins, whereas the sucking vitality shtick was targeted at wardens. If enough of the poison entered your bloodstream it could be toxic to the point of death. Even a small scratch poisoned a paladin's system, making them feverish, sick, and unable to function for days. Not to mention the scarring. Ryker's face had been proof of the damage those noxious claws could do. He still didn't know how his Captain had managed to survive such a wound without a liege to heal him. As for himself, Lark had taken a swipe here and there over the years and he had no desire for a repeat today.

"Knox!" he yelled and couldn't believe it when the chade came to an abrupt halt, claws extended but still as a statue. The chade's eyes were practically boring holes through him but he forced himself to take another step closer, motioning Dex and Ivy to stay back. "Knox," he repeated, "that's your name, isn't it? Knox? You were once an Air Warden," he stated, knowing it was true based on the abilities the chade had shown.

The chade – Knox, he corrected himself – started opening his mouth wide once again and Lark quickly clapped his hands, "Stop! None of that, Knox," he hoped repeating his name would somehow help the chade focus. At the moment, it only seemed to be pissing him off further if the curled hands clenching and unclenching was any indication. Still, he persevered. Max had made a specific point of telling him the chade's name. It had to be for a purpose;

"Knox," the chade tilted his head to the side a fraction and Lark hoped it was an indication that he was listening, "We're not here to hurt you. We want to help you," he spoke softly but with conviction, hoping the chade could hear the truth in his words.

Knox shifted his eyes to Ivy and the very shiny sickle, eyeing it in a way that made Lark think he was pointing out the flaw in his argument. Lark turned a fraction in Ivy's direction and muttered from the corner of his mouth; "Can you put that thing away?"

"No."

That was it. Just no. Lark repressed a curse, something he rarely did. He wasn't really a swearer. He supposed he shouldn't have expected anything more from the ranger. She was probably itching to bring the blade down on Knox's neck. He shifted his attention back to Knox, saying, "Don't you worry about her. She's a total pussy cat, gentle as they come."

Dex laughed and he thought he heard a small snort of amusement behind him from the direction of Ivy too. "I know you can understand me, at least a little, so I need you to try and focus on what I'm saying. We are going to help you but I need you to want to help yourself as well. I'm going to try something with the help of my liege –" Lark broke off when the chade hissed at the word liege – seemed it was a sore spot, "I know you were once someone's liege too. If you want the opportunity to serve nature again and for others to serve you, then I need your permission. And your cooperation," he added.

The chade didn't respond but it also didn't hiss again. Lark wanted to take that as tacit agreement but he checked with Dex to get his thoughts, "What do you think? Is he compliant?"

Dex waved his hand and the swirling shackles released

from Knox's feet. The chade immediately moved forward, arms outstretched menacingly in Lark's direction, "Hey!" Ivy yelled, brandishing her sickle, "Quit it! This guy here is your best bet. Either let him try or I'll put you down right now. It would save us time and put you out of your misery. Choose," she demanded.

Hmm, sexy, Lark thought, *who knew authority could be so sexy?* Dex's smirk quickly had Lark looking away from Ivy and desperately hoping that smirk didn't mean Dex could read his thoughts. The mirth glinting in the other man's eyes didn't bode well, however. The chade seemed to appreciate Ivy's authority too, for it had ceased its forward momentum and was now standing unnaturally still.

"Is that a yes?" nothing – no response, "I'll take that as a yes," he decided.

'*Let's do this thing,*' he said to his Order.

Max took a deep breath, '*Okay, everyone, hold onto your hats.*'

Lark felt the familiar pull on his vitality as Max drew upon the bond between herself and her paladins, gathering energy in preparation to disburse it. The feeling was nothing new and as the seconds ticked by, he wondered if this was even going to work, '*Max ...*' he prompted.

'*I know, I'm trying but the energy keeps wanting to split evenly between all of you. I need to focus it just in your direction, Lark. Ryker, drop the link between all of us,*' Max commanded her Captain.

'*What? But if you're concentrating on funnelling your energy through Lark and into the chade, there's no way you can also maintain the link. I'm the only one who can,*' Ryker argued.

'*It will work. Just trust me,*' Max responded and Lark was grateful when she didn't explain herself any further.

There was a brief grumble of unease through the link as

the rest of his family chimed in with their discontent but he quickly felt Ryker dropping his hold on the mental bridge that kept them all connected. Although he could still feel the energy from the others, they were no longer in the loop so to speak.

'You okay to maintain the link, Lark? Because Ryker was right, no way I can concentrate enough to do both at this distance,' his liege asked.

He felt himself start to sweat but firmed his jaw and nodded his head. He may not have had much practice at this but he could do it, *'I got this, Max,'* he assured her. *'You just do your thing. Let's help Knox.'*

He felt her mental assent even as a warm tingling spread rapidly through his body. It was like being injected with pure adrenaline; his heartrate increased, his skin flushed pink, his blood pressure rose, and he felt like he could jump buildings in a single bound. Lark shook his head, the sheer power he felt was unbelievable. Being metaphysically bound in the Order and with his soul bonded to Max's for as long as they lived, he had assumed he was now accustomed to the huge energy Max emitted and kept contained in her compact body.

But he was wrong – very wrong. The overwhelming potential of her powers was unfathomable and he wondered if even she knew what her full capabilities were. But now wasn't the time to ponder such questions, for the chade in front of him was now eyeing him like he was a stuffed and trussed Christmas turkey.

And just like that, Lark went from *this is so cool* to *holy shit, this is awful!* Knox quite literally flew at him, his cold, spindly arms wrapping around him with a strength that belied the thinness of his limbs. The warm tingling sensation in his limbs and torso quickly morphed into a bone-chilling coldness and within seconds he felt himself falling down into a bottomless abyss that held no light, no laughter, no love ...

no life. Lark felt himself shake as he realised this was a part of his nightmares – but this time – it was his reality. He saw the gaping, misshapen mouth yawn widely in front of his face and his last thought before he tumbled into oblivion was;

Bad idea. VERY bad idea!

TEN

"How are you feeling?"

Lark looked up from the book he was reading to find Max hovering in front of him, bouncing from one foot to the other in nervousness. He patted the bench next to him, indicating she should take a seat but she just eyed the spot as if sitting down might cause him injury.

He sighed in exasperation and solved the issue by reaching forward, grabbing onto her arm, and yanking her down beside him. "Will you relax already? I'm fine," he told her firmly – for about the hundredth time that day.

His liege only eyed him sceptically and he reminded himself that she could see, taste, and probably even smell a lie, so he amended his response; "Not one hundred percent yet but far better than I was."

Max nodded, biting at her bottom lip, "I'm sorry, Lark. I didn't know it would hurt you so much. I –"

"No apologies, Max," he interrupted her – something paladins in other Orders would never dare do to their lieges, "This isn't your fault. I'm fine, truly. Besides, it's my –"

"Duty," Max interrupted, sounding frustrated, "I know. You've all told me, like, a thousand times."

He placed his hands on either side of her head and waggled it from side to side, hoping to make her smile, "Then why don't you listen?"

"I listen," she blatantly fibbed, before grinning, "I just choose to ignore you."

"Uh huh," he sent her a mock-frown, glad to see her smiling again. But her next words had his own frown returning.

"It was a bad idea. I should never have agreed to it."

"It was not a bad idea. It was a great idea – one that worked, by the way. How cool is Knox?" he bumped her shoulder, companionably.

"You were in a coma, Lark," Max reminded him, expressly ignoring his point about Knox.

He held up his thumb and forefinger, "Just a wee coma, like, three itty bitty days. I just needed a good nap, that's all."

His attempt to lighten the mood fell flat this time and he sighed, wondering what he could do to get Max out of her guilt-induced funk. If he were being honest, he had been a little disconcerted to wake and be told he had been unconscious for three days. The last thing he remembered had been the feeling of the chade drawing his life from him. Next thing he knew, he was in his bed and feeling like warmed up dog shit. Over the last week, he had been slowly regaining his strength – thanks to Max – and other than some residual fatigue, he was pretty much back to normal, including his body weight.

It had been truly frightening to see his own emaciated state in the mirror the first morning he had woken up. Being a paladin, he had never been on the receiving end of a chade taking so much vitality before. Whenever he thought of wardens as wizened husks after being drained completely now, it made him shudder on a whole new level. This was one of his rare times he had been allowed to venture outside on his own during his 'convalescence'. The whole damn household had practically had him on lockdown for the past ten days and the bunch of them had been hovering around him like mother hens. And while it warmed his sentimental side, it was also driving him absolutely insane. If Darius tried to force feed him his home-made chicken soup one more time ...

A genuine laugh broke into his reverie and he saw Max shaking with mirth next to him. He was glad for it but he had no idea what had prompted her amusement; "What's so funny?"

"You are! Complaining about the team hovering over you. Now you know how I feel when you all do that to me," she poked him in the ribs.

His lips quirked up – maybe he could see her perspective more now. But it still wasn't the same. Max was their liege and she was theirs to protect. He was a grunt, a soldier. When he got hurt it was collateral damage.

"You're not just collateral damage to me, Lark," Max spoke, softly. "Maybe I was wrong about this whole chade thing. I don't want you going after the others. I –"

"Don't even go there, Max. You're only saying this because you have misplaced guilt. You were right about the chades; they need us and we're going to need them. Now we know what to expect, we'll be more careful next time. And don't say there won't be a next time because there has to be. After the success with Dex and now Knox? We have no other choice," his voice was soft but firm. "Unless you think I can't handle it?" he asked, only just considering that just now.

Max waved a hand, "Of course you can. That's not the point."

Her immediate confidence in him warmed him and made

him feel stronger than he had in days, "It's the most important point to me," he assured her, picking up her hand and kissing the back of it.

The rosy blush that tinged her cheeks made him smile. For someone so outspoken and hard-headed she was still painfully shy whenever any of them offered her casual affection. At first, he thought she was reciprocating with the touchy-feely when she placed her palm on his cheek. But when warmth immediately began to infuse his body, he quickly pulled back;

"Max," he scolded, gently, "we agreed this morning; no more healing. I'm good now and none of us want you overexerting yourself between Knox and me."

He had checked in on Knox before coming out into his favourite garden with his book an hour ago. The now ex-chade was slowly making his way back to the man he was before – not that any of them actually knew who that man was. He still wasn't speaking but he had lost the creepy stick-man look and instead, now looked like a man who had been on a year-long bender. He was still terribly pale, hair still black as ink and overly thin but he could no longer unhinge his jaw and didn't try to kill Max every time he saw her.

In fact, Darius had informed him that Knox successfully recharged from him two days ago when the air paladin had volunteered his services. Out of all his comrades who would volunteer, he would have assumed Darius would be the last on the list given his hatred of the chades just months ago. But apparently Max worked miracles with her healing in all shapes and forms, regardless if it was the mind, body or soul. Speaking of which …

"Max, why haven't you healed me completely?"

"Huh? You just said –"

He shook his head in her direction, silently telling her that wasn't what he was talking about, "You healed the scar on Ryker's face, his perpetual grumpy mood, Darius's hate, and Dex's soul," he explained. "I know you know my history, Max. I know you've seen my scars. Why haven't you offered to heal me?"

He watched her turquoise eyes widen and he knew he had surprised her. But what she said next shocked him even more;

"Because you don't need healing. Lark, you are perhaps one of the most whole and undamaged people I have ever met," she paused and considered for a moment, "Other than Diana, that is. That girl totally has her shit together."

"You can't be serious? Whole? What about my scars?" he laughed with no small amount of bitterness.

And when he said scars, he was talking about the literal kind – not the metaphysical. Although, the Mother knew, he likely had his fair share of those too. He was always careful when he worked-out with his fellow paladins. He always wore a shirt or singlet of some kind and was careful to shower at the Lodge only when no-one else was around. At first, the others had teased him about his so called 'modesty' before finally giving up when he refused to rise to the bait. Control. His father had taught him control if nothing else.

He was pretty sure most of his Order had discovered his dirty little secret by now but they were all circumspect enough to pretend otherwise. The only person he had overtly discussed it with was Beyden and that was only because the larger man had been concerned Lark's modesty had sprung from the rumours surrounding him. Lark had swiftly and completely put the idiocy of that notion to bed. He wasn't worried about being naked in front of Beyden because of Bey's supposed sexual orientation, but because of his back.

The skin on his back was a testament to the viciousness and cruelty of his father and was a crisscross of scarred tissue. Some were flat and pale, others raised and still angry looking, despite the number of years which had gone by. Most were the result of his father's belt, but some had been acquired from blades, flames, whips, and canes. His father and his father's Order, including the Earth Warden liege, Terran, had been into variety.

He reached a hand behind his back and fingered a particularly ragged scar running from shoulder to hip. That one had been acquired from his own father's scythe. He noticed Max was watching the motion of his hand curiously, her head cocked to the side, thick hair tumbling in chaotic waves over her shoulder. He was going to make some excuse, laugh the whole thing off but Max held up a finger. She twirled it in the air and the gesture was easy to interpret; *turn around.*

Considering he was the one to bring the whole thing up, he steeled himself and turned, pulling up his shirt and exposing his bare back to the all-knowing eyes of his liege. "Still think I'm undamaged?" he asked, mockingly.

He resisted the urge to flinch when he felt warm fingers trace over the network of scars littering his back from shoulder blades to waist. The light touch didn't hurt ... but it also didn't soothe, so he assumed she wasn't making his back a flawless expanse of pink skin like she had done for Ryker's face. She smoothed his shirt back into place and then moved around in front of him as he braced himself for her reaction. He was definitely surprised to see humour in those turquoise depths instead of the pity he had expected to see.

"Um, you think my scars are funny?" he asked, completely confused and disarmed by her reaction.

"No, honey. Not at all," she assured him, rubbing his arm affectionately, causing his coat of arms to leap merrily at the contact. "I think it's funny that you refer to them as damage. Oh, I know that's what a scar is in the very literal sense, but that's not what these are – not really."

He groaned, "Please don't tell me you think they're badges of courage or some such bullshit ..."

"Of course they are!" she enthused.

"Then why did you heal the scar on Ry's face?" He wasn't angry or even disappointed that she seemed so set on not healing his but he was definitely curious as to her reasoning.

"Ryker's scar was worlds apart from yours. Every time Ryker looked in the mirror, he was transported back to the most horrific time of his life. That scar was the very real manifestation of his failure as a Captain, as a paladin, and as a friend. It was still an open wound, stopping him from moving forward," she explained, her eyes lit with indulgent affection as they peered back into the house as if she could see her lover from here. "He hated it and he hated himself."

"And you don't think I hate mine?" he questioned with blatant interest.

Instead of answering him, she asked him another question; "What do you see when you look in the mirror? What do you feel? Do they disgust you? Do they make you feel like a failure?"

He didn't have to think about his answer because it was an easy one, "No. None of the above. They just remind me how much of a dick my father is."

He saw Max's unusual irises go cold and flat, "Oh, he is that. And he'll get what's coming to him, mark my words. Anything else?"

He reached back once again, feeling the puckered edges of a different nasty scar, "They remind me what it's like to feel pain, what it's like to feel hate. They remind me that I never want to feel that kind of hate again. And more importantly, that I have a choice not to feel hate. They remind me that I'm not weak, that I'm more than what that miserable bastard and his Order tried to make me. They remind me that I beat him – that I won."

Max was smiling at him even as she pulled his head down, kissing him rather soundly on the lips, "See; one of the most undamaged people I have ever met."

Lark opened and closed his mouth a few times, completely at a loss for words for once. Max laughed at his dumbfounded look;

"Your scars don't hurt you, Lark. Not like Ryker's, or Darius's, or even Dex's. You're not a vain person, so they don't even bother you aesthetically. The reason you keep them covered is to spare others; you don't want to make them uncomfortable. Plus, you don't want to elicit questions. I don't blame you, you're entitled to your privacy. But you're not ashamed of them like the others were with theirs. You don't need me to heal you, Lark."

"Well, I had no idea I was so well adjusted. How boring," he said, making Max laugh once more.

"Never that, I promise you," she assured him. "For example, I know one person in particular who finds you very interesting – despite themselves."

He perked up at that, "Really? But is it, interesting like dog shit on the bottom of her shoe? Or interesting as in; *hmm, I'd like to tap that fine, green-eyed man's arse.*"

His liege burst out laughing, "You're not even going to try to play it cool with me?"

He grunted, "No. What would be the point? You can read my mind and see the future," he pointed out. Besides, before now he had only seen evidence of dislike and indifference from the ranger. He was more than thrilled to hear differently.

"I can't see the future," Max rebutted, still stubbornly denying what they all knew was true now.

But he waved that away; "Whatever. Tell me more about Ivy's unrequited love for me."

Max snorted, "Don't get cocky on me. I'm giving you

some insider info because I'm rooting for you. Be patient, take your time to get to know the real her. Too many people only glance over the surface," she pointed to the ratty, plain book he was holding. "You know not to judge a book by its cover. Employ that same philosophy to Ivy."

He opened his mouth to question her more but decided not to push his luck. Besides, Max had given him plenty to think about this afternoon. He pushed to his feet, placing a chaste kiss to the top of her head, "I'm going to go work-out for a while. I feel stiff."

"Okay. But don't overdo it, please?"

"I promise," he swore as he crossed his heart.

Max pursed her lips at him but stood and headed into the house, "Oh," she paused, "Ryker installed a new sound system in the gym."

"He did?" Lark perked up at that. For years they had nothing but a retro CD player with one speaker to pound out a tune as they were exercising.

"Yep. When you were sick, he asked the others what he could do to make you feel better. Beyden said you'd been after a decent sound system in the gym so Ry went and ordered a state of the art surround-sound unit."

"Damn, I wasn't whinging at Bey or anything. Ryker shouldn't haven't bothered. I don't need the music that badly," he said, feeling a little guilty.

Max looked at him knowingly, "Yes, you do. And you know Ryker; if his team has a need, he makes it happen."

"Big softie." He scoffed but deep down he was flushed with pleasure, knowing his Captain would do such a thing for him. But then, Ry wasn't just his Captain, was he?

He was family.

ELEVEN

Lark barely restrained himself from shouting with joy when he saw the new sound system, complete with subwoofer and at least half a dozen speakers already well-placed around the matted floor area of the gym. He had the space to himself for now but he wasn't sure how long his alone-time would last, so he quickly plugged in his MP3 player and browsed his selection of songs.

Dex, Ivy, and Darius had taken Knox out of his makeshift cell-slash-guest suite which connected to the gym about an hour earlier. As far as he knew, they were still trying to coax the former chade to speak as well as trying to get him used to human contact once more. Dex and Darius were also attempting to hone Knox's once-lost skills with his element – Air. And as far as Lark was aware, Ivy was playing babysitter in case Knox needed a spanking in the form of his head being removed from his shoulders.

Seeing one of his all-time favourite songs, he hit play to reacquaint himself with the music as he stripped off his shirt and shoes and began to stretch out his still-sore muscles. The music blared out in the large space, the acoustics perfect for what he had in mind. No doubt Ry would have researched the perfect places to hang the speakers in order to ensure the sound quality was perfect. He bent forward, placing his palms flat on the mats whilst keeping his legs straight. It still shocked him whenever someone went out of their way to do nice things for him. It wasn't a comment about the people in his life – no, it was because his self-esteem could be a little sketchy at times.

Although he had dedicated his whole life to ensuring his father didn't win, it had been more out of spite and stubbornness rather than strength. Or so he had always believed. But recalling his conversation with Max just minutes before, knowing he had a goddess who thought he was strong and capable and undamaged, was a definite boost to his ego. Feeling the beat of the loud music echoing in his body thanks to his Captain also helped. Ryker had already given him his garden and his library, not to mention somewhere to park his disgraced butt when he had nowhere else to go four years ago.

Technically, a paladin couldn't complete the training and the trials to become a sworn paladin until they were thirty years old. With the ability to live longer and the maturation from child to adult a slower process, the age for being considered an adult was older than in the human society. But thanks to his father's strict training regime, Lark had been well advanced both physically and intellectually compared to his peers. He had therefore undertaken the trials when he was just twenty-six years old.

And he had failed them miserably.

He laughed out loud in remembrance of his father's face when his trainer had informed Isaac that his one and only son had failed the Paladin Trials. The shock and absolute horror had been worth every beating and cruel word. It hadn't been his first act of defiance but it had been his most public – and the one with the greatest repercussions.

Sitting down now, he spread his legs and stretched them out to the sides, lowering his torso flush to the ground as he considered those consequences. The first one had been when his father and his father's liege, Terran, had beaten him to within an inch of his life for daring to humiliate them in society. He had already been a disgrace in so many ways; he wasn't tall enough, broad enough, or sadistic enough for his father. He looked and acted nothing like the Captain of the Order of Tor and as the only child his father had been able to produce in a thousand years, it was one of Lark's greatest faults. But his father would have been able to forgive his auburn hair, his green eyes, and his smaller frame, if only Lark been born a potentate like him. But alas, he had failed to maintain the psychic bridge within his father's Order when his father had pushed the issue, let alone create such a connection.

Lark smiled when he thought of the silence and stillness he was met with when he had attempted to lock onto the Order's link when he had been a mere teenager. The silence had been pure music to his ears because there was no way he had wanted to be connected to the Tor Order in any capacity, let alone in such an intimate way. He had been terrified the cruel and violent tendencies of its members would somehow seep through the link and he would be contaminated. So he had prayed with everything within him for the bridge to remain closed and detached. It was the first time any of his prayers had been answered. The second time they had come to fruition? When he had failed the renowned Paladin Trials. He had failed them in a spectacular fashion too, he remembered. And he had made sure his father had been front and centre during every test.

The testing process for a paladin to become eligible to

join an Order was just as extensive as the training. Usually, an aspiring knight would be posted to a variety of training lodges around the world for years before they were permitted to undergo final exams. He hadn't been to any of the training facilities nor had the opportunity to learn from any paladins other than those in his father's Order. So, when he had entered the training lodge to undertake the Trials, he had been completely overwhelmed. He had been kept so isolated as a child, that he hadn't understood the easy comradery and banter going on around him. His clear discomfort and naiveté had added to the very big target already on his back because of his father's reputation. Terran's Order was not well liked. But they were very much feared.

So, he had decided to play the role of the too-young, too-skinny, too-short paladin and had no problem finding motivated contestants to beat him in every single test. Written and oral exams, shooting, archery, scythe-handling, hand-to-hand – he had placed last in every single one. Every time he was teased or berated, every black eye, every time he had been spit on, it had all been worth the resounding *FAIL* on his final report, for his father had disowned him the same day.

And he had finally been free.

That was until the head trainer who had been holding the trials had questioned his results. It seems the trainer was more than just a cantankerous meathead as Lark had assumed. The man had found him behind one of the makeshift residences after his father and Terran had left him for dead. He had been a mass of bruises and cuts, his face so swollen he could barely see through his puffy eyes. Even now, more than four years later, he could still feel the phantom pains twinging along his ribs and he sucked in a breath as he remembered the conversation that changed his life;

He was dying, he was sure of it, he silently moaned to

himself. He couldn't believe his luck. His plan had worked and his father had finally publicly washed his hands of him. He'd had about an hour of pure bliss to revel in his joy and new-found freedom, only to be brought back down to earth by Terran and dear old dad jumping him as he had walked the bushland bordering the training lodge. For years he would have welcomed death as a respite from his life but not now. Not when his liberty was within his grasp.

"Hey, kid."

The deep voice and the hated moniker startled him enough to pry his eyes open and wheeze out a painful breath, "I'm not a kid," he informed the tall stranger. He was unable to make out any features due to the blurriness of his vision.

A grunt met his ears, "You gonna die?"

Lark chuckled, despite the fire it caused to spread throughout his body, "Probably. It'd be just my kind of luck."

Rustling followed and a large but gentle hand tilted his face up. Lark squinted, groaning once again when he finally recognised the large scar running down the left side of the man's face; Ryker. The managing paladin and head trainer at the lodge. Just his luck, Lark repeated to himself. The huge guy was almost as much of an arsehole as his father was.

"I'm going to ask you a question," Ryker said, releasing his chin, "and I want you to answer honestly."

Lark was positively exhausted, so he merely flapped a hand with three broken fingers in the man's direction, "Shoot."

"Did you throw the trials?"

Now, that wasn't the question he had been expecting. But given he literally had nothing to lose, he answered honestly, "I did."

"Why?"

Failing in one's duties as a knight was the height of shame in their society. And failing on purpose? Well, Lark figured it was a probably an offence punishable by death. But regardless of that and even though Ryker was a complete stranger and looked just as formidable and unrelenting as his father, he didn't censor his answer;

"Because I hate my father and his Order with everything that I am. It was the best way to flip the piece of shit the bird."

Ryker continued to stare at him, that horrendous scar on his face twitching in time with the clenching of his jaw and Lark prepared himself for another arse-kicking of epic proportions. He knew Ryker's reputation. But the man only asked for clarification;

"You failed the most prestigious examination process in society, making yourself a shameful outcast for the rest of your long life, just so you can stick it to your father?"

"Damn straight," Lark confirmed.

Ryker nodded, "Fair enough." He stood up, dusting off his hands on the seat of his pants, "If you live, I have a spare room available at my house. It's thirty minutes north of here, converted barn by the sea. You can't miss it."

Ryker had then left him there in mute shock. But he hadn't been alone long. Two absolutely gorgeous female paladins had rushed to his side and administered the first kind words and gentle touches he had ever received in his quarter of a century of life. That had been the first time he had met Diana and Cali. A few hours after that, after struggling his way into the backseat of the duo's car, he'd also had the privilege of meeting Darius and Beyden.

He knew the others had similar stories to tell surrounding how they had come to live in the beautiful log cabin by the ocean. Somehow, the surly, half-dead potentate with the scarred face and the hostile countenance had managed to collect one stray paladin from every domain. He was as bad as Max when it came to saving the underdogs and the downtrodden – not that he would ever admit it. But Lark knew Ry's compassion was as deep as his grouchiness. He and Max really were the perfect match.

Standing up and shaking out his limbs, he picked up his device again, looking for the perfect song for his current mood. Seeing Hozier's, *Take Me To Church*, he promptly hit play and let the beat roll over him before he made any attempt to move. Dancing was his secret joy. Whereas reading allowed him to escape his feelings; dance allowed him to express them. He didn't know if the others knew he could move like a professional ballet dancer. Ryker and Max knew of course, and Axel had also stumbled upon him one day in the midst of a particularly graceful lyrical routine. He had feared the fire paladin would tease him but he had been wrong. Axel had been spellbound and had asked if he could play the piano for him one day as he danced. It was something they now did routinely as a part of their bromance.

With the music and the lyrics now soaking into his skin and his childhood firmly in the past where it belonged, he leapt into the air ... and danced.

TWELVE

It had been almost two weeks since the incident with Knox and Ivy regarded the maiden voyage for chade redemption as a half-win. The victory half was the amazing progress the now former chade had made since his enforced stay at the camp. She had just spent an hour with Knox, Dex, and Darius, trying to stabilise Knox's powers once more. The chade had stopped trying to consume Max's energy whenever she was within touching distance a few days ago and was now able to recharge like a normal warden once more.

If she hadn't seen it with her own eyes, Ivy never would have believed it. It was something everyone had been told was impossible for centuries. The chades were purported to be power-hungry traitors, bastardising their birthrights and bringing ruin to nature's balance deliberately. After taking so many lives – too many to count – she had begun wishing for an alternative. Well, the alternative was finally here and its name was Max. Or, apparently, members of Max's Order who volunteer as conduits. And that was why she considered their initial efforts only a half-win. Because she had watched

Lark's ever-present vibrancy wither to grey skin, hollow cheekbones, and rattling breaths.

When he had collapsed so silently to the ground, she had feared they'd all made an irrevocable mistake. The sharp pain she had felt in her chest seeing him lying half dead on the ground had shocked her and she had found herself rushing to his side instead of burying her sickle into the chade as her years of training should have demanded. Even now, the memory of seeing those sparkling green eyes go dull and lifeless made her pulse kick up and her stomach drop. And that thoroughly pissed her off just as much as it terrified her. She was now afraid these people with their acceptance and their fun and their steadfast loyalty were highly contagious.

All the mushy, warm-fuzzies must be like an airborne virus or something, she told herself. She rubbed at her arms as if that would help remove the contamination. The sooner she got out of here the better, she knew. She'd rather take on a horde of rabid chades and face an eternity of near-death experiences than the butterflies she felt every time she thought of the young earth paladin coming to harm. Luckily, the paladin in question was now almost back to full health and they would be able to head out on the extended mission to retrieve as many chades as possible.

There had been many a war council over the past couple of weeks and a plan had finally been decided upon; Lark, Ivy, and Dex would travel to all the known chade haunts. Dex and Max, through her connection with Lark, would determine which chades were redeemable. Lark would then volunteer as tribute again (his words) and act as Max's magic wand but on a much smaller and more controlled level. Max would only hit the chade with just enough juice to 'humanise' him and she would also keep the link open between her entire Order. Everyone would shoulder the burden.

It sounded viable in theory but Ivy had her reservations.

They still had a few details to iron out, like where were all these chades going to stay? How would they get back here? Nikolai had agreed to look the other way and basically keep the area clear of rangers so they had time to fully bring the chades back into the light again. Her Commander had big reservations but he trusted her. Ivy only hoped his trust wasn't misplaced and they weren't all making a huge mistake.

That feeling was compounded by the information Nik had given her during their phone call just minutes ago. He told her the number of rumblings regarding Max was increasing in volume, frequency, and type. There was a decided shift from shock and awe to suspicion and fear from the local wardens and paladins. And it was spreading. Ivy had no doubt specific factions were responsible for the perpetuation of the negative rumours and the fear mongering. In her opinion, it was something they needed to get a handle on – and soon. Ivy hadn't put much stock in Max's silly referrals to her squirrels but she was now worried she was turning into a believer.

Stepping up to the door of the gym, she was about to open it and unceremoniously interrupt Lark's workout when she heard the loud music. It surprised her because she didn't take Lark as the type to listen to music at such a volume. She would have thought he'd be more of the silent exercise type. But then, what did she really know about him? Other than the fact that he was willing to sacrifice his own health and safety for his liege's wishes – so typical of a paladin. It was another reason why being a ranger suited her. She sacrificed her safety all the time but it wasn't for one specific person. Nobody was that important – until now.

Glancing down, she saw the seven, small black elemental symbols in a perfect circle on her upper arm and guessed that was proof enough that Max was that important. It had been

Max who had pointed her in the direction of Lark this morning. Ivy really didn't want to spend too much one-on-one time with him but they needed to discuss their next steps. She could only be grateful Dex would be accompanying them on their mission. For now, her curiosity got the better of her and instead of going through the main door of the gym, she walked around the side so she could see into one of the windows.

And damn near swallowed her tongue.

He was stripped from the waist up, bare chest glistening with the evidence of his exertion. His feet were also bare and he was in a scrappy-looking pair of red cut-offs that made his pale skin look like smooth ivory. But the real kicker? He was dancing. Not the kind of bump and grind you'd see on the dance floor of a nightclub, nor the ballroom dancing her own brother preferred. But the type of dancing with lots of leaps and stretches and pirouettes. Even as she watched, Lark shifted his weight fluidly from the ball of one foot to the next and he executed a perfect leap in the air with both legs out straight. He then collapsed his front knee when he landed, letting the floor absorb his weight as he tumbled, effortlessly regaining his feet again.

She had known the guy was flexible from the yoga session she had seen but this was another level altogether. But it wasn't his undeniable skill or even his pretty chest which had her eyes glued to his frame. It was the soul he put into every movement. Lark in motion was the singular, most beautiful thing she had ever seen.

She'd noticed he didn't parade around half naked like most of the other male soldiers. She'd had to keep telling herself that it didn't bother her. Why should she care if her eyes were never given the treat of seeing his perfect, pale skin stretched taught over lean, corrugated abs? It hadn't bothered her – not in the least – she assured herself, even as she continued to watch the half-clothed paladin. She had just assumed he was shy or maybe a prude but as he turned away from her, she automatically cringed, her body sucking in a shuddering breath.

His back! By the Goddess, his back! It was a mass of scar tissue from shoulder to waist. So, the man wasn't a prude. He was likely ever-cognizant of the markings on his skin. And here she was – some kind of creeper in the bushes, spying on him when he was obviously engrossed in a very private moment. She kept telling herself to walk away and leave the man in peace but her body wouldn't obey her brain's command. Her eyes were too enraptured by what they were seeing. His body was poetry in motion.

"You know, if he wanted an audience he would have asked for one."

Ivy spun quickly, leading with her sickle as was habit whenever someone snuck up behind her.

Ryker merely eyed the lethal blade blandly, "Planning to take my head off, Ivy?"

She blew out a breath, lowering the weapon, "Not today."

Ryker glanced past her where Lark was still dancing. He was clearly tracking Lark's movements as he leapt and tumbled and spun his way across the matted floor of the gym. She struggled heroically with herself not to turn around and glimpse those lithe muscles and sensuous movements just one more time. Ryker's eyes re-focused on her and she could easily see the censure in them.

"This is Lark's private time. He doesn't dance for an audience; he dances for himself."

"I wasn't spying," she hastily defended, cursing herself for her automatic response. She didn't need to explain herself to Ryker, he wasn't her commanding officer. But she did feel guilty knowing she had witnessed something intensely personal, not to mention those scars ... "Max sent me out here," she added. She had no problem shifting the blame to the whacky custodian.

Ivy watched Ryker's dark brown eyes narrow, "She did, did she?"

She almost smiled when she recognised the look on the Captain's face; pained resignation. "That's right. So, if you'll excuse me ..." she motioned with her sickle but the man didn't budge. Instead, he crossed his arms over his chest and narrowed his eyes;

"Are we going to have a problem?" he asked.

"No," she answered automatically, before pausing to consider the situation more fully. After a moment, she shook her head and finally relaxed back against the wall. "No," she repeated, "No problem. I'm just feeling bitchy I guess. We never had a problem," she added.

"That's good. I never thought we did. No, that's not the whole truth," he admitted, "I didn't really care if we did. When I woke up the next morning, I was more concerned about how Beyden would react than how you would."

She watched as he scrubbed both hands over his crop of shaggy dark hair in clear agitation, leaving it appealingly messy. His jaw was shadowed with a couple of days' worth of growth and he was wearing his usual black cargos and plain white tee. *Definitely a fine specimen,* she mused. Too bad her taste in men had undergone a sudden shift lately. She noticed Ryker still looked uncomfortable and contrite, and because she hadn't lied to him when she said there was no problem, she decided to put him out of his continued misery;

"I was a virtual stranger. Bey is your friend. Why wouldn't you be more concerned for his feelings than mine?"

Deep brown eyes watched her for a few seconds before Ry's mouth kicked up in a genuine, friendly smile, "Why is it the women in my life never react the way I think they're going to?"

Ivy smiled – very briefly and very small – but a smile nonetheless. Because she knew exactly what he was referring to; the women of the household weren't your typical touchy, hormonal, sensitive divas. "Just lucky I guess," she told him.

"Oh, I am that. Very lucky," he was quick to concur. "But seriously, we should get a move on before Lark finishes and sees us out here. I was serious before; he doesn't like to be watched. Unless it's Max ... or Axel" he amended. "He doesn't seem to mind them watching him dance."

Ivy nodded, pushing herself off the wall. She hesitated only a moment before voicing the question that had been plaguing her since she first set eyes on Lark's shirtless form, "How'd he get the scars?"

Ryker's face shut down completely and she was looking at the stoic, pissed off knight she had known pre-Max, "That's even more private than his dancing and a sore spot I don't suggest you poke at."

She felt her irritation levels rise again, largely because she felt guilty, "I'm not trying to garner gossip here, Ryker. I'm about to head off alone with the kid. I need to know I can trust him."

"First, Lark isn't a kid. Second, you can trust him. You have my word on that – for what it's worth to you. If mine's not enough, you have Max's. I'm pretty sure that brand on your arm means you trust Max's judgment. If you don't – there's your brother. Lark is one of his best friends."

Ivy barely contained her grimace as Ryker listed all the exact same reasons Dex, Max, and even her brother had given her during their conversations. Either they had all teamed up to get their stories straight, or they all believed in the same thing; Lark. After watching him in the field with Knox, Ivy was inclined to believe the latter. Her questioning of Ryker regarding Lark's history really had been more about satisfying her curiosity. But one thing kept playing on her mind;

"I just don't see how he can have enough real-world experience given his age. Six months as Max's sworn paladin in a time of peace ..." she let her comment trail off.

Ryker surprised her by not immediately jumping to Lark's defence once more. Instead, he merely eyed her curiously; "You haven't investigated him? Or any of us for that matter? I would have thought it'd been the first thing you did when you learned your brother was living here."

"Oh, it was," she assured him. "But Lark wasn't living here then, was he?"

When Beyden had first moved into the large, isolated house, Ivy had looked into the backgrounds of all of its occupants. She'd had to ensure her brother wasn't going from one bad situation to another. Ryker, Darius, Diana, and Cali had passed muster – to a certain extent. They were all adrift in a society where everything was based on one's connections and rumours were rampant. But she had the ability to see through most of the ludicrous gossip. Beyden's situation had taught her not to believe everything you hear. Both Axel and Lark moved in years later and by then she had learned to trust Bey's judgement as well as the other occupants in the household.

Besides, although she had researched the practical aspects of each individual, like their skill level with a blade, their Order histories, and their training records, she had purposefully not delved too deeply into each of the knights' personal histories. The main reason why was because she didn't want to get to know them on an intimate level. She was a ranger and had no interest in being friends with any of them. She rolled her eyes at herself; because whether she liked it or not, Max was determined to bring her into the fold. But Ivy wasn't going to give in too easily – resistance was never futile.

As for Lark, all she really knew about him was that he had failed the entire paladin examination process and was deemed unfit to become a sworn paladin. By rights, he would never have been indoctrinated into an Order if Max hadn't come along and ridden roughshod over their laws and traditions. Max hadn't given the IDC any choice in the matter whatsoever. If anyone else had attempted to bind a paladin without first seeking permission and then having it formally witnessed, Ivy and her fellow rangers would have been called in to administer punishment for unlawful conduct. But the IDC were too concerned with the ramifications to charge Max with anything – outwardly anyway. Those rumblings Nikolai had warned her about weren't only in the general populace, but also within the very foundations of their society.

"All I really know is that he failed the Paladin Trials," Ivy told Ryker, getting back on track.

Ryker nodded once, "He did. Quite spectacularly I might add. And I would know, I was the paladin trainer in charge of the results."

Now, that was interesting to her. Ryker had witnessed Lark's ineptitude firsthand and yet he still had no problem entrusting his lover's life to the kid. Something fishy was going on.

"If it really matters that much to you, why don't you ask him?" Ryker suggested.

She eyed him, drolly, "I may be rude but I'm not that insensitive."

"You're not rude – just socially inept," Ryker pointed out. "Kind of like me. Max tells me I'm socially stunted all the time."

Ivy felt her lips twitching again and wondered what the hell was happening to her. Two smiles in as many minutes? And not only were her lips tilting upward but she had also talked more in the past five minutes than she usually did in a week. Her earlier hypothesis must be correct; *definitely a highly contagious, fast acting, insidious virus,* she confirmed silently.

She could only hope there was a cure.

THIRTEEN

When Ryker finally left, she decided to wait for Lark near the back door of the house so she wouldn't miss him but also so he wouldn't suspect she had seen him in the gym. Her mind wanted to focus on the very graceful and very limber paladin but she forced her mind back where it should be; her duty. It was a mere ten minutes later when Lark, now fully clothed minus his shoes, walked down the stone path connecting the large exterior building which housed the gym and pool to the homey, converted barn. She saw the moment he noticed her presence because he slowed his gait, his face morphing into a happy and welcoming smile.

"What are you smiling at?" she asked a little breathlessly. *Was that soft, warm smile for her?*

"Looks like you've got a little hitchhiker," he said, pointing to her left shoulder as he came to a stop in front of her. "I still find it hard to believe we have a slater bug as a pet," he chuckled.

Ivy looked at her shoulder and saw a tiny, grey beetle clinging happily to her shirt with his numerous miniature legs. She felt herself flush; *Smiling at you, was he Ivy? You're pathetic. That look was for a bug!*

"Something wrong?" he queried with a frown.

"What? No, of course not," she quickly guaranteed him.

"You sure? Because if it was anyone else, I'd say that look was … chagrin. But on you, I'm not so sure. What could you possibly have to be embarrassed about?"

Ivy didn't answer, hoping the question was rhetorical. Instead, she put her finger out and Bert the beetle climbed on board. He really was a cute little thing; small grey body very reminiscent of an armadillo, only Bert was about one-centimetre front end to end. He had over a dozen tiny, pale, hair-thin legs, and two little grey antennae. When she had first arrived, he and his little Woodlouse friends would immediately roll into their trademark balls whenever she approached. But over the weeks, even the little beetles had warmed up to her and Bert no longer used his defence mechanism when she was near. She smiled at the little fellow but restrained herself from cooing like an idiot at him. Lark squinting up at the sky and then bending down to feel the ground had her refocusing;

"What are you doing?" she asked, truly stupefied.

"I'm seeing if there's a blue moon and checking to see if Hell has frozen over. Because I swear, that thing you just did with your lips … it was a smile."

She immediately scowled in his direction. This is what she got for being nice – sarcasm. Lark's demeanour quickly changed from flippant to serious and he took a step closer to her. She forced herself to stand her ground.

"Hey, I'm sorry. I was just joking. I didn't mean to hurt your feelings," he apologised.

"You didn't," she quickly guaranteed him. His emerald peepers remained on her face for a few moments and she stayed completely still – a trick she had learned when Nik was trying to do his Jedi-mind-meld thing.

"Whatever you say," he soothed and quickly changed the subject before she could defend herself again, "Were you waiting for me?"

She straightened her shoulders, feeling on much safer ground discussing business, "Yes. I wanted to see if you were feeling up to getting on the road. My Commander informed me of some troubling rumours and I think we're running on borrowed time."

She watched in fascination as his bright, green eyes darkened in unison with his frown, "What kind of rumours?"

"The kind that says Max is a fraud and an evil usurper."

"Shit! They're getting worse?" he queried, worryingly.

Ivy nodded, "Yes. I have real concerns this whole thing is going to blow up in our faces. If Max wants redeemable chades, we need to find them asap."

Lark firmed his jaw in determination, "Well, I'm pretty much back to normal. As soon as Max gives us the go ahead, we'll leave. And between you and Dex, we should have no problem finding more chades. You both have a built-in radar where they're concerned," he added, looking like he wanted to say more but restraining himself instead.

She didn't know why that bothered her so much so she half-prompted, half-demanded; "Just ask."

He shrugged, not bothering to deny he had something to say, "I can understand Dex's affinity with the chades but not yours. You seem to have a connection with them almost, as well as a deeper connection with your element."

She chewed the inside of her lip as she contemplated the best way to answer him. The curiosity from both Dex and Lark had been palpable when she had said the earth alerted her to the chades when they had been hunting Knox. She could tell they believed she had an unusually strong connection with her element for a paladin, but that wasn't strictly true. Still feeling the sting of guilt for invading Lark's privacy, she decided to reveal some little spoken about facts;

"The earth speaks to me – tells me where they are. I think that's true of all rangers. Our elements seem to be more in tune with chades than other paladins. We have more of a connection to them. It's why we become rangers and not just sworn paladins."

His eyebrows arched, "I didn't know that."

She shrugged negligently, "It's not something that is spoken about."

"Another secret from the council?" his voice held disdain.

She sighed, knowing she was going to have to explain herself more, "It's not that we're told not to talk about it. But who would we tell? We don't socialise with anyone other than rangers much. Wardens see us as workers and paladins see us as some kind of monster. We're the bogeymen of society, doing the dirty work that no-one else wants to do."

"But that's not all there is to it," Lark encouraged.

Ivy hesitated for a second and then figured it was in their best interest to get to know each other a little. Besides, perhaps he would reciprocate and share some of his confidences, like his ability to dance or his scars ... "No. That's not all there is to it," she confirmed, "Tell me, what did you feel the first time you saw Max?"

If he was surprised by the apparent shift in topic, he didn't show it. Instead, he smiled cheekily, revealing a set of even, white teeth; "Now that's a loaded question. But I think I know what you're alluding to. You're talking about the instinctive bond that exists between a warden and their paladins when the connection is organic."

She nodded, "Correct."

Lark shifted his gaze above her head, a wistful smile transforming his face and reminding her how appealing it was, "When I first walked into that bar, the earth literally shifted beneath my feet," he began. "I looked up and saw this short woman sitting on a too-tall chair and my heart started beating faster, my breath became shallow. I felt an immediate need to be near her and if Axel and Darius hadn't followed her out of that bar – I sure would have." He arched a look at her, "I thought it was love at first sight."

That confession had Ivy literally sputtering and an incredulous, "What?!" flying from her mouth.

He laughed – a self-deprecating laugh; "I know, hilarious right? But what was I supposed to think? I'd never been in an Order before so I had no idea what a natural bond felt like. I've experienced an instant attraction to women before but again, this was different. The only logical conclusion in those initial few moments was that it was love." His smile was crooked as he angled his face half away from hers, "Don't worry, after just minutes in the car with her I knew it couldn't be that. By the time we were back at the camp, my feelings for her were already firmly in the platonic category. She was so sick and sensitive and there was such a vulnerability to her then. I wanted to hug her – not sleep with her."

Vulnerable? Max? Ivy couldn't reconcile the outspoken, fiery, powerful woman with the picture Lark was painting. Despite her brash behaviour and outspoken opinions, there was a definite sweetness to Max. But vulnerable? Not that Ivy had seen.

Lark held up a hand, "I know, I know. Max doesn't exactly give off the vulnerable vibe. But there's more to her than what you see on the surface ... as is the case with everybody," he added.

Was he trying to make a point about himself, or me? Ivy wasn't sure but she knew the comment wasn't a benign one.

"Anyway, we're getting off track. We were talking about the bond between paladins and wardens. I assume you asked because it's similar for you? But instead of that instinctual bond with a warden, you feel that way with chades?" he asked, and the surprise in his voice was obvious.

"Yes and no," she answered, slowly – still unsure how much to reveal. She should have known someone with his intellect wouldn't be satisfied with a half-answer. But all this talking was getting to her; first with Ryker this morning and now with Lark. She was not garrulous by nature, preferring to let others waste their words while she sat back and watched. And she most certainly didn't share her thoughts and feelings easily. So why was she about to reveal something so intimate about herself and her fellow rangers to what amounted to a complete stranger?

Because we have to be able to trust each other in battle, that's why, she assured herself. There was no other reason, like the fact that she felt comfortable in his presence or actually enjoyed talking with him. Nope, that wasn't why she continued to explain;

"As paladins – or rangers – we don't feel our elements as much as the wardens nor can we actively manipulate or create them. But they still talk to us; the earth comforts me, it warns me when I'm in danger, for example."

Lark was nodding, "Sure. It's the same for me. The earth is integral when it comes to helping with Max."

"Well, instead of the earth telling me when my liege or a warden is in need, it warns me of a chade's presence; where they are, how many there are. I can't feel them – don't be mistaken – but my element can. It creates an instinctive need for me to seek them out."

"Huh," Lark tilted his head to the side, "So, you've always known you were going to join the rangers and not an Order? Like a calling?"

Exactly like a calling, she silently acknowledged. And knowing Max shared that calling with the chades had been one of the primary reasons Ivy had pledged her loyalty to her.

But all she said to Lark was; "Yes."

"And that's the same for all rangers?" he pressed.

She gave a negligent shrug, "Pretty much." As she watched him, she could almost hear the wheels turning in his head. He was a thinker, she'd give him that. She only wished she didn't find that trait so appealing.

"I owe you an apology," he said, presently.

"Huh?" She had no idea what he was talking about.

"An apology," he repeated, before clarifying, "When I asked you if you were going to be able to save the chades instead of killing them? That was clearly an insult. You've always wanted to save them ... haven't you?"

Ivy quickly ducked her head, knowing there was no way she'd be able to hide her emotions from his sharp eyes and analytic mind. She felt exposed for some reason, as if someone was seeing the real her for the very first time. People didn't bother trying to figure out what made her tick and some of the onus of that was on her. She wasn't a big fan of people as a rule and she knew she kind of had a *fuck off* vibe about her. But she still couldn't deny the twinge of disappointment she felt when others made assumptions about her. So, for someone to recognise that she actually did have a few layers and a beating heart ... it made her feel all warm inside. She thought, maybe, the warmth was a little heightened because it came from the man standing in front of her. Perhaps that is why she answered truthfully;

"I guess I always believed – always *hoped* – the purpose for the connection wasn't to hunt the chades ... but to save them."

The admission was a hard one to make out loud, despite the current comfortable circumstances, and she found herself bracing for Lark's response. He had apologised but now that she had confirmed his theory would he laugh at her? Show derision? It wouldn't be the first time. She had only spoken her secret dreams to two other people on the planet; Nikolai and Alex. Nikolai was easy – he shared her views – but Alex had been a different story.

She had been seeing the older ranger for a couple of months – practically a long-term relationship for her – when she had told him about her feelings concerning the chades. The man had laughed his arse off and then told her she was delusional and soft. He had capped it off by saying; *"And this is why women shouldn't be soldiers – you're all weak."* She hadn't been in love with the other ranger but she had thought they were at least friends and she had trusted him. His words had not only made her feel like a fool but they had also made her second guess herself. After all, it was pretty laughable that the executioner wanted to heal rather than hurt. But she hadn't given the chauvinistic bastard the satisfaction of seeing the blow to her confidence. Instead, she'd done what any self-respecting female would have done; she'd kicked his nuts into his throat. Chancing a glance at Lark, she saw that his face held acceptance and curiosity – nothing more.

"That makes sense. Do other rangers feel the same way?" he asked, his question laced with curiosity.

"I can't speak for anyone else," even though she knew of at least one other ranger who felt the same way – Nikolai.

Her commanding officer was her best friend – her only friend if she was being brutally honest with herself. He had been a ranger before she was even thought of, being on good terms with Dex – formally Charlemagne – for hundreds of years. What had started as respect between colleagues had slowly but surely turned into a friendship. They had never been lovers. Once she discovered their potential for friendship, she hadn't been interested in complicating that by sleeping with him. That was despite the fact that Nik was one of the sexiest men she had ever had the pleasure of ogling.

"Hmm," was Lark's response.

Now, why did that one non-verbal sound hold such a wealth of knowledge? Like he had read her thoughts and knew all that she hadn't said. Despite his easy reaction to her admission, she still needed clarification, "So you believe me?"

He looked surprised, "Of course. Why wouldn't I?"

"Because I'm a killer. You've said so yourself in the past," she pointed out, the reminder cooling her feelings a little.

"Well, sure. But that was before you explained yourself. I mean, if someone told me my connection to Max was only to cause pain and harm, I wouldn't believe it either. Why should your bond with the chades be any different?" he eyed her closely.

Ivy took a physical step back, feeling as though he was seeing just a little too much now, and she felt herself begin to panic a little. She should never have opened up to him in the first place.

FOURTEEN

Lark watched Ivy as she took a wary step back. He could practically see her walls going up brick by brick and told himself not to be disappointed. Rome wasn't built in a day. After he finished dancing, he had spent the remainder of his cool-down time thinking over what Max had said. She'd made it sound as if Ivy was interested in him. He had never seen a hint of such a possibility, even with his ability to analyse even the tiniest nuances in a person's expression.

At first, such a skill had come about purely for self-preservation; knowing when a sociopath was finally going to snap their leash and beat the holy hell out of you, sure came in handy. But over time, he had been able to refine it and he had since discovered that silence often exposed more than words. Thus, observing Ivy's face – something he did ridiculously often – should have exposed her feelings to him, no matter how hard she was trying to hide them. So how had he missed her interest in him?

What's more, listening to her divulge her motivation for being a ranger had shown him that she was far more sensitive and vulnerable than he had given her credit for. Once again, he wondered how he could have missed the signs before now. After all, he had noticed the exact same traits in Max almost immediately. But he didn't need to think too long to have his answer – he had let his ego get in the way of his natural instincts.

His initial reaction to the lovely ranger had been attraction but that hadn't been all. He had seen a distinct sadness and also compassion behind all that determination and grit. That was why, just minutes after sitting at the same table with her, he had resolved himself to making her smile. But over the weeks, he had allowed her derision and seeming distaste for him to prick his male ego. He thought he was above such primitive flaws but turns out he was just as susceptible as the rest of his species. *Max would have a field day with that,* he snickered.

But now he had seen the shining glimmer of the *real* Ivy and he was determined to peel back her layers. The woman wouldn't know what hit her. But *subtle* – he had to be subtle. He had a feeling Ivy wasn't the type to respond to brute strength. She would only push right back.

"So, if other rangers feel the same way you do, why hasn't anyone spoken up before now? It would certainly go a long way in humanising you to the general population. To be honest, I always thought you guys liked the badass rep," he said, trying to ease Ivy back into a conversation with him. He considered it a small success when she smirked;

"We do."

He laughed out loud and this time he caught the small flicker in her dark eyes as they travelled over his tilted lips. Feeling another victory, he leant casually against the veranda railing, "Rep aside, it still might be nice to tear down some barriers. That's what Max is all about, after all. I've no doubt she'd be willing to speak with the council about how isolated rangers are."

Ivy frowned, "I'm not sure it would matter. The council and most of the wardens are very set in their ways."

"One word: chades," Lark pointed out.

Ivy nodded at that, "Good point. She has had success in convincing the council as far as recognising chades as being ill. But I guarantee you, they are falling back on old habits and doing their own testing to try and replicate what Max has successfully accomplished naturally and easily."

He felt his good mood disappear upon hearing that news, "More experiments?"

Ivy merely shrugged and he knew he was looking at the ranger once more instead of the woman. He sighed;

"I wish we could speak openly with the council about the whole thing, share information, swap stories. But ..." he trailed off.

"But, Max thinks there's a conspiracy within the council," Ivy filled in.

He nodded, cautiously. They were getting into dangerous territory now.

"What do you think?" she asked him, bluntly.

Lark chose his words carefully, wanting the opportunity to gauge her reactions. He knew Max trusted Ivy implicitly and he certainly wanted to do the same. Especially now, after he had seen those tantalising glimpses of the interesting woman hidden underneath those green robes. But at the same time, he couldn't allow his attraction to her to impact his good sense. On the small chance they were wrong about her and she was indeed a plant from within the council itself, any comment he made in the affirmative could very well see him imprisoned for treason. Unfortunately, the only way to know for sure where she stood was to be honest – to a degree;

"I think there are a lot of things that don't add up. Thousands of years of research and tests trying to determine the origins of the chades and yet no definitive answers. And that is despite the fact that chade numbers have been increasing and their behaviours seem to be changing. As far as I'm aware, there have been no new attempts before now. Why is that?"

"Because they already tried and failed? It was an expensive, time consuming, and resource-intensive endeavour over the span of literally hundreds of years. They weren't getting any results and nothing was changing. Why would they invest in that again?" she asked her own question.

Although she offered a well-reasoned and rational response, he couldn't help snorting, "Because their people were dying? Seems like a good enough reason to expend some more resources to me."

She merely shrugged and he could see she was closing herself off even more. But not before he saw what he was hoping to see; agreement. However, he could also tell that although she agreed with what he was saying, she also still seemed to agree with the council. More curious than annoyed now, he questioned her further;

"You don't really agree with the IDC and the way they do things, do you?"

Her dark gaze stayed on him for a moment before she spoke, "I believe in the institution of the council. In a world where everything is disposable, I believe it's important to have something enduring. The council and their rules provide that stability."

He agreed with her and liked he was finding more and more in common with the pretty, reticent ranger. But there was one important thing he felt she was missing; "But how stable and enduring can our foundations be if there are cracks? If there is rot at its core?"

She opened her mouth to answer but he didn't get a chance to find out if she was about to admit there was decay within their society or if she was about to oppose him because a masculine throat cleared behind them. He instinctively reached for his absent scythe, his hand coming up empty. Ivy didn't have the same problem however, and her sickle was up and ready to remove heads before he could even turn to see who the intruder was.

Leo and Lawson hastily stepping in front of Caspian with their own scythes at the ready, had Lark quickly invading Ivy's personal space. He placed a light hand on her arm, "Easy. It's just Cas." He ignored the stiffness in her posture, turning to smile at his three friends, "Hey guys, sorry about that. You startled us. What brings you here?"

"It's not a problem. We thought you heard us," came Cas's muffled reply. An indignant huff could be heard before Caspian pushed his two paladins out of the way, "Would you two move?"

"Just doing our jobs," Leo pointed out.

"Whatever," Caspian rolled his eyes.

The action was so reminiscent of his own liege, Lark couldn't help laughing out loud, "I feel your pain, guys," he said to the brothers.

Caspian looked pained when his paladins looked smug, "Don't encourage them, Lark. I was hoping for an audience with Max. I know I don't have an appointment ..." he said.

Lark straightened, trying to look professional even though he was wearing holey clothes and was shoeless, "Of course, my Lord. After you ..." he invited, sweeping his arm out and nodding his head in deference as was custom.

The Water Warden ruined the moment when he merely rolled his eyes at Lark before sweeping past. Lark stifled a snicker; he really did like the guy.

FIFTEEN

Saved by the warden, Ivy thought in relief as she followed the four men into the house. Although she happened to agree with everything Lark had said regarding the IDC and their society as a whole, she was not prepared to admit it out loud. Until a few theories could be proven without a shadow of a doubt, Ivy was not prepared to reveal what her stance was. It wasn't necessarily that she didn't trust Max and her crew but she had also spoken the truth when she'd said she believed in the institution of the council. When certain deceptions came to light, there was going to be a lot of hurt and betrayed citizens to deal with – Ivy included.

"Caspian! Hi, how are you?"

Max's cheery voice broke into Ivy's introspection and she watched with no small amount of humour as Max threw convention to the wind and hugged the young warden to within an inch of his life. She then did the same to his two paladins, asking them how they were and how they were finding their new home. Caspian's fair, angelic face flushed with a mixture of embarrassment and pleasure.

"My Lady, I apologise for coming over unannounced ..." he began, only to have Max wave away his apology, dragging him further into the busy kitchen, so the others could say their hellos.

"No worries. You're always welcome," Max assured the trio.

Caspian bowed formally in thanks and his two paladins quickly followed suit.

"Will you three stop that already? It gives me the willies," Max groused as she mock-shuddered, causing Caspian to grin. Max cocked her head to the side, studying him intently for a moment, "Is everything okay, Cas? You seem a little stressed."

He did? Ivy thought he looked as happy and bright as always. That was until he began to shift from foot to foot nervously and his partner Lawson, placed a comforting hand on the small of his back.

"Did you happen to pay us a visit last night?" Caspian asked.

The question had Max's Order standing to attention and casting suspicious looks in the direction of their liege. Max scowled at them before turning back to Caspian; "No. Why would you think that? Did something happen?"

"Yes and no," he replied, slowly. "The evening was quite unremarkable. This morning however ... I woke up to this," he pushed his sleeve back to reveal a circle of small symbols on his left bicep that looked highly familiar to Ivy – and to everyone else if their quick indrawn breaths were any indication.

Max ignored her paladins, stepping forward and running a light hand over the black symbols. She raised an eyebrow, looking at Leo and Lawson; "What about you two?"

Both paladins nodded their heads and pushed up their sleeves to reveal their own brands. Max hummed over those as well for a moment before turning back to the room at large; "I got nothin'."

"Max!" Ryker's one word was clearly a reprimand and Max knew it too, for she stiffened;

"What? I didn't do anything!"

Ryker crossed his arms over his chest, a deep scowl on his face, "No? It has to be you, Max. Who else?"

Max clenched her jaw and threw her lover a filthy look. Ivy saw the entire Order wince – with the exception of Ryker who stood his ground, stubbornly. She saw her brother rub at his coat of arms, which was now writhing angrily on his flesh. The vines and leaves moved as if a strong wind blew over them and the druidic symbol for his element, beast, glowed a bright, luminescent orange. Looking around, she saw his fellow knights also fidgeting uncomfortably. Ivy figured their own heraldries were also doing the tango and understood it was a sure sign their liege was getting pissed off.

"I don't know who is doing it, Ryker," Max's voice was soft and sugary sweet, "Maybe it's the branding fairy. Did you ever think of that?"

Ryker's eyes narrowed at his love and liege but before he could antagonise her further, Diana stepped forward; "Now Boss-man. Let's not provoke the wrath of the goddess, hmm? After all, the last time I heard that tone from Max she was threatening to squeeze Marco's neck until blood leaked from every orifice. And I do mean *every* orifice. Remember?"

Ivy managed to suppress her grin of delight over that happy little reminder. Although she hadn't been there to witness the spanking of the paladins from the Order of Vulcan, the whole thing had fast become the stuff of urban legend.

Dex, not having been privy to the earlier encounter, choked on his mouthful of food; "She did what? You did what?" he repeated in Max's direction – who merely shrugged, never taking her gaze off her lover.

"The Captain of the Order of Vulcan and his sad little knights gave Lark a beating. So Max threatened to squeeze his neck so hard his dick slit would bleed," Cali commented, almost lazily.

Dex barked out a laugh, "You did what?!" he echoed, once again.

Cali patted her lover's hand, "She –"

"We don't really need to keep repeating it, do we?" Darius chimed in, looking a little rosy around the cheeks.

Dex just laughed at his staid brother, turning to Max, "Could you really do it?"

"I don't know. Shall we find out?" she asked mildly, tension thick in the air as she gazed at Ryker.

Axel snorted out a laugh, ambling over to his liege and throwing an arm around her shoulders, "As if you would break your favourite toy. What would you do without Ry's meatcicle?"

The room erupted into a series of splutters, guffaws, and cackling. Ivy could only shake her head; *they're all nuts!* Axel's depraved levity had the desired effect though, and Ryker pushed Axel away from his woman as he drew her into his large chest;

"I'm sorry, honey. I don't mean to be an arsehole but I'm scared for you. Your display at Cas's went a long way in proving your legitimacy to many wardens and paladins. Unfortunately, the opposite is also true. There are those who believe your display of power was a scare tactic, an attempt to shock people into following you," he explained.

Max looked curious but not alarmed, "Following me? For what?"

"World domination," Darius volunteered, deadpan.

Max laughed, clearly believing the air paladin was joking

but unfortunately, Ivy knew he wasn't. There really was a bunch of wardens and paladins who believed Max had ulterior motives.

"He's serious, Max," Beyden spoke up. "You're powerful. The most powerful being on the planet. A lot of people are worried you will abuse that power."

Max looked shocked, "But it would be impossible for me to do that. My purpose is as deeply ingrained in me as it is in you to be a knight. I could never use my abilities for harm – well, not in that context anyway," she amended.

"We know that," Ryker assured her, rubbing her arms in comfort, "But there are already pockets of paladins and wardens who think you are some kind of evil genius planning to take over the world. And I know for a fact at least three members of the council feel the same way. Do you see why it's important that you don't create any more brands?" he implored.

"I honestly didn't do it!" Max gestured wildly to Caspian, Leo, and Lawson, who were trying to remain as still and as inconspicuous as possible. Max turned pleading oceanic eyes to Ryker and Ivy saw his brown eyes soften as he pulled her to his chest once more;

"Okay, sweetheart, I'm sorry. I believe you. Any theories?" he then asked the room at large, walking Max over to sit down next to Ivy herself at the table.

Ivy wanted to move immediately but knew that would be rude and also draw attention to herself. She would usually stand against a wall, ensuring she was well out of any conversation. But everyone else had been standing, so she had sat down instead. She felt a warm weight press against her lower leg and knew the mottled pup must be leaning against her. She didn't bend down to scratch him outright but she did lift her foot to give him a solid rub on his rump near the base of his tail. She knew he loved that.

"I've got a couple," Lark volunteered in response to Ryker's question.

"Of course you do," Axel snorted, turning to the room, "Egg-head always knows something we don't."

Ivy felt herself bristling at Axel's words. She may still have concerns regarding Max's choice of a partner for her but she had felt herself softening towards to the earth paladin the more time she spent in his presence. And for some reason, she now took exception to Axel picking on the guy.

"Don't worry. Axel is just teasing. He doesn't mean any harm and Lark certainly won't take offence. They're as close as brothers," Max patted her hand as she spoke quietly.

"I'm not worried," Ivy responded, rather shortly. Had she been so obvious with her thoughts?

Max held up her hands, as if in surrender, "Of course not," she agreed. "And, no. Your thoughts weren't obvious," she said, in direct contradiction to her words.

Something had sure been obvious, Ivy thought, *unless Max could read my mind ...?* Which she couldn't, Ivy assured herself, because Ivy was not bound in her Order. But sure enough, Max was clearly correct regarding Axel and Lark because Lark merely grinned at his brother-in-arms;

"Aw, don't be jealous just because I can read books that have words and not just pictures ..."

Axel shook his head, "I've already told you – *Playboy* has articles too."

The room laughed once again and Ivy felt herself relax, reminding herself that this wasn't a typical Order. This was also a family.

"Children ... focus," Darius reprimanded, raising his eyebrows at Lark.

Lark nodded, turning to Caspian, "Did you happen to be talking about Max last night?"

Caspian frowned a little but nodded his head, "Yes. We

were talking about how grateful we were for the new home, the new garden ... the new friends," he added, smiling sweetly.

Lark nodded, "And did you happen to make any comment about being loyal to Max?"

The three visitors looked at each other, Caspian confirming, "We did."

"That's why then," Lark stated, as if it was obvious. "Although the new brand is clearly all about Max, given it's made up of Max's symbols for all seven domains, it's not the same as her Heraldry. Her coat of arms is a manifestation of her power and therefore all about her – the giver. In contrast, I believe the brand is a manifestation of loyalty and is thus, all about the recipient."

"So, I did it to myself?" Leo asked.

"Yes and no. Max's power must have brought it to fruition – unbeknownst to her," he quickly added before Max could interject. "But, I think if you're loyal and you're worthy ..." he trailed off.

Ryker started pacing, "Loyalty brand makes sense. We already figured that anyway. But, you're telling me Max doesn't have to personally give this brand to people? She doesn't even have to be around?"

Lark shrugged, "It's just a thought. But ... the proof's right here."

Ryker swore, "*Fuck!* So, people only have to think they are loyal and they could start popping ink?"

"No, I don't think it's as simple as that," Lark said quickly. "I think they have to mean it."

"Oh well then, as long as they mean it ..." Ryker groused and Ivy could tell he wasn't comforted in the least.

"You think I'm right?" Lark asked.

Ryker waved a negligent hand at him, "Of course you are. You're always right with stuff like this."

Ivy watched as Lark quickly ducked his head as if he were embarrassed by his Captain's words. She knew how much such absolute faith from your superior meant. It was just more evidence of how much all these people believed in the young paladin. Ivy felt her previous low opinion rising more and more with every little titbit she learned. *A good thing? Or a dangerous thing?* She wondered.

"So, paladins could be waking up all over the world with a new brand. That's not going to go over real well with their wardens," her brother commented, chewing on his lower lip.

"Or the council," Diana noted.

"No, it's not," Ryker's frown was dark as he finally stopped pacing. "I'm worried this is going to cement their opinions ..."

"Perhaps it's time we tested some of our fellow citizens?" Darius suggested, "We've all heard the rumblings, we all have our suspicions but I think it's time we were a little less subtle about determining what they are and where they're coming from."

"Less subtle?" Dex asked, his voice full of shock. "Who are you and what have you done with my brother?"

Darius flashed his older brother a droll look, "Funny. I'm serious. What if there *are* other wardens and paladins waking up out there with Max's unique domain symbols on their arm? This could very well start some serious in-fighting ..."

"What do you think we should do?" Ryker asked his second in command.

"We set a trap," Darius responded, decisively.

"Now you're talking my language. Let's trap the bastards! I hear bear traps are particularly effective and painful," Max crowed, rubbing her hands together. Zombie, who had still been sitting happily and quietly at Ivy's feet, joined in Max's jubilation, jumping around and barking happily.

Bloodthirsty little animal, she thought, liking the dog even more.

Darius shook his head but laughed, "Not a physical trap, you malicious little goddess. A mental one. We get them to expose themselves so they are forced into the open. Not only for us to see but for other wardens and paladins as well. We'll be able to identify our allies and our enemies in one fell swoop."

Ivy could have sworn Max was pouting at having her bear trap plans flushed down the toilet but a few moments of thought had her nodding her head, "Mind games. I like it," she finally decided.

"You think we should dangle Max's power in their faces? See how they react?" Dex asked, years of shared strategy making the brothers think alike.

Darius nodded, "Precisely."

"I'll do it. I love mind-fucking people," Axel volunteered.

"No. Not you," Ryker shook his head, "Lark."

"Lark? What? Why? Lark already has a secret mission!" Axel whined, "I wanna annoy arseholes until they snap like rubber bands!"

"We all know you're the master of irritating people, Axel," Ryker soothed the fire paladin. "But you're also known for your snark and your strength. You don't let anyone get away with shit."

"And I'm known for being weak, a pushover, and a victim," Lark stated.

Ivy eyed him, expecting to see resentment on his face but instead all she saw was calculation as a smile began to bloom upon his lips;

"And they say you're all brawn, Captain."

Ryker sniffed, "I have my moments."

"Fine," Axel pouted. "You look more like a squirrel than I do anyway. All that red hair," Axel pointed out.

"It's not red, it's auburn," Lark corrected, quickly.

"Whatever you say, Ed," was Axel's quick and obscure response – to Ivy at least.

Lark merely rolled his green eyes at the fire paladin and turned to Ryker; "You want me to head out now and start making some waves?"

Ryker nodded his agreement, "I think this is something we need to deal with immediately. I know you, Ivy, and Dex need to be moving out again very soon – as soon as possible. But this needs to be dealt with too. With three fewer soldiers in the house, we need to know what and who we're up against."

"It's cool. I'll check out the lodge first and if I don't have any luck, I'll hit Lonnie's," he said, naming the paladin-frequented bar where Ivy knew he'd had a violent encounter in the past.

"Let me get my scythe," Bey said, preparing to leave the room.

"What for?" Lark asked.

"So I can come with you, of course."

But Lark was already shaking his head, "You can't."

Beyden's lion-gold eyes narrowed, "You need back-up."

Uh oh, Ivy thought. Her brother was a soft-spoken man but he was loyal and protective down to his marrow. She recognised the hard line of his jaw for what it was; stubbornness.

"Seriously, Bey. You can't. The people we're trying to expose are bullies. They pick on the defenceless. I need to make them believe I'm vulnerable. If I bring six-foot-three of hulking muscle with me, no-one is ever going to make a move."

Beyden merely crossed his beefy arms over his chest.

"He's right, Beyden. He needs to be flying solo for this to work," their Captain chimed in.

"I don't like it," her brother was still stubborn and she could see he was genuinely worried for his friend. Before she could even think about the consequences, she opened her mouth;

"I'll go with him." All eyes turned to her and she made sure to keep her face blank. The looks of surprise on the various faces had her wanting to sink into the floor.

Lark cleared his throat, breaking the awkward silence, "Not that I don't appreciate the offer but your presence would be worse than Beyden's. You're our law enforcement. Nobody's going to pick on me with you around."

Ivy kept her mouth shut this time and let someone else fill in the silence;

"We'll go," Caspian spoke. "Nobody will think twice of me being there and they certainly won't worry about insulting me or others in my presence," he added, sardonically.

Ryker blew out a breath and Ivy realised he was just as concerned for his paladin's safety as her brother had been for his friend, "That would be perfect. Thank you, my Lord," he said, formally.

Caspian smiled, "It's the least we can do. Why don't you give us a bit of a head start?" he asked Lark. "No point being obvious about it ..."

"Good idea. I'll go shower real quick and get changed. That should give you guys enough time to already be there, acting all casual-like," Lark offered to Caspian and his knights, who nodded. He then began to leave the room but stopped briefly in front of her, "Thank you," he said softly, his eyes smiling and sparkling under his shaggy mop of hair.

Ivy felt her heart give a giddy leap and she questioned herself once again; *A good thing? Or a dangerous thing?*

SIXTEEN

He tried the Lodge first. Given it was a Sunday, there was nothing formal going on but many paladins still hung out in the large recreation room. Especially the trainees and the unbound paladins. It was also a popular place for wardens and the local council, given it was the council meeting place as well. Leaning over, he sighed a little as he stowed his scythe under the seat. Rules were rules and there were no weapons allowed in the common areas of the training centre. It was something even the most rebellious paladins adhered to; Ryker's rules were not to be messed with. Although, he knew Max took her tanto sword everywhere. Some habits were hard to break.

Catching his reflection in the mirror, he forced himself to wipe the subconscious smile from his lips and dim the sparkle of warmth in his eyes. He was still feeling all glowy-like from Ivy's offer to watch his back. The look on her face when all eyes turned to her was priceless. Oh, he knew most people wouldn't have noticed but he had her number now. He was confident the woman had had a whole bunch of: *what the hell did I just say?* rolling around in her thick skull. She may have regretted it as soon as the words had left her pretty mouth. But the automatic offer spoke volumes to him. He now found himself eager to set out with the lovely, pixie-faced ranger so he could see what else he could coax out of her. But first; work.

One glance was all it took to satisfy him that he would not have to make another stop. The training lodge was filled with no less than fifteen people and he was glad to see there was a good mixture of pleasant and *unpleasant* individuals present. Some he knew had been outspoken against Max in the past and had apparently changed their tunes since her Custodian status had been proven and accepted by the IDC. Some had been kind and supportive all along, and there was a good number of pricks who he already knew had issues with Max. In fact, his job was going to be easier than he anticipated because he could make out a familiar broad back by the pool tables.

Ignoring him for the moment, he made his way around the room, stopping to nod respectfully to the few members present from the Local Warden Council, including Lake, Hades, Ray, and Fawn. He knew Lake and Hades had been less than polite to Max at their first meeting and their attitudes had scarcely improved since then. Although, Lake really was just a glory chaser, he also thrived on gossip and Lark's initial instincts told him the man was a douche but hardly an evil mastermind. There was no secret where Fawn's support lay – she had always been kind to Max and she was a good friend of Beyden's. Lark trusted his friend's judgment implicitly. If Bey said the Beast Warden was cool, then she was cool. Ray, one of two fire wardens seated on the local council, was a soft-spoken, older man and had likewise always shown respect for Max. Lark was confident the man and his paladins would also prove to be allies.

He made a show of unlocking and stepping into the office so he could pretend he was there for something work-related rather than Max-related. He rearranged Ryker's desk draws, his pens, and even changed the password on the man's computer. Ry was very protective of his office. Unfortunately for him, Lark and his fellow paladins received great joy from constantly pranking the man. Lark made sure to set the password to: #AxelRulz! His fellow knight would get the blame and Lark will have killed two birds with one stone, so to speak.

Satisfied with his ten minutes worth of work, he stepped back into the common area. Catching the eye of Caspian, he nodded his hello and thanks for the back-up. Three sets of identical faces also drew his attention and he waved at Kai, Kellan, and Kane. The three air paladins waved back and Lark decided to go and talk to them as he waited for his presence to have the desired effect. He really liked the three men. They were a little older than him at seventy-five and had been very young men during the Great Massacre fifty years ago. He knew they were the current Lotharios of their society but Lark knew most of the tales were likely just that – tales. *Nobody could make their way through that many women, could they?* Although, if you divided the number by three, it was more realistic ...

"On your own today, boy?"

Lark came to an abrupt halt and gritted his teeth at the tone as much as the content of the question. This was why Lark knew it wouldn't be hard to stir things up; Carlos was here. The fire paladin was directly associated with one of the most powerful and respected families in their society. The family he was referring to had always been a bag of arseholes but they had certainly upped their game since Max came on the scene. Cinder was the family matriarch and a member of the IDC. Her daughter, Magda, was the head of the local council. And her grandson, Ignatius, had recently gone off the reservation and had been given chade-status. Regardless of the fact that Max had assured everyone Ignatius was not turning into a chade and was 'merely' a sociopath. But the council did not recognise mental illness and had imprisoned the fire warden in one of the chade encampments.

Months ago, Ignatius had taken it upon himself to try to kill Caspian and his two paladins because of who they loved. Homosexual relationships were likewise not recognised in their narrow-minded society. But Max and his own Order had stepped in and they had all barely made it out with their lives. Ignatius had abused his powers over his domain and had turned the element into something twisted. Darius had damn-near been fried alive and Max had turned into a cold, vengeful Goddess, rather than the warm, fun woman they had all grown accustomed to. If Diana hadn't been able to talk Max down, he was sure Ignatius and his paladins would have been nothing more than piles of goo on the ground.

And that's where Carlos came on the scene. His brother, Marco, had been the potentate of the Order of Vulcan and had likewise been sentenced to prison with his liege. Needless to say, Carlos now hated anything and everything to do with Max and her Order. Not that he didn't have issues with them all before – it seemed to be hereditary. Marco had always gained a perverse enjoyment in picking on Lark. Lark could only speculate it was because of his shitty reputation as a paladin – thanks to the failed trials. But then again, bullies rarely needed an excuse. In fact, it was Marco who had ordered his fellow knights to hold him still as he had used him as a punching bag when Max had first arrived.

Lark shook his head; *Yep, the whole bunch of them are arseholes.*

"What's the matter? No pithy comeback today? That lame excuse for an Order of yours always seems to have something ridiculous to say," Carlos griped, obviously not liking being ignored.

Lark saw the triplets frowning as they began to weave in and out of the crowd that was already gathering for the show. *Perfect,* Lark thought, *this is almost too easy.* He gave his helpers a small shake of his head, indicating they should stay back. Kane dipped his head minutely but his frown stayed firmly in place.

"Carlos," Lark began, jovially, "always such a pleasure. Tell me, what about my Order and my liege is ridiculous?"

Carlos scoffed, as did at least handful of other paladins, "You're kidding, right? Everyone knows the whole thing is a farce."

Lark allowed his features to morph into cluelessness, "A farce? I have no idea what you mean."

"Bullshit! You really think we all believe the most pathetic paladins in history are now a part of some special Order? You're all a bunch of rejects; no wardens, dead wardens ... take your pick!"

Lark didn't allow himself to react to the slight against Ryker's and Diana's deceased lieges. Instead, he answered calmly, wanting to appear to be the victim in the scenario; "We're not rejects anymore. Now, if you'll excuse me ..." Trying to step around Carlos was fruitless when the bigger man stepped in his path.

"No, I won't excuse you. Do you think we're all stupid? That the council is stupid? Your *liege* had better watch herself."

The tension in the room was steadily rising as Carlos began to show his true colours. Now to see how many others held the same beliefs; "Is that a threat?" he asked for clarification.

Carlos puffed out his chest, "You're damn right it is! You think I'm the only one who's suspicious? A woman shows up with all this power, insisting she's the daughter of a goddess, and just expects us all to blindly follow her?"

As calmly as possible, he responded; "Max is not some kind of mad usurper. She has no ulterior motive other than to help maintain the balance between the domains. She was simply lost and now she's been found. That is all, I assure you."

"Oh, well then. Because *you* assure us, that's fine then."

Carlos's sarcasm was not lost on him but Lark smiled innocuously nonetheless, "Excellent. I'm glad we got that all sorted." He made to walk around the idiotic paladin but a tight grip to his forearm halted his forward motion.

"You think you're safe now? You think that midget bitch is gonna protect you? Everyone knows what you are – a pathetic failure as a son and as a warrior. You're a miserable excuse for a male, let alone a knight," Carlos hissed, loud enough for the entire room to hear.

Lark took a deep breath, feeling his anger rise. It wasn't the slurs that bothered him – such defamations were old school to him. It was the way he spoke about his liege that had his blood boiling and his hand itching with the urge to uppercut the pig. But he was supposed to be a coward, so he merely locked eyes with the piece of shit in front of him, "Let go of me."

Carlos smirked, "Or what? Is the itty-bitty paladin gonna hit me?" he laughed.

Lark heard the accompanying snickers from other paladins in the room and raised his head to make eye contact with each and every person who deemed this scenario okay. Many immediately lowered their eyes, shifting uncomfortably, while others seemed to be thriving on the supressed violence. He was relieved to see at least a handful of people looking upset by the display – even if they were too chicken shit to stand up and put a stop to it. Caspian was watching him avidly and he saw a small pocket of who he assumed were supporters all congregated around the water warden; Fawn and her four paladins, the triplets, Ray and his three paladins, and two new trainees.

Lark dipped his head at the group, subtly asking them with his eyes not to move. To his surprise, Fawn nodded back, touching her upper left arm briefly. He didn't react outwardly but he knew what the pretty, golden Warden of the Beasts was telling him; she carried Max's loyalty brand.

"What's the matter, Larky-boy? Cat got your tongue?" Carlos taunted, eliciting another round of laughter.

Now Lark was seriously contemplating if it would be worth the ensuing chaos to wipe the self-satisfied smirk off Carlos's face. He had the information they needed; names and faces of over a dozen likely combatants, as well as some newly marked friends. He had just managed to talk himself out of it when he heard a voice in his head;

'You totally have my permission. I love chaos just as much as I hate smirkers.'

Lark grinned – his liege had decided to chime in.

'Break his nose. I wanna see some blood.'

The voice belonged to Cali and he chuckled silently; pregnancy was making her even more bloodthirsty than usual.

'No, go for the throat. I'm sick of hearing this guy talk,' Axel added his two cents.

'Pfft! The throat? The balls – go for the balls!'

Lark shuddered over Diana's recommendation; the females in his life were damn vicious.

"What the hell are you smiling at?" Carlos demanded, giving him a small shake.

"My Order seems to think you need to be taken down a peg," he felt satisfied when the arsehat in front of him paled a little, looking quickly around the room. The jerk may refer to them all as pathetic when they weren't around but everyone knew their team was a force to be reckoned with.

"Uh huh, nice try. I know you're here alone. And the Order link doesn't reach that far."

Well, he was finally right about one thing. The mental links within Orders were strong between wardens and their paladins over short distances only. It was never really a problem, given paladins were rarely far from their lieges. Those that did venture away from their wardens were from those Orders where the warden was very powerful. The greater the power, the stronger the link with their knights. Given he was a good forty kilometres away from his liege, Carlos was right in assuming the mental connection couldn't reach this far – if he was in a normal Order, that was. Unluckily for Carlos, Lark wasn't a part of a normal Order.

Deciding to fuck with the man in front of him a little, he made another attempt to free his arm as he spoke, "Maybe your inferior Order link doesn't reach that far but I assure you, my superior one does. And I gotta say, Carly, the females in the gang are rather unimpressed with you." Heat infused Carlos's cheeks as snickers now became directed at him.

"It's bullshit, man. Don't let the twerp get to you," Lance decided to join the party. He was in the same Order as Carlos.

'Twerp?' he questioned silently, *'Do you guys think I'm a twerp?'*

'Twerp is so eighties. I would have gone with nerd,' his very own Captain suggested, making him sputter his amusement via the link. Not many people knew Ryker actually had a wicked sense of humour. Most people just figured he was nothing but a stoic arsehole.

'You know I can still hear you right?' his Captain enquired, dryly.

'Stop wasting your time with them, Lark. We have a better idea of who is against Max and who might be behind

those rumours. Just get back here.' The voice of reason belonged to Darius.

He would be more than happy to but Carlos still had a hold of his arm, "Do you want a date or something?" he enquired, pleasantly.

Carlos looked confused, "What?"

"My arm," Lark clarified, "You've been holding it for at least five minutes now. Didn't know you swung that way dude."

Carlos snarled and practically flung Lark's arm back at him. "I ain't no filthy homo."

Lark narrowed his eyes now, "Watch your mouth, Carlos. It's going to get you into trouble just like your brother."

Carlos snarled at the reminder, "The perfect example of how dangerous that woman is," he said, turning to the room. "A well respected, noble paladin from an honourable family line ... now imprisoned like an animal thanks to that fake bitch Lark is harbouring."

Lark shook his head, Darius was right; he was wasting his time here. There was no talking to people like Carlos. Their minds were closed and no amount of logic would expand their beliefs. "Whatever, man. You will all bear witness to the truth in time," he spoke softly but knew his voice could be heard in the tense stillness of the room.

When no-one said anything, he just sighed and turned to walk away. When Carlos began talking again, he had every intention to keep walking. But as Carlos's vile words registered, he felt an unnatural stillness and rage building over the calm veneer he had honed over the years. He was across the room and on top of Carlos in less than a second. A swift right hook to the jaw floored the man and Lark had Carlos's arms pulled high behind his back as he pushed all his weight into the back of his neck, smashing his face into the floorboards;

"You just made a very big mistake. You think I'm a twerp huh? A miserable excuse for a soldier who let his father down by failing the Paladin Trials? Let me enlighten you; I flunked that test on purpose, you fucker," he hissed the words into Carlos's ear as he thrashed ineffectively in his steely hold, "Newsflash; I let your brother and his goons beat me up that time *on purpose*. Everything I do is deliberate and calculated. You know why?" Lark pulled roughly at the hair at the man's nape, ensuring he had his full attention, "Because if I don't think before I act, everyone gets dead. I was trained by the best – and the worst. I was my father's best student. Do you know what that means, arsehole? It means I can hurt you in ways you've never dreamed of. When I stop thinking, I make Max look like a fucking kitten. Don't threaten my family again, or I'm going to introduce you to Isaac's son."

He released the hair he was holding, gaining immense pleasure when Carlos's nose made harsh contact with the floor. He stood up, dusting off his hands, glaring coldly at the stunned occupants in the room. *Cowardly bastards,* Lark thought.

Lark could still feel his temper seething as members of Carlos's Order rushed to help the jackass to his feet. Looking down he found his fists still tightly clenched, wishing for nothing more than to slam them repeatedly into Carlos's face. Making eye contact with Caspian across the room, the warden gave a small shake of his head. Taking a deep breath, Lark forced his tense muscles to relax. He nodded to Caspian, acknowledging his superiority and also thanking him as well. Caspian was right – now was not the time and he had well and truly achieved what they had set out to do. Time to leave before he killed the fucker.

SEVENTEEN

Lark seethed all the way back to camp and he fought the instincts that were pushing him to turn around and permanently remove the threat to his family. But he continued on, finally coming out of his rage long enough to notice that the closer he got to camp, the darker the sky became. It was close to dark – despite the midday hour – when he pulled to a stop in the driveway. Stepping out of the car, he realised the shadowy veil was the result of a swirling sail of wind high above the house.

What the hell? he thought, staring in cautious wonder at the spectacle of the wind rushing feverishly some one hundred metres above his head. Looking around, he saw the ground and the trees were completely untouched by the fury of the air above it. It was almost like a reverse tornado.

"Well, this is new, even for Max," he commented to himself.

'It's not me,' was the quick rebuttal in his head.

'No? Then what?' he asked, only to catch on in the same breath, *'Dex. This is Dex,'* he stated, cursing himself even as

he bolted to the house.

How could he have been so stupid? Dex may not be in their Order and therefore unable to hear his thoughts, but his brother was and so was his fiancé. They would have divulged Carlos's hateful words the moment they left his lips. He hadn't thought to censor the link when he had been reading Carlos the riot act because he hadn't been thinking at all. All he had seen was red. And that was precisely why he always strived to keep his shit together. He hadn't just been blowing hot air back at the lodge – he was damn lethal.

Opening the back door and racing into the kitchen, he saw that the entire household was occupying the space ... and so was one pissed off ex-warden in full-on chade mode. The black in Dex's eyes had completely swallowed his irises and they were now bottomless pits of rage and anguish. His feet were hovering off the ground and Lark knew the spectacle outside was a direct reflection of the man's inner turmoil. Searching the room, he quickly found Ivy in her usual casual pose against the wall. He was surprised to see the woman was weaponless. He would have thought the ranger would have grabbed her sickle at the first sign of any chade-like behaviour.

Sensing his scrutiny, she gave him a nod of acknowledgment. Feeling happy inside from that small token, despite the circumstances, he nodded back – adding in a small smile as a bonus. Moving cautiously closer to the action, he spoke; "Hi team. How's it going?" His forced casualness worked for the most part, with the majority of his family looking in his direction.

"Oh, it's just peachy here, man. Good job acting as bait-boy."

Axel may have sounded flippant, but Lark knew he was anything but. There was a cold rage shimmering in the depths of his blue eyes. Looking around, he saw almost identical looks everywhere – except Cali's. Hers just looked scared and worried.

"Calm down, Dex. Don't make me kick your arse," Ryker threatened. But they all knew it was an empty threat. Ryker was just as pissed as everyone else.

As for Dex, he merely snarled and flexed hands tipped with nails which looked alarmingly like claws. After seeing Dex in action when they had retrieved Knox, Lark knew and accepted that Dex still retained some of the more peculiar traits of the chades. But seeing him now, had him worried that maybe his new friend was regressing.

"Dex ... please," was all Cali said from where she was wrapped securely in her brother-in-law's arms.

Dex seemed to soften when he looked at Cali but then he yelled; "He threatened our baby!" The words were practically roared out and although they vibrated with fury, they were also laced with fear.

Yes, Lark agreed silently, *and in a spectacular fashion.* It was why he had lost control of himself and revealed some of his true strength to all the gawkers back at the lodge. Thinking about the hateful words made him want to gut the son of a bitch;

"You think we don't know about the abomination that whore of a paladin you live with is carrying? She'd best be careful, someone might do the world a favour and cut the little monster out."

"I know he did," Cali swallowed audibly, cradling her distinct baby bump with both hands. "But he won't hurt our son – nobody will. Right?" she asked Max.

Surprisingly, Max was the only person in the room who didn't look furious. She responded to Cali calmly but with confidence, "That's right. Nobody."

Lark felt the tension in the room drop by a few degrees. Max's voice had resonated not just with determination but also with power. He felt his coat of arms heat on his skin and although it wasn't moving, he saw his druid symbol flare to life with light.

Max moved around Ryker and Diana, who were partially blocking her from Dex. She simply walked up to the angry man and placed a hand on his forearm; "Dex ... calm," was all she said. But he deflated as if he were a balloon and Max had stuck a pin in him.

The lashing wind immediately ceased, Dex's feet hit the floor, his eyes immediately lightened to their now dark hazel hue. He didn't say anything to the custodian who had restored his light. He just walked to Cali and swept her into his arms. She buried her face in his neck and Lark felt a lump form in his throat; the two were perfect for each other. Dex had saved Cali just as much as she had saved him. And the life they had created was a true miracle. There was no other explanation for the little guy other than a greater power being involved as far as he was concerned. Looking around and seeing all the shiny eyes and clenched fists, he knew each and every person in the room would fight to the death to protect their little nephew.

"I would never let anyone hurt Hitch, Dex. I promise you," Max repeated her words again and they were once more filled with power.

Dex took a deep breath, sitting down with Cali held firmly in his lap, "I know, Max. Thank you." He looked around, a little sheepishly, "Ah, sorry about all that ..."

"All what?" Ryker asked, patting the man on the back as he took his own seat at the table.

Dex smiled and Lark heard Cali give a happy little giggle before she finally raised her head. Her eyes were a little red but she looked relaxed once more as she proceeded to kiss the breath out of her fiancé.

Darius cleared his throat, looking pointedly away from

the make-out session involving his brother, "Yes, well. How about we discuss what Lark kicked over?"

"I'd say we have confirmation about who the instigators and perpetuators are," Lark volunteered, going to the fridge for a bottle of water. Emotional drama always left him thirsty. "Carlos and his Order – very likely his Warden, although Victoria wasn't there; Hades and his paladins; the two paladins from the Order of Aquarius; three unbound paladins; and definitely Violet and her Order, although she didn't say anything. The look on her face said it all. In fact, I'm pretty sure she and Carlos are lovers," he added. He had seen the look in the earth warden's eyes when Carlos started talking – pride and lust.

"That's over a dozen, just in the one room," Axel pointed out.

"I don't understand what I've done wrong. Why don't they like me?" Max asked, sounding like the vulnerable, sick young woman they had all met eight months ago instead of the powerful, strong goddess they had grown accustomed to.

"It's not about you. It's about their own insecurities. Get over yourself," Ivy said in a bored tone.

Ryker, Axel, and Cali scowled at the ranger, while Beyden just rolled his eyes.

Max huffed at Ivy, "*You* get over *yourself*! Insensitive cow."

Max's words sounded a little pouty but she was smiling, all evidence of sadness and vulnerability gone and Lark knew Ivy had handled the situation perfectly – even if most of the others couldn't see it. Comfort would have reinforced Max's insecurities; facts grounded her in reality.

Lark cleared his throat, "Ivy's right. Their opinions have nothing to do with you personally. They're scared and easily manipulated. It's the perfect combination for a mob."

"Dangerous," said Ivy, nodding her head at him.

"Very," he confirmed, knowing they were on the same page.

"But there was also as many supporters," Beyden pointed out, optimistically. "And some we didn't know about. Those two new trainees for starters ..."

"And Lake," Lark told them.

"Lake? You sure?" Ryker asked, looking unconvinced.

Lark nodded, "I'm positive. He was revelling in the situation a little because he can't help but thrive on drama. And he didn't step up and put a stop to it but his frown was definitely directed at Carlos – not me."

"That's good, I guess. We need more wardens on our side," Darius muttered, looking thoughtful. "Did I see Fawn hint at you about a brand maybe?"

Lark nodded, "Definitely. Her paladins too."

"We'll need to talk to them all eventually," Dex pointed out. "But first, why does that Carlos guy have such a hard-on for you?"

Lark snorted out a laugh, "His brother hates me. Now that he's in prison, I guess Carlos feels like it's his duty to carry on the tradition."

"Prison?" Dex's wheels were obviously turning as he looked at Darius, "His brother is from the Order who almost killed you?" Dex demanded.

Darius nodded, "That's him – great family. Though to be fair, he was aiming for Max."

"Not funny. It's not funny, Darius," Dex scolded, "I can't believe you've finally decided to get a sense of humour. It's decidedly warped."

"It's the company he keeps," Max smiled warmly at her Order.

EIGHTEEN

Ivy felt the last of the tension drop from the occupants in the room as they continued to discuss the success of Lark's little mission. She listened with half an ear as she thought back over the past hour or so. She hadn't been privy to Carlos's words firsthand but Beyden had filled her in when Dex had started to go ballistic. Her automatic reaction had been to grab her sickle from next to the back door. But then she had thought about everything she knew and weighed up the situation subjectively – rather than objectively. Even though it went against all of her training. She could never be subjective out in the field. But right now? After spending so much time with the motley crew? She knew Dex would never harm any one of them. And if someone had dared to threaten her child? Well, there would be no safe place in all the worlds for them to hide.

So, she had stayed casually by the wall and let Dex rage. The power the man controlled with his combined warden-chade skillset was phenomenal. Nothing to equal Max of course but she knew Dex had been one of the most powerful wardens before he had gone off the reservation. He'd had twelve paladins – twelve! The number was unheard of. In fact, Max now had the largest Order with her seven knights. She idly wondered what had happened to his other paladins ...

"Ivy?"

She jolted, "I'm sorry, what?"

"I asked if you're okay to head off tomorrow? Lark is back to full health and my kiddies have the answers they need to fortify this place and start bringing in the good guys for some frank conversations," Max explained.

Ivy just nodded, "Fine by me."

"Great. Dex –"

"I'm not going."

Silence met his harsh interruption and Ivy watched Dex clench his jaw so hard she wouldn't be surprised to hear his teeth crack.

"Dex –" Max began again but the irate man was already shaking his head;

"I'm sorry, Max. I know how important the mission is and I know I'm yours to command but I –"

"Dex! Will you shut up for one damn minute?!" Max finally yelled, interrupting his tirade. He snapped his jaw shut. "Thank you. Now ..." Max continued, "of course you're not going. Your place is here with Cali and your baby."

Dex stared at her for a moment before croaking, "Huh?"

Max huffed, the noise sounding ill-tempered, "Do you really think I would ask you to leave Cali when there was a threat to her and your son?"

Dex looked half dumbfounded, half contrite, as he stuttered, "Well, I ..."

Cali smiled sweetly at her fiancé, wrapping her arms around him. Ivy saw her mouth the words, *thank you*, to her liege and Max's dipped head of acknowledgment in return.

"So, what now? Ivy and Lark can't go on their own. Not only is it too dangerous but how will they identify the chades they need to?" Beyden voiced the question Ivy herself had been thinking.

"Two of you can accompany them and –"

"No, Max," Ryker interrupted. "I'm sorry but after what Lark discovered today, there's no way I'm willing to lose more of your protection. I don't even want to spare Lark and Ivy. The threat to you is very real, Max."

Max sighed and instead of getting annoyed or pushing the issue like Ivy expected her to do, she crossed the room to stand in front of Ryker instead, placing her palms on both his cheeks;

"I know it is, babe. And that's why we need to bring these wardens home," her voice was soft and as serious as Ivy had ever heard. But the woman quickly ruined the moment by adding; "I need my squirrels."

The room seemed to relax with the exhalation of quiet laughter from its occupants. The moment of levity lasted about two seconds because a new voice spoke, startling everyone;

"I'll go."

Everyone spun at the same time, facing the intruder in the doorway. Max and Cali were firmly pushed behind a half a dozen paladin bodies and the sound of scythes singing from their harnesses was sharp in the air. Ivy had to give the guy credit, Knox didn't even bat an eyelash at all the lethal steel pointed in his direction. He just stood silently and waited for a response.

Ivy had to admit, the ex-chade looked like a whole new man. He was still lean but his six-foot-one frame had bulked out nicely and he was now carrying a decent amount of muscle mass – his previously emaciated appearance nothing but a memory. His hair was still black but Diana had given him a very nice haircut and the healthy-looking strands were now cropped close to his skull. His skin was also still pale but it flushed with healthy colour with his changing moods. He had sharp cheekbones, a straight nose, and square jawline. Even his eyes were no longer black. Although they were still a dark shade of grey, making her wonder if his original eye colour had been grey or perhaps blue. There was one thing she couldn't deny; the man was very good looking.

She couldn't believe that sexily shadowed, chiselled jaw was the same one which had unhinged grotesquely, ready to kill, just weeks ago. He was like a whole new person and she realised Dex must have undergone the exact same transformation to get to where he was today as well. She hadn't been here to personally witness the before and after that was Dex, only the end result. Seeing Knox's redemption served to strengthen Ivy's belief in Max. Knowing that, and realising Knox was the only way they were going to help others like him, she stepped forward and spoke up;

"He's right – he should come."

She knew her words surprised the majority of the group if their incredulous expressions were anything to go by. The only people who didn't seem shocked were Max and Lark. The reason behind Max's acceptance was easy; the darn woman knew every bloody thing. But Ivy couldn't help but wonder why Lark didn't seem bothered by her support of the chade. But then again, she had stupidly bared her soul to the guy, hadn't she? Maybe he thought she had a soft spot for all chades now. That certainly wasn't the case. Yes, she wanted to save any who could be saved. But she had no problem putting down any others who were solely bent on maiming and killing.

Ryker shook his head, "No way! No offence, man. But I don't know you. Not from before and not now. I'm not comfortable saddling my team – my *family* – with an unknown."

Ivy blinked at that; surely he was just referring to Lark? No way was Ryker including her as family. But his small nod in her direction seemed to belie her automatic thought. Instead of feeling uncomfortable by his inclusion, she felt ... grateful. As for Knox – he didn't say anything. In fact, Ivy was pretty sure those were the first two words he had uttered since coming back from the brink.

"I'm with Ivy," Lark said into the silence of the room. Ryker opened his mouth to speak but Lark held up his hand. And strangely enough, Ryker closed his mouth and let Lark speak. He turned to his liege; "Max? What do you think? Is Knox completely healed?"

Max smiled in the ex-chades direction and Ivy saw him blush a little. Yep, seems no person was immune to the charms of the turquoise-eyed custodian. "His murderous tendencies have resolved, he can recharge normally, and he's sporting some cool new ink. He's as healed as anyone can expect him to be," she vouched.

Ivy thought Max's last sentence was a bit off but she couldn't put her finger on why. The important thing was that Max trusted Knox and as strange as it sounded, Ivy did too. The small pockets of time she had spent with the man, had showed her a man with true grit. He was much further gone than Dex had been and yet here he stood. She wondered what kind of motivation he must have to have held on to his tiny piece of soul for so long.

"Max ..." Ryker sounded aggrieved but also resigned.

"Ryker ..." Max mimicked, "Knox is good to go. He can sense chades the same way Dex can. He'll be able to communicate with them to the same extent. He's also the guardian of Air and will be able to travel swiftly in that form and cover long distances if needed. He'll take the other car, so the chades can be transported back when they are found.

157

And Ivy and Lark can move on to the next location in the meantime."

Ryker looked to the other members of his Order and one by one they all nodded. Ryker sighed, "Fine. You sure you're okay with this? You two are going to have to provide Knox with vitality when you're on the road."

Lark shrugged in response to Ryker's question, "Won't bother me. Ivy?"

She kept her face blank, "Whatever. What's one more chade-warden hybrid?"

"Fine then – sold," Ryker stated, seeming to gain a measure of satisfaction from her grumpy response. He walked over to Knox and held out his arm, "Thank you. You all look after each other out there and we won't have a problem."

Knox eyed the outstretched arm for a moment before he clasped it in a traditional warrior's grip, "I'll look after them," he promised.

Before Ivy could assure the man she could look after herself, he was gone as quickly as he had arrived.

NINETEEN

Silence reigned for a few minutes, everyone lost in their own thoughts – including Ivy. Presently though, Axel spoke;

"Looks like we're all sorted – except for one small detail ..."

"And what's that?" Max asked.

"What are we going to do with all of these new chadey-wardens while they're healing and becoming reaccustomed to the land of the living?" Axel asked. "I mean, we're going to need paladins for a start. And don't volunteer us, Max. We're already in an Order – your Order. We will obey your wishes if you command us to serve others but our priority and our duty is to you. We can't be spread thin by sharing vitality with a bunch of recovering chades."

Max shook her head, "I'm not going to ask you to share your vitality with them, let alone command it. I've already considered the dilemma and have a solution."

"Oh, really? Who?" Beyden asked.

"Well ..." Max began slowly, "there are three of them and their names all start with K."

Ryker's reaction was loud and very negative, "No. Hell no!"

As was Darius's; "I do not believe that will be necessary."

The reactions from the other two females in the room were quite different, however; "Hells to the yes," Cali crowed. "They would be perfect."

Diana's grin was huge as she chimed in, "I agree. Kane, Kai, and Kellan are more than ... *fit* for the job."

Darius crossed his arms over his chest in what Ivy had come to recognise as 'serious Darius', "I know that look, Diana. You aren't going anywhere near those three playboys."

Diana raised her eyebrows and widened her eyes – the very epitome of innocence. Ivy had to suppress her smirk of approval, she knew as well as the rest of the men that the females in their group were many things, but innocent wasn't one of them. The curly-haired beauty was gearing up to fuck with her man.

"What look?" Diana asked, voice dripping with virtue.

"Don't give me that. Those three revel in tormenting me about you – and vice versa! I think it's time you told me just how well you know those idiots."

Darius's tone was all 'master of the manor' and Ivy winced, no way would any self-respecting, independent woman put up with that tone. Even as she watched, Axel, Beyden, Dex, and Lark were edging their way backwards. The only male stupid enough to stay in the line of fire was Ryker. And that was clearly because he thought Darius was in the right. No doubt he was threatened by the undeniably delicious identical specimens of manhood as well.

"Oh, you do, do you? Don't narrow those hazel eyes at me, mister," Diana quickly reprimanded, seeing her man's changing expression. "I didn't enter a convent any more than you entered a monastery in the years it took you to pull your finger out of your arse and finally touch me. I had me some sex – sometimes good sex, sometimes bad sex – so sue me. Besides," she huffed, "you're in no position to talk. I know you slept with Eboni."

"What?" Darius sputtered, eyes positively bugging out of his head.

Diana waggled her finger at her lover, "That's right. Eboni with the boobs made from the finest of silicon and the Venus flytrap masquerading as a vagina! I'm surprised your dick didn't get frostbite after sticking it into that ice queen."

"I – I – I ..."

Darius's stuttering was pathetic and Ivy somehow found herself standing in solidarity with the women. How she had migrated across the room to be standing in line with Cali, Max, and Diana, she wasn't sure. But by the nervous looks on the men's faces, she was pretty sure they made a formidable-looking team.

"You, you, you ... what?" Diana asked, archly.

Darius frantically looked for help but received none. No-one was stupid enough – even Ryker. But Zombie chose that moment to enter the room. He stilled, cocking his head to the side and then padded his way over to Darius, sitting loyally at his feet. Ivy knew Darius had been the one to rescue the abandoned dog and no doubt Zombie remembered too. It seemed feminine pride was no match for two sets of puppy-dog eyes – Zombie's and Darius's included – because Diana huffed out a breath;

"Fine, fine. You two look pathetic. I'm sorry for teasing you but you dug your own hole with your assumptions," Diana wagged a finger at her man.

Darius was looking relieved and he patted Zombie enthusiastically in thanks, sending the dog's back leg kicking in ecstasy. "Wait? Assumptions?" Darius abruptly asked, finally computing Diana's words.

The woman smiled, twirling a strand of curly hair around her fingertip, "I said I had me some sex over the years. I did not, however, say I had sex with any of the triplets."

"What? But you – they –"

"Were fucking with you, sweetie," Diana pinched his cheek, grinning at the look of incomprehension on his face.

"What did all of us girls agree on the first week you met me?" Max asked, "We don't fuck our friends," she reminded them.

Darius's eyes rounded, "You knew? And you let me think she'd had some kind of triplet orgy?!" Darius yelled at Max.

Max didn't even bother containing her laughter, nor did the others – including Ryker – who now found the entire scene hilarious. "Oh, I knew. But you needed a little extra push ..." she trailed off, chuckling.

"If you think this changes anything, you think wrong," Darius informed Diana. "I'm still going to kill them – just for a different reason now."

"You'll do no such thing. They did you a favour. Who knows? If it weren't for their teasing, I could have been waiting another thousand years for you to make a move," Diana pointed out.

"So true, bro. That was just ridiculous," Dex added his two cents, earning a glare from his brother.

"No-one is hurting the brothers. And they will be helping us with the chades. They are loyal, honourable, and good fighters. What's more, they are unbound and have no liege. They are perfect for the job," Max informed the room at large, her firm voice leaving no room for argument. Although, Ryker gave it one last try;

"They're immature –" he began.

Max rolled her eyes at him, "They are not. You've told me how much you approve of them as paladins. You just don't like how pretty they are. Besides, they're harmless. They just have a high play-drive – like Zombie."

Hearing his name, the playful pup looked up from his toy bunny and gave a happy yip. He stood up and began chasing his own tail until he ran into the centre island. Max winced;

"Okay, perhaps not a ringing endorsement ... But it's decided. Full stop. I'll contact them later. Now, as to the other problem Axel raised – where to put them? I haven't figured that out yet," she admitted. "I know they can't stay here. If Ivy, Lark, and Knox are as successful as I hope they're going to be, there's going to be too many."

"They definitely can't stay here," Ryker confirmed, "But I know a place."

Max looked surprised, "You know a place? Really?"

Ryker pinched the bridge of his nose with his thumb and forefinger, "Must you look so surprised? I have good ideas sometimes."

Max shook her head, "I didn't mean it like. I –"

Ryker grinned, tweaking her on the nose, "Relax. I'm just exerting *my* play-drive."

Max grinned in appreciation, grabbing his tee shirt to pull him in for a deep kiss that had the ambient temperature in the room rising by a couple of degrees. A few weeks ago, Ivy would have rolled her eyes at the display in front of her. Now she just felt ... wistful. Unable to help herself, she sought out Lark. Eyes of sparkling green met hers and the zing she felt was almost physical in its intensity. *Trouble,* she told herself, *big trouble.* Perhaps he sensed her thoughts because a small crease formed between his eyes and he broke contact with her.

"Okay, you two, break it up. Ry, about this place ..." Lark prompted.

Ryker gave Max's arse one more decent squeeze before setting her free and facing the room, "Have you seen the old hotel behind the back of Dave's?"

Max looked positively horrified, "You mean the one that looks like the Overlook Hotel from *The Shining*?"

"It does not look like ... hmm, you know, it actually kinda does," Axel acknowledged.

"Anyway," Ryker cut in, loudly, "I think Dave would let us use it."

"Use it? I know these guys are used to living rough, but that hotel is completely abandoned, Ryker. Does it even have running water?" Max asked, still looking less than keen with the idea.

Ryker was frowning, "It's not abandoned. It still sometimes gets guests."

"What?" Max looked dismayed, "Guests? But what about *REDRUM* painted on the walls? Doesn't it turn the guests off?"

Lark laughed, the sound tickling something loose in Ivy's stomach.

"Funny," Ryker replied, looking amused despite himself.

"I'm not joking, Ry. Is it really still a functioning hotel?" Max asked.

Ryker nodded, "It is. The same way the bar is still a functioning bar despite its outward appearance."

"Yeah, the place looks like a dive from the outside – and from the inside too, to be fair," Beyden added. "But Dave runs a decent place. The drinks aren't half bad, even if his usual clientele is a little ... colourful. But it is super clean."

It was at that, Ivy acknowledged. Dave had a kind on unnatural obsession with glass polishing. She had frequented the establishment a few times over the years. She much preferred it to the other local watering hole; Lonnie's. There were too many paladins and wardens there for her liking.

"Question: if it's a working hotel, how are we going to hide dozens of pale stick-men there? They are going to be a little conspicuous for a while," Axel added.

Ryker shrugged, "It doesn't exactly get a lot of traffic. I'm sure Dave would close it down to the general public and allow us the use of it for the indefinite future."

Max was watching Ryker closely, "Why would he do that? And what is he going to think when his guests are a bunch of black haired, black eyed, phantoms?"

Ryker shifted, looking a little uncomfortable. "He knows all about chades. It won't be a problem."

Max's blue-green eyes narrowed, "He knows all about chades? How? And does that mean he knows about paladins and wardens too? I thought we were a secret to humans."

"We are – for the most part. Of course there are some slips here and there and a few humans have been trusted with the information," Darius rushed to assure her.

"And Dave is one of them?" Max looked sceptical and Ivy couldn't blame her.

"Kind of. I met him here, at his bar over thirty years ago. He had just opened and I was living at the Lodge. I had finally agreed to become a trainer at the behest of the council. They'd been bugging me for a long time after Flint and my Order was killed," Ryker explained.

"But Dave isn't that old," Max protested.

Ryker shared a look with his Order, "He's older than he looks."

Max gasped, "He's a paladin?"

It was Darius who shook his head, "No. But he is the son of one. His mother was a normal human. He's not ageing as slowly as a full paladin but it is more gradual than a full human."

"What? How come you never said anything before?" Max demanded.

"Don't go getting all sensitive, Max. It's his business, not our secret to tell," Cali said.

Max clenched her jaw for a minute before exhaling and nodding her head, "You're right. How do you know about him, then? Oh my god! Don't tell me he's your son!" Max gasped, pointing a finger at her lover.

"What?! No! Don't be ridiculous, woman. Your imagination ..." Ryker shook his head before continuing, "Some chades popped up outside the bar one day when I was leaving. I was a little, um, intoxicated ..."

"You were completely wasted, drowning your sorrows and being a major bastard, as per usual in those days," Diana jumped in.

"I'm telling the story," Ryker glared at Diana.

She held up her hands, "Whatever you say, boss."

His scowl remained in place, a direct contrast to the grin on most everyone else's, "Anyway, I'd decapitated two of them but a third caught me by surprise and I was flat on my back in the dirt when its head goes sailing off and it disintegrates into dust. I found myself staring up into the eyes of the hairy bar owner. To say I was surprised was an understatement."

"He could see the chades," Max said.

"Yeah. Anyway, we got to talking. He knew a little about who and what his father had been. Seems his father told his mother all about us. After putting in his twenty years in the military he came here, looking for his father. The man was already dead, unfortunately, but Dave decided to stay."

"That's why you hang out there instead of Lonnie's," Max stated and Ryker nodded before she tilted her head at him, "Did you tell him who I am?"

Ryker hesitated before nodding, "Yes. He knows."

Max slapped her hand hard on the tabletop, "That's why he was so protective when I met Nikolai that night! You told him to watch out for me, didn't you?"

But Ryker shook his head, "I didn't have to. He may not

be fully entrenched in our society but he is a soldier and he has his own code. He understands duty. It's in his blood."

Max crossed her arms over her chest and Ivy thought she may have been pouting a little, "You men and your duty."

Everyone ignored the sulking custodian, Dex turning to Ryker, "You really think he'll allow the chades to stay there? It sounds like the perfect solution."

"I do."

But Max hesitated, "I don't know, Ry. It's a risk."

"I trust him. He wouldn't betray our secret," Ryker promised.

Max waved an impatient hand, "Obviously. You would never entrust my safety to someone you didn't trust implicitly. That's not what I meant. It's a risk for him – dangerous. The chades won't be fully healed. Plus, if the council finds out or even the rangers, he could be in real trouble."

"We'll discuss it with him. But like I said; it's in his blood," he said as if that was all that mattered. And in essence, it was.

Being a paladin, a ranger, or a warden was a birthright. Their duty and sense of responsibility were like a compulsion within all of them. Even though Dave was only half paladin, Ivy had no doubt his sense of honour was just as deeply ingrained.

"Okay, we have a location and we have sources of vitality," Beyden stated, ignoring the twin grumbles from Ryker and Darius over the veiled mention of the triplets. "But what about monitoring them? We're going to need someone – multiple someones – to make sure they stay in line."

"Well, obviously we have Caspian, Leo and Lawson as well. With how strong Cas is, he'll be able to spank them if they need it. Leo and Lawson will ensure their liege's safety.

We also have Dex," she turned her eyes to the man in question, "It's closer to home, you'll be able to keep an eye on Cali easily enough and be back here every day. What do you say?"

Dex bowed his head in her direction, "I'm yours to command."

Max grinned, "Mm-mm-mm, just how I like my men."

"Behave devil-woman. If everyone's in agreement ...?" Ryker cast his eyes around the room, receiving unanimous nods. "Then we have a plan."

TWENTY

"How come you didn't go all executioner-ninja ranger on Dex when he went a little skitz yesterday?"

The voice of her companion had her turning to him, only to find his eyes on the road and both hands responsibly on the steering wheel. As she watched, his hands flexed a little and she couldn't help but wonder what they would feel like against her skin.

Dammit! Not even one day in and I'm already picturing us naked together! She really wanted to bash her head against the window but opted for a vocal response that would at least prove she was listening; "Executioner-ninja?"

He shrugged, "If the shoe fits ..."

"You know I don't slaughter everything I see, right?" she asked. Her voice was laced with sarcasm but she genuinely cared about his answer. Did he really only see her as a killer?

"I know that. After all, you haven't taken my head off yet," he teased her.

"We've only been on the road ten minutes. Don't get too comfortable," she informed him.

He chuckled, "Jokes, Ivy? Me likie. But you didn't answer my question."

How to answer without coming across as soft or revealing too much about herself. "He wasn't a threat," she finally answered.

He finally took his eyes off the road to look at her askance, "You're kidding, right? The man made an upside-down tornado and was floating off the ground like some he-witch!"

"Fine. Amendment: he wasn't a threat to me," she revised her response. He was silent for so long, she thought he was satisfied with her answer and she felt herself relax a little more into the seat.

"Is it really so hard for you to admit you like him? That you trust him?"

She tensed at his words and inquired quietly; "What?"

"I know, I know – badass ranger. But are you honestly saying that you haven't come to care for anyone in that house even a little over the past few weeks? And especially Dex. I mean, as a ranger I know you don't share your vitality as freely as us general paladins do. But I know that under the right circumstances, that sharing creates a certain bond – a relationship. You have a relationship with Dex whether you're willing to admit it or not."

His words annoyed her and she had to clench her teeth together to stop the immediate denial that sprang to her lips. But she knew it wouldn't do any good – the annoying pest would be able to see her lie. If she was being honest with herself, she knew she had bonded with Dex to a certain degree and she was headed in the same direction with Knox too. Lark was right; you couldn't share life-giving energy without a sense of trust – and even like. She liked Dex and she liked Knox. But she wasn't about to admit that to anyone, let alone someone she wanted to see her as hard, aloof, dangerous, and professional at all times. In the end, she admitted to the other reason she had allowed Dex to vent;

"I thought he was entitled to his temper tantrum. Someone threatened his baby. I would have done the same," she added.

He glanced at her, "You like babies?"

She glared at him now, insulted by the shock she heard in his voice, "Yes, I like babies. What's so strange about that?"

"I'm sorry. I just didn't picture you as the baby type ..." his voice trailed off.

"Well, you're wrong. I like babies just fine," she informed him, a little primly. And it was true. She had absolutely adored having a baby Beyden in the house. His amber orbs peering up at her with complete trust as he sucked on his bottle; his strong little grip on her fingers every time he grabbed them and dragged them to his mouth; and those pudgy little arms and legs that never seemed to stop moving. Hell, Beyden had the cutest little butt she had ever seen.

"I stand corrected," Lark soothed. "I bet Bey was a darn cute baby, huh?" he then asked as if he knew her thoughts were centred around her brother.

"He was," she confirmed.

"I can't wait to see what Cali and Dex's baby looks like. Poor little guy is going to be royally screwed though. All those overprotective aunts and uncles, including the daughter of Mother Nature?" he ended with a chuckle, the happy sound filling up the whole car.

Ivy only shrugged in response, her nerve endings tingling with warmth from the sound. Although, she wholeheartedly agreed with him. That little guy was going to be one of the most spoiled but also the luckiest baby in history. And she had a feeling Max was going to be the worst of the bunch. Thinking of Max had Ivy remembering their send-off.

Lark had received multiple kisses to the cheeks, slaps to

the back, and also the traditional man-hugs. Just before he had stepped into the vehicle Max had called him back. She had wrapped her arms around him and held him tight as she whispered into his ear. After listening intently, he had nodded sombrely and then kissed her square on the mouth. The action had brought a smile to his liege's lips and a growl to his Captain's.

As for herself, she had been pleasantly surprised and more than a little embarrassed when every member of the household had gripped her arm in the way of the knights and wished her well. Beyden had of course, hugged her right off the ground and she had hissed in his ear about it being demoralising for a ranger like her to have her baby brother picking her up so easily. He had merely laughed, given her a good shake, and sternly told her to 'not get killed' or she'd be in trouble. She had then opened her own door, only to be called back by Max as well.

Expecting to hear words of wisdom, or perhaps a glimpse into the future, the crazy red-head had instead looked into her eyes and said; *"Can I hold your sickle before you go?"* Ivy had shaken her head and responded with her customary one-word response; *"No."* But somehow, the playful exchange had meant a lot to her – though she couldn't figure out why.

"What did Max say to you when we left?" she asked, abruptly.

"I'm sorry, what?"

He sounded surprised by the question and Ivy couldn't blame him. Not being privy to her internal thought process, it would sound as if she was asking him something completely random. "Never mind," she muttered, feeling foolish.

"Hey, I don't mind. Anything to keep you talking. I like the sound of your voice," he added, aiming a charming smile in her direction. Before she could process the compliment, he continued, "It wasn't any great words of wisdom or anything. She was giving me dating advice."

The answer floored her, "Dating advice? Why would she be giving you dating advice?"

"Because I want to date," he answered, easily.

He wanted to date? Who? And where could she find the bitch? Her thoughts turned jealous and violent before she could stop herself and she felt her carefully erected brick wall beginning to crack. She was going to need to repair those cracks before the whole damn thing fell down around her ears and she was left with nothing to shield herself from the wiles of a baby-faced, green-eyed knight.

"Why would you want to date?" she asked, stiffly. "Just because there's something in the water at your house ..."

He barked out an appealing laugh, "I guess there is."

She turned to him, "And you're not worried?"

"Why would I be worried?"

"Other than the commitment-heebie-jeebies? You really think the council is accepting of all these relationships? How many rules do you think they are willing to let you all break before they take action?"

"Is that a warning, Ivy?" Lark's voice held a coldness she had never heard him use before and she frowned for a moment, wondering what had caused it. But then she realised how her words could be taken in the wrong context.

"No. It's not. I haven't heard any specific rumblings about all the love going on in the house. I was just suggesting ..."

"That the council are not as fine with the situation as we've come to believe?" Lark finished, his tone back to normal.

She nodded once, "Yes."

He was frowning now, "Do you think we need to worry about this as well as the issues associated with Max's appearance and power?"

She thought about it for a moment and finally shook her head, "No. I think you've got bigger fish to fry."

He was silent for a moment as if considering his words, "Are you really a fan of the council? Considering everything we're slowly piecing together, has your opinion changed?"

The territory was beginning to get a little dicey but she decided to answer anyway, "I am a fan – of some of them. The establishment of a governing body is critical for a functioning society. It provides structure and order – integral for citizens to feel safe and secure."

He looked at her from the corner of his eye, looking impressed, "You like politics, huh?"

She shrugged, saying nothing. But truth to be told – yes, she did. She enjoyed the intricacies of politics, as well as the law system. Perhaps in another life she would have aspired to be a lawyer. She was about to tell Lark that when she realised something – she was enjoying the conversation so much, she wanted to keep it going a little longer. Before she left, she was worried the atmosphere in the car would be tense and awkward and had prepared herself for an uncomfortable few weeks. But, turns out Lark's steady and unobtrusive presence was easy to talk to. In fact, she was pretty sure she had spoken more in the past twenty minutes than she had in the past month.

And therein lies the problem, she reminded herself. The guy was observant and perceptive enough at the best of times and yet here she was, providing him with insight into herself which she never allowed anyone to see. Relationships? Baby talk? Politics? It was getting too personal. And the worst thing? She was honestly enjoying herself. She had to shut down their budding dialogue before it was too late. Before she liked him even more than she already did.

"We need to head north for one hour and then turn inland. Nikolai said there have been some chade sightings in that area."

"Changing the subject?" he enquired,

"Didn't realise we were playing twenty questions," she snapped back.

He threw her a startled glance, "It's called conversation, Ivy. You know, getting to know each other."

"I know enough," she assured him, turning her head to look out the window. She heard him sigh, the sound full of disappointment but he didn't say anything and the rest of the trip was made in silence.

She found she missed his voice after the first five minutes.

TWENTY-ONE

They arrived at their first scheduled destination in a little over ninety minutes. The first twenty minutes had been very pleasant and Lark had enjoyed talking with Ivy. The woman was bright and calm and had a healthy sense of humour buried beneath the stoicism. He had been happy to realise she was passionate and stood up for what she believed in. And it was obvious she was quite well-read – another plus in her column. Too bad she was also as stubborn as the day was long.

As soon as they had developed an easy dialogue, she had shut the conversation down. He knew she didn't have a problem with him as a human being anymore but she still clearly *wanted* to have a problem with him. And that amounted to the same thing in his estimation because the end result was the same; Ivy acting like a cold, closed-off bitch.

The car door opening and closing interrupted his ruminations and he looked over to see Ivy throwing her dark green ranger cloak on. By the time he joined her at the front of the vehicle she had the hood pulled up, obscuring her features. The damn cloak may as well have been a suit of armour, for it achieved the same purpose. Another car door shut and booted feet made their way over to them. Knox nodded at him but didn't say anything as his dark grey eyes quickly scanned the wooded area they were in. Nikolai had told Ivy he had sent ranger units to this area three times in the past two months. For some reason, it seemed to be a popular location for chades. Although, Nikolai also reported the execution of all chades in the area the last time rangers were sent so Lark was unsure how many they would find.

"Knox?" he questioned.

Knox nodded, "Three."

That surprised Lark. Maybe this was going to be easier than he thought. "Are they on the Dark Side or do they follow the ways of the Jedi?" he asked, wondering if Knox even knew what *Star Wars* was.

Knox looked directly at him and smiled and Lark could have sworn Ivy drew in a sharp breath. Because she hadn't believed the guy could smile? Or because the man was undoubtedly good-looking? Even a straight guy like himself could recognise and appreciate male beauty when it slapped him in the face. Not that he appreciated Ivy doing the same right then.

"One Jedi, two Dark Side," was Knox's response.

"You sure?" Ivy asked.

Knox nodded and before Lark could even blink let alone connect with Max and the others to give them an update, Ivy had her sickle out and was striding to the trees. Sure enough, three chades appeared from the darkness of the leaves just as the air cooled and the earth rumbled beneath his feet. Swearing, he palmed his own weapon and ran for the chades who were already in a battle with Ivy. All three of them engaged her at once and Lark couldn't determine which one was redeemable. At that moment, he didn't even care. All he cared about was saving Ivy's butt so he could kick it later.

A well-placed kick from Ivy sent one chade flying to its back but there was still two against one. Even as he watched, he saw Ivy evade a swipe of sharp claws by mere millimetres. Throwing his scythe, he sent it tumbling end over end, hitting its target precisely. The clawed hand of the chade sliced off in one clean cut. Lark took a running dive, sliding under the chade's legs, picking up his scythe and decapitating it in three smooth motions. He remembered himself at the last moment and suppressed the dark glare he wanted to aim in Ivy's direction. She wasn't looking at him anyway, but at the two remaining chades – who appeared to be transfixed with Knox.

Knox was planted like a wall in front of Ivy and it seemed his appearance had cooled the other two down a little. One looked at him curiously, as if trying to puzzle him out. The other looked at him like it wanted to slice its fingernail across Knox's belly, open his intestines, and watch them spill across the ground. No guesses needed as to which one was the evil one. Ivy must have arrived at the same conclusion he did because she promptly cut the now-advancing chade off at the knees. The miserable creature went down hard but uttered no sound and didn't look as if it felt a thing. It continued to pull itself along in the direction of Knox – very *Dawn of the Dead* – and Ivy easily severed its head, causing a splash of putrid water to hit the ground. The chade had obviously once been a Water Warden.

The remaining chade hadn't moved in their direction but it wasn't looking particularly friendly now that its companions were dead. A quick flick of the wrist from Knox and the chade found himself immobilised by the same tornado shackles Dex had used.

Knowing the chade was secured, allowed Lark to feel the

emotions he had steadfastly cut off the moment the fight started. It was something his father had taught him and a rule he still adhered to; don't take emotions into a fight. And the feeling? *Rage.* Ivy had purposely put herself in danger. But before he could call her out on her behaviour, she turned to him with a look of arrogant expectation;

"Well, do you have Max on the line or what?"

Censoring his violent words, he closed his eyes and reached for the link; *'Max? We have one that Knox says is cool,'* he notified his liege, trying to sound casual and calm instead of pissed off and frustrated.

'Already? That's good news. Just the one?'

'There is now,' he said.

She didn't question him at all, just said; *'Okay. Take two. Everyone ready? I'm going to balance the power through all of you this time. Lark, you just think happy thoughts and focus the energy at the chade. Capiche?'*

Assent came from every member of his Order and Lark forced his body and mind to relax so he could focus on the important task at hand. Five minutes later, his butt was on the ground and his head was spinning but he was not unconscious and the chade was sitting a few feet in front of him with a look of awed peace on his face. Lark would consider it a success and light years better than last time. In fact, within only a few minutes he was back on his feet with nothing more than a niggling headache as he waved Knox and the new recruit off.

As soon as the taillights were out of sight, Lark wheeled on Ivy, allowing her to see his anger, "What the hell was that?"

"What was what?" she asked in that indifferent tone of hers. She didn't even bother to look at him, just continued to examine her sickle as if she had never seen it before.

"Don't give me that. You know what I'm talking about,"

he knew his voice was a couple of octaves deeper – anger did that to him. Ivy obviously picked up on that too if her next words were anything to go by.

"What are you so pissed about? Did you want to try talking to them or something? Knox said they couldn't be saved. Even Max agrees those types of chades need to be put down. I'm sorry if your do-gooder sensibilities were hurt."

He was incredulous, "You think I care about the chades you put down? You're an idiot! I care that you didn't wait for back-up. I care that you were reckless and put yourself in danger," he informed her, coolly.

She didn't even spare him a glance, "I was never in any danger. I've been doing this before you were even born."

He felt his hold on his control becoming wobbly as she blew off his concerns like they were nothing. He drew in a deep breath before speaking again; "I don't know how you work within your ranger units but that lone-wolf bullshit won't fly with me. We work as a team. If you can't or won't do that, we're wasting time."

"Really? You're going to lecture me about how to work within a unit? You've been in an Order for less than a year! You've had, what, one battle together?" her voice held an insulting amount of condescension.

"Experience doesn't override stupidity. And what you did was stupid," he growled at her, pulling her arm around so she would look at him. That damn cloak was still blocking her face and he yanked it back. Her dark brown eyes were narrowed in anger and colour was high on her cheeks.

She looked deadly and so beautiful it took his breath away.

Ivy yanked her arm free, scowl deepening, "Listen kid –" she began.

And that's what tore it for Lark. His famed control finally snapped and before he knew it he had Ivy pinned against the car behind her. Grabbing her hand, he forced it over his growing hardness, "Do I feel like a kid to you?"

He expected her to sucker punch him or at least push him away but the woman shocked him, cupping him firmly and causing him to stutter out a half curse, half groan. Ivy's dark eyes actually lightened as her pupils dilated and her breath began to come out in short bursts. Unable to stop his body's wild reaction to such a sensual display, he tangled his hands in her ponytail, forcing her head back and her neck to arch. He brought his mouth close to hers and felt their breaths mingle. But instead of slamming his lips against hers like he wanted to with every fibre of his being, he waited.

TWENTY-TWO

Ivy felt her breath stutter out when Lark's lips hovered tantalisingly close to hers. Anger, arousal and an ever-increasing affection raged within her and she fisted her hands in the material of his shirt, thinking to push him away. But her anger was drowning under the seductive feel of Lark's body against her own and she found herself gripping his shirt for purchase with her one free hand instead. Her other hand was more than occupied feeling the hefty weight of his package through his pants and she was helpless not to cup her palm over him, learning his size and shape.

More than a little impressed about what she was feeling and riding high on courage and lust, her fingers dived for Lark's zipper. Not wasting any time, she lowered the small metal tab and reached inside, gasping when she felt nothing but hot skin. Lark went commando and he had been absolutely right – he did *not* feel like a kid.

A guttural groan was her only warning as Lark slammed his warm, soft lips against hers and proceeded to lay siege to her mouth. Their tongues fought for dominance for a few heartbeats before he slowed the sensual dance, his mouth coaxing hers to follow his pace. She took advantage of the change in tempo to fill both her hands with him and give him a few solid strokes. His hard, heated flesh jerked in her grasp and she smiled against his lips, loving the feeling of feminine power that swept through her.

As focused on her task as she was, she jumped and let out an excited gasp when large hands abruptly engulfed hers, pinning them high above her head against the smooth metal of the car behind her. Loving the difference in their height, she came up onto her tiptoes so she could press her chest more firmly against his. He may be the shortest guy in the Order, but he was still a good six inches taller than her five-foot-five frame and she revelled in the feeling of being surrounded by him. She knew the moment those strong arms stopped surrounding her, she was going to kick herself for this act of weakness. She knew she would regret. But for now, for right now ... she was going to indulge.

She knew her earlier actions were reckless and dangerous and everything else Lark had said. It had been an act of defiance to prove to herself – and to him – that she was strong and capable and disciplined. Unfortunately, it had only served to prove the opposite. She had regretted her immature decision the moment the three chades converged on her simultaneously. Sure, she was good but taking on three chades on her own was like begging for an arse-kicking.

But Lark had swooped in, severing the chade's hand with a precision she could only be jealous of. Then watching his fast and nimble movements to slide under the chade and pop up behind him ...? Well, his hours of yoga had been more than evident. Her eyes had been spellbound by the display of masculine power and her body had been humming in appreciation and yearning ever since. Which was why, when Lark had pushed her against the car, her brain had shut down and her body had decided to take the wheel.

When a calloused hand skimmed over her bare stomach, she felt goosebumps break out over her skin and she squeezed her legs together to try to relieve the ache she felt between her thighs. Cold air helped to cool her heated skin a little as Lark exposed her flesh an inch at a time. He pushed her top up enough to reveal the practical black sports bra she was wearing but he soon had that pushed up and out of the way too. She moaned when he bit down none-too gently on one hard nipple, before quickly soothing it with a rasp of his talented tongue.

With one hand still holding her own hostage above her head, he trailed the other back down her waist as his mouth continued to play havoc with her sensitive nipples. When his hand reached the waistband of her pants, he didn't even hesitate, opening them and delving a hand into her underwear immediately. He groaned against her breasts and his hips thrust against her when he found her wet and needy.

"Please," Ivy wanted the word to be a demand but was fairly certain it sounded more like begging. Lark didn't seem to mind either way because he finally stopped teasing her mound, plunging a thick digit into her hungry depths. She moaned and pushed herself harder against him, seeking deeper contact, even as she tugged against the hold on his hand. He finally relented and she hissed in triumph when her hands found his hard length once more.

After that, all bets were off. There was no more seduction. No more teasing. No more power games. It was just a race to the finish line as they touched and caressed in time with each other. Feeling pressure begin to build in her womb, she managed to gasp one word, "*More*", and was rewarded with another finger stretching her wider. That was all it took to have stars exploding in front of her eyes as her body erupted into a series of small explosions that skirted that sweet edge of pleasure and pain.

She had just enough coherent thought to continue the stroking movement of her hand and recognise the faltering motions of his hips for what they were; impending release. She teased the opening on the broad head of his cock once, twice, and was rewarded by a guttural groan above her. Then they were both shuddering through their pleasure, their pulses wild, as they tried to catch their breath. The vast array of happy little lights was still dancing behind her eyelids when her brain decided to check back in. And the first thing she thought?

What the hell have I done?

TWENTY-THREE

"Well, this is it. Casa de Chade," Dave said as he opened the main doors to what could loosely be called a hotel.

Max squinted through half-closed eyes because she was a little afraid to look. But as it turned out, the place wasn't as much of a pit on the inside as it looked from the outside. She hadn't been joking when she said the building looked like the kind of place serial murderers went to find their next victims. From the front of Dave's pub one could be forgiven for not even noticing the large building at the back. Even at the back, the densely populated bushland obscured it somewhat and she had barely even given it a glance the first time she had been back here. Though to be fair, she was being attacked by chades at the time.

Looking around the reception area now, she was pleasantly surprised to see the large space was sparse but clean. It housed one sad looking desk, no computer, a surprisingly very green and healthy looking potted plant, and a washed-out green lounge that had seen better days.

"There are forty-one rooms – twenty on the first floor

and twenty-one here on the ground floor. One of those is the manager's quarters and has a living room, two bedrooms, and its own kitchen. There is a large dining area and also a professional chef's kitchen but it hasn't been used in years," Dave explained, walking them through the doors to the left of the desk.

Max was relieved to see the restaurant area was likewise clean and furnished with the bare necessities. It was obvious the place did not see a lot of traffic. She stayed next to her host as Diana, Cali, Dex, and Darius quickly checked out the large space for security risks and other such boring details. She started to space out the second Darius and Dex began talking about blind spots, locks, and man-hole covers. Turning to her companion, she asked;

"Are you sure you want to do this?"

"Don't insult me, woman," was the hairy man's gruff response.

Max felt herself smile and fall half in love with the taciturn man on the spot. He was gruff and borderline rude more than half the time but she knew now that he had been watching out for her best interests practically from the moment she had stepped her weary feet into his bar. In fact, as she continued to observe him now, a small piece of information revealed itself to her, direct from his thoughts to hers. She hadn't meant for it to happen – she rarely did. But such occurrences were happening more frequently and with greater ease now than ever before. It was something she wasn't really a fan of, considering the things she often discovered.

Take now for example, what she had just learned from Dave had her taking a few shaky steps backwards. Her feet tripped over themselves and she would have done a decidedly non-graceful face-plant if large, steady hands hadn't gripped her upper arms tightly.

"Okay?" the reticent man asked gruffly, quickly removing his hands.

"I ... you ..." she stuttered.

Dave frowned at her, that creepy mono-brow of his dipping low over his eyes, "What?"

But she could only continue to stare at him as things about their first encounter began to make more sense to her.

"Max, are you okay?" Diana asked her, gripping her by the elbow.

"It was you," she said, sure she was making sense to no-one but herself. "That day in your bar – the day I met Lark, Darius, and Axel. It was because of you. You rang Ryker and told him I was there!" her voice rose several octaves before the end of her sentence.

Dave's face went blank and he shrugged his shoulders. Max found herself turning to her paladins, who were now all congregated around her, "Did you know about this?"

Diana frowned, "No actually ..."

"Darius?" she questioned. Darius had been there that day. He would know.

He shifted uncomfortably from foot to foot for a moment but he did speak, "We were driving past on our way home from the Lodge when I felt a certain shift in the air. It wasn't really anything big but it was enough to catch my attention. We were already there checking the place out when Ryker sent us a message saying there could be some trouble at Dave's. We assumed chade or paladin trouble – that's why we stopped in any way. Dave always gives Ry a heads-up when mischief is afoot," he added, nodding his head in thanks at the other man.

"But when we arrived, we didn't see any disturbance, so we figured it was nothing. To be honest, to this day, I had no idea he was referring to you. I honestly assumed he was referring to real trouble. It didn't even click with me that it was about you – even when I saw you."

Max didn't need to look at Darius's see-through counterpart or use her other skills over the elements to determine he was telling the truth. She could tell by the look of contrition and chagrin on his face that he was ... and kicking himself that he hadn't put two and two together before now.

"Dave, man. Is Max why you called Ry that day?" he addressed the bar-owner directly.

The man in question gave a mix between a nod and a shrug like it was no big deal.

"Damn," Darius exclaimed. "Why didn't you ever say anything?"

"Thought it was obvious," Dave grumbled, causing Cali, Diana, and Dex to laugh.

"Wow," Cali breathed. "Thank you so much."

Dave shrugged bulky shoulders again, "No big deal. Been keeping an eye on unusual things for Ryker for years."

"And I was unusual?" Max asked, finally getting her swirling thoughts back into order.

Dave huffed, "Darlin', you're about as unusual as they come. I might not be one of you magical folk, but I know special when I see it."

That had her mouth closing and her frenzied thoughts quieting, "Special?" Was it only her imagination or was the big, hairy man blushing?

"You heard me," he grunted.

Max felt a slow smile bloom on her face and the other half of the love she had been holding onto joined its counterpart. She was a little concerned that she was now emotionally invested with yet another gruff, testosterone-filled soldier but she wouldn't change a thing about her new life. That was despite the overprotectiveness of her new family, who were now pushing her behind them because the rear doors were opening. She could have told them not to bother – it was only their invited guests – but she knew it would be a waste of breath.

The wall of human flesh relaxed somewhat when they recognised the three faces that stepped into the room. Well, if she was being accurate, it was only the one face. But there were definitely three different bodies. Three very fine, very ripped bodies to be exact. She both heard and felt the feminine approval from Cali and Diana when Kane, Kai, and Kellan smiled and began heading their way.

"Hi guys!" Max greeted, trying to push Darius out of the way, no easy feat considering he was a solid six-foot-three to her petite five-foot-three. "Thank you for coming on such short notice," she grunted, finally succeeding in squeezing past him. Even herself, having no shame, fought a blush when three identical sets of dimples flashed her way.

"Anytime," Kellan purred.

Max cleared her throat, "I wanted to ask if you would all do me a favour ..." she began, only to be interrupted by a subtle cough from Darius. She turned to him, eyebrows raised.

"Max does not have a favour to ask in the strictest sense. She has a job for you – a duty," Darius pointed out, formally.

Max would have rolled her eyes but she knew it would do no good. Darius had lightened up a little since allowing himself to love Diana and since his brother's return. But he was still a compulsive rule-follower and his duty was the foundation of his being, so she let him posture and lecture a little as she considered the three young men in front of her.

The three men with the dark brown, short-cropped hair, chiselled jawlines, smoky grey eyes, and adorable dimples were now standing to attention, looking the very epitome of soldiers. Max knew for all their cheekiness and flirtations, they were highly skilled paladins – albeit relatively young by warden society standards. Even Ryker, who scowled every time he heard their names, vouched for their skill and professionalism in the field. She had no idea why they were as yet unbound. She knew they had passed the entire paladin examination process with flying colours and many wardens had petitioned the IDC for them to join their Orders. The three men had so far declined every offer. She knew their polite and diplomatic refusals would not be tolerated for much longer. As civilised as the International Domain Council appeared to be at times, they were a dictatorship.

She also already knew they were trustworthy and reliable. She'd taken it upon herself to check out their colourful shadows when they had stepped into the room. All three were predictably vibrant, the men full of life. She was a little surprised to see a shadow of grey hovering around their hearts but supposed no-one was safe from some form of heartache in their lives. But what had sealed their fates, was the new circle of symbols their cheeky souls had avidly pointed out. The three men were loyal and had been deemed worthy.

She'd be lying if she said the magic brands didn't freak her out a little. She hadn't been lying to Ryker and the others when she'd said she had no idea how she was making them. She had no intention, let alone any recollection of transferring the brands – other than to Ivy and Dex, which she had witnessed first-hand. These others – Caspian, Leo, Lawson, Fawn, and now the triplets – it was news to her. But Lark's explanation made sense and she had no choice but to trust that the universe knew what it was doing and the people being selected to be marked were indeed loyal and worthy recipients.

She was going to need them.

As Darius's lecture wound down, Max refocused her attention on the brothers, "Will you three relax? Darius is just being dramatic," she informed them. Kane's lips twitched but he didn't change position and she knew they were taking Darius's firm words to heart. Or they were attempting to at least. Feeling a little nervous, she looked to her friends. And after receiving five individual nods she took a deep breath and began talking.

As suspected, the triplets took her 'job offer' in stride and had all professed to be willing to aid her in any way possible. Outwardly they seemed totally fine but Max couldn't quite shake the feeling that they were holding something back a little. It was something to do with that little grey smudge over their hearts ...

'Max? What is it?' Cali asked, picking up on her tension.

'They're withholding something,' she admitted, not wanting to get them into trouble but needing to be honest with her Order.

"Okay boys, fess up," Cali commanded, her fingers firmly enlaced with her fiancé's.

They looked genuinely startled, "What?" Kane asked.

"You're not telling us something. What is it?" Cali asked in her typical blunt fashion. "And before you try to deny it, remember; Custodian," she pointed at Max.

The brothers looked at each other before Kane sighed and slumped a little in the seat he was sitting in. They had all migrated to the dining area when her long-ish tale had begun. "We're sorry. We didn't mean to offend. It's just ..."

"This kind of thing hits a little close to home," Kai finished. "Our father is a chade – or was a chade. No doubt he's long since dead."

Max closed her eyes, cursing herself silently. Suddenly those little grey patches of pain and hurt made sense. If only she didn't cling so stubbornly to her aversion to reading people, she could have seen this coming. There was no way she would have asked them had she known. Clearly sensing her distress, Kai placed a large, warm hand on her arm;

"I can see what you're thinking and it's not a problem. We meant what we said – we're happy to help. More than that, we're honoured to be entrusted with such an important task."

"Besides, Kai's right. It was a long time ago – the Great Massacre to be exact," Kellan added.

"Close to half a century," Dex murmured, clearly thinking of his forty years spent in exile and darkness.

"That's right. That's how we know he must be dead by now. It's just too long. And if he weren't. No chade could come back from that," Kellan shook his head.

"But, that just makes this even more significant to us. If we can help save someone else's father, then we want to do everything we can to make it happen," Kane vowed.

Dex clapped him on the back and even Darius now appeared to be looking at them with less hostility. And then Max felt it. It was a tingle of warning, a split second of premonition in which all she could do was gasp before the back doors slammed open once again. Burying her face in her hands and wishing she would have seen this coming, she could only close her eyes in defeat when she heard three voices cry out simultaneously;

"DAD?!"

TWENTY-FOUR

For once, his liege's advice had proved useless. The irritating woman had been right about everything since the second they had met and when she finally decided to be wrong, it just had to be about him and Ivy. Three weeks. Three weeks and nineteen chade redemptions later and Lark was about at the end of his rope. Max had told him to be patient, to show her he wasn't like every other arsehole out there bent on getting into her pants. But he had been patient, dammit! He had been funny and kind – he was great company! He had also been totally kickarse with the chades – fighting and killing those that couldn't be saved and acting as the conduit for Max to those that could.

But was the woman impressed? No! If anything, with every passing day, she became more closed off and distant. It was really pissing him off. He didn't know what else he could do – other than molesting her against the car again, that seemed to work out pretty well the first time. But then, he knew that was likely the reason she had shut down on him. The situation reminded him a little of how Ryker had been with Max – always blowing hot and cold. Although to be fair, Ivy had never been hot – lukewarm maybe – on her good days. But still, there was only so much ice he could take before he got frostbite … And he was feeling pretty frickin' cold!

And when he wasn't feeling the cold, winter chill that was Ivy? He was feeling horny – like, all day, every day, kind of horny. He was forced to watch her wield that sexy, lethal blade of hers all day long. And that sinister cloak of hers that made him picture the subtle curves on the short frame hidden underneath? He was getting a serious case of blue balls. Suddenly, his Captain's predicament when he had first met Max was no longer so amusing. Popping wood a dozen times a day was not his definition of fun.

As for his other companion, Knox couldn't exactly be called chatty but his one-word responses still held more warmth and interest than any of Ivy's. He had seemed a bit thunderstruck after his first trip back to the hotel but his demeanour had continued to improve upon each round-trip home, so Lark wasn't concerned. That first week, Knox had followed them in the second car, ferrying the partially-healed chades back to Max and the hotel. It had been a rather time-consuming process because he and Ivy had been forced to wait until Knox returned before they could make further attempts to identify chades.

It had been Knox who had suggested an alternative. He would travel in his 'other' form, basically as the air itself. Because the others could also revert to the pure states of their domains, Knox could guide them back in the same manner. It had definitely saved time and the last couple of weeks had consisted of he and Ivy travelling in the car while Knox caught up with them as the wind. They would locate chades, identify who still clung to their souls, give them a hit of vicarious Max, and move on to the next location while Knox escorted the chade-wardens back.

It had been a very successful process and he knew by his daily check-ins with his Order that things were progressing very well back at the camp and the hotel. Nearly all the chades sent back were already sporting some new ink and were slowly reacclimating to being wardens again. As far as he was aware, there had only been one instance when one of the survivors had tried to get a little too close to Caspian. Leo had promptly removed his head – a decidedly messy experience because the chade in question had been healed enough that he didn't just go 'poof' anymore. Leo had been unrepentant under Caspian's scolding but no-one else, not even Max, had reprimanded the paladin.

As for Lark and Ivy now? They were headed down another stretch of highway, en route to their next possible chade sighting. Picturing another cheap motel, with dust-filled pillows and who knows how much random human DNA clinging to the mattress, Lark made a sharp turn onto the next highway exit. He had caught sight of a big sign advertising a five-star hotel just ten minutes from here. If he had to travel with shitty companionship and stay in an even shittier hotel one more night, he thought he might just snap. In fact, it took Ivy a good five minutes to notice they were no longer on the scheduled route. It just proved how hard she was focusing on ignoring him and he felt his temper flare to life once more.

"What are you doing? The next location is still two hours away," she said, looking out the window.

"I know," he said. See? He could do short, snappy sentences too. He didn't always have to be happy and full of conversation.

"Do we need petrol?" she queried.

"No."

"Do you need to go to the bathroom?" she tried again.

"No."

"Then what are we doing?" she asked, sounding frustrated now.

"We're stopping here for the night," he stated, already turning into the driveway of a truly beautiful old Victorian-style hotel. It had five, yellow shiny stars above its name and Lark felt like whimpering in gratitude.

Ivy's head was whipping back and forth from him to the window, "Here? What? Why?"

"Because I want to," he informed her.

She looked incredulous and more than a little confused by his odd behaviour, "Because you want to? What are you – ten?"

He flashed her a look filled with heat, "Really, Ivy? Another comment about my age? Be careful, I'm sure you remember where that got you before." The warning had the desired effect and her mouth closed with a snap.

Gazing out his window, he noticed that the hotel was not only big and beautiful but it also nestled into the surrounding landscape like it had sprung from the rainforest itself. Oh yes, they were definitely staying here tonight. His body was practically vibrating with the need to reconnect to his element – as well as a feather-down pillow.

Putting the car in park, he pocketed the keys, "Come on," he threw over his shoulder. He didn't bother to wait for a response, just hopped out and began striding to the entrance. He heard a car door slam and stomping footsteps as they hurried to catch up – he didn't bother tempering his longer strides to match her shorter ones.

"Wait a minute. What the hell is going on?" she huffed out.

He came to an abrupt halt, causing her to crash into him. His mood was so dark that the full-body contact only made his dick twitch to half-mast, "Look, I don't know about you but I'm tired, I'm sore, I'm cranky, and I'm starving. I'm taking the night off and asking for a late check-out and pretending there are no such things as chades."

Less than ten minutes later, he was leaning back against a solid oak door, his bag at his feet and a pouting Ivy stashed away in the adjoining room. His eyes scanned the room from the high ten-feet, tray ceilings to the gorgeous crown molding lining the walls and over to the king-sized canopy bed with the mahogany-coloured comforter. It was even better than his tired brain could have imagined. But he was still a knight and the twinge of guilt he felt had him groping for the Order link;

'Max?'

'S'up?'

Lark grinned, even hearing his liege's voice was enough to make him smile. The distance away from Max had also been a strain on him. That was another reason why paladins were never far from their wardens; the bond. It was a bond that was literally soul deep. His need to ensure to Max's safety, health, and happiness was so entrenched in him now, that he couldn't remember what it felt like to be un-bound. If it weren't for the daily connection with her and his Order when they healed the chades, he was sure he would have needed to turn back long before now in order to satisfy his sense of duty.

'I'm taking the night off. Check out my digs for the night,' he crowed, scanning the room again so Max could 'see'.

'Oooh, nice! I bet a place like that has a spa bath. Enjoy. You deserve it,' his liege said.

Max didn't even hesitate. Not one question about why he was there or what he was doing or when he would be leaving. No scolding about getting the job done. Just: *enjoy!* Was it any wonder why he adored the woman? *'Thank you. We'll be back on the road tomorrow,'* he informed her even though she hadn't asked.

'*No probs. Oh, and Lark?*'

'*Hmm?*'

'*Patience, remember?*'

He growled at that, '*What the hell do you think I've been doing?! Max! Max!*' But it was no use, his liege had closed the link. *Damn aggravating woman,* he grumbled silently, *no more adoration for her!* he promised himself. After a few more grumbles he availed himself of the facilities and noticed Max had been correct, there was indeed a spa bath.

Although the claw-foot tub called to him like a siren, he was famished and he made his way out the door. Despite himself, he paused at Ivy's door, listening for any signs of movement. Hearing nothing through the thick wood and feeling like a creeper, he raised his fist to knock. As soon as Ivy cracked the door open he began to speak;

"The menu from the restaurant looked amazing. And I saw they have live entertainment with a dance floor. I don't care what you do but I'm going to go and sit at a restaurant and eat like a civilised person while listening to some relaxing music," he informed her and headed to the elevator, not waiting to see if she came or not.

Seeing the suspicious look in her eyes when she had opened the door had brought his temper flaring to life once more. He knew whatever else was on the fancy menu, a decent scotch would also be included.

TWENTY-FIVE

Ivy was left standing in the doorway of her truly spectacular suite, watching Lark's truly spectacular arse flex and bunch as he marched purposefully away from her. Although she couldn't be positive what had prompted his sudden change in attitude, she could make an educated guess. It was because of her. After that first day when he had pushed her up against the car and given her the best orgasm of her life, she had reverted back to the old ranger who was cold and unfeeling. Why? Because the fact that he had given her a blinding orgasm without even taking her clothes off had terrified her as much as thrilled her.

She had known there was something special about him the moment she laid eyes on him. Attraction, yes, but after so long on the road with him, she knew there was so much more. When he had touched her, never once looking away, as if he saw the *real* her – as if *wanted* to see the real her ... Well, it had given her something she knew she couldn't afford; hope.

She was a ranger, her duty was to imprison, punish, and kill. Lark was all happy, warm, and fun. Basically?

Everything she wasn't. She hadn't wanted to tarnish that shine he had and she knew that is exactly what would happen if she let that hope keep blooming in her chest. So she had cut off their budding friendship and easy comradery at its knees and proceeded to only talk shop for the last three weeks.

It had been hell, pure and simple. She had been forced to sit next to him in the car day after day, his fresh scent driving her crazy, and his warm attempts at conversation and humour making her melt inside. She was dying to respond to him, to ask him questions, but she had held back, figuring he would give up in time. He hadn't – until today. She had never seen him like this – so closed off, so cold. It was like he was channelling her or something. Her knees buckled with that thought and she had to hang on to the doorframe for support when she realised she had done the exact thing she thought a relationship with him would do; take away his shine.

Thinking quickly, she wondered what she could do to repair the damage she had caused – if he would even be receptive to reigniting their fledgling, friendly relationship. She wasn't looking for anything further, she told herself. She just wanted the happy Lark back. Picking up her phone, she dialled the one person she knew would give her unconditional help.

"Bey? I need your advice."

*****

Apologise? Ivy thought as she made her way downstairs to where she knew the restaurant was. After listening carefully to her tale of her poor attitude and even poorer behaviour, Beyden's golden advice had been to apologise. She supposed to anyone else the solution would have been obvious but like Ryker had suggested; she was a little socially stunted. Her brother had broken it down in his customary, sensible fashion;

"Let me get this straight. Lark has apologised to you countless times now for his assumptions, his words, or his actions. From what I understand, your assumptions and faults have been far worse than his and yet, how many times have you apologised to him?"

Ivy hadn't answered, letting her silence speak for itself. But she knew he was right. Her mother would have kicked her butt by now; stoic was one thing but rudeness was something else entirely.

Spotting him at a table by himself close to the man playing a black baby grand, she took a fortifying breath of humble and made her way to him, "Do you mind if I join you?"

His green eyes flicked up, looking her over with disinterest, before settling once more on his menu. He shrugged, "The seat's free."

Not exactly the warmest of welcomes but at least he hadn't said no. For want of anything better to do, she picked up her own menu and began to scan its contents. Her eyes nearly bugged out of her head – fifty dollars for a starter! She didn't even want to know what the main courses ran for. Quickly looking around, she noticed for the first time how fancy the place was. Every other occupant in the room was dressed in formal attire of dresses and suits. Patting her hair, she suddenly remembered she hadn't taken a brush to it since that morning and she had been hacking off heads all day. What's more, she was still wearing her plain black cargo pants and shirt. She wished she had the protection that was her ranger uniform. She had never felt so exposed before.

"You look beautiful."

His voice startled her as much as his words and her eyes flew to his. She was able to witness first-hand how his eyes lost their coldness and the lines of tension bracketing his mouth smoothed out. "Huh?" she managed to stutter out.

"I said you look beautiful. You outshine every woman in this room."

Ivy ducked her head, feeling her face flame. But not from embarrassment – no, it was from pleasure. Lark thought she was beautiful. Nobody had ever told her she was beautiful before. Well, other than Beyden and her mother but they didn't count. And although she hadn't heard them from any man in the past, she knew they couldn't possibly have meant more to her than they did when spoken from the man in front of her right now.

Apologise, Beyden had said. But Ivy thought she could do one better and appeal to him on a deeper level – show him she had been listening every time he spoke. And prove she had been watching every time he moved. Standing up, she held out her hand, "Will you dance with me?"

He stared at her outstretched hand so long she began to think he wasn't going to take it and she felt a small ball of dread settle in her stomach. But just as she was about to lower her hand, he grasped it firmly, allowing her to pull him to his feet;

"I'd love to," he assured her, softly.

There were three other couples on the dance floor, so she didn't feel like a complete moron but it took her all of ten seconds to step on his foot, "Sorry," she hastily apologised. "I don't dance often – or ever."

Warm fingers caught her chin, tilting it up and she found herself ensnared by the jade depths of his eyes, "You're doing fine. Although, if you stopped trying to lead ..." he quirked a smile at her.

"Oh," she exhaled, loosening her steel grip on his hand and beginning to follow his steps as he moved her slowly but surely in a circle across the dance floor. By half way through the song, she had relaxed enough to close her eyes when she heard him whisper;

"Apology accepted."

She smiled into his chest where she knew he couldn't see, feeling an insurmountable pleasure knowing he had read her actions for what they were; a request for forgiveness. As the last lines of the song came to an end, she found herself in an unusual predicament; she didn't want to step out of the masculine arms that surrounded her. One song. One dance. That's what she had allowed herself. One tiny moment of whimsy where she could just be a woman and not a killer. She knew better, she reprimanded herself, for now here she was, her body aligned with a lean frame that smelled of freshly cut grass in the spring time ... and muscles that wouldn't quit.

He had been the perfect gentleman, guiding her through the dance with one hand securely on her waist and the other covering hers on his chest. He didn't step into her personal space at all, just moved them together with the beat of the music. She found the casual brushes of his body against hers even more arousing than if they had been slamming naked against each other. Although, she was sure that would be damn arousing as well.

She felt him inhale, bringing them into even closer contact, rather than letting her go. Seems she wasn't the only one disinclined to part ways. Although, judging by the large bulge behind the zipper of his standard issue cargo pants, she was confident his reasons weren't so innocent. Another inhale accompanied a nose brushing against her hair. Was he sniffing her?

"Are you sniffing me?" She demanded, frowning at him but still making no move to step out of his arms – because she was clearly a glutton for punishment.

He shrugged, "Yes. Your hair smells amazing."

She quickly lowered her head, lest he see how much the comment warmed her. Her one vanity was her hair. It would have been far more practical to cut it all off. After all, anything an opponent could grab and use against you in battle was a hindrance. But she just couldn't do it. The memories of her mother brushing her hair before bedtime every night were her favourite ones. Before she could formulate a response that didn't make her sound like a weeny, Lark spoke again;

"Do you know what I wanted the first time I saw you?" he murmured, this time skimming his chin across the top of her head.

She smirked at that, pushing herself against the hardness at her hip, "I think I can guess."

She fully expected a bawdy comment in return or a lewd gesture – the typical male response to such a blatant sexual innuendo. But when none was forthcoming, she glanced up at him again. Bright green eyes, the colour of the freshest of fields, met her own dark gaze. Those emerald orbs mapped her face, even as he raised a hand to trace her lips. Despite herself, she felt them part in anticipation – so sure he was going to lean in and lay siege. But the earth paladin only quirked his own and shook his head;

"I wanted to see you smile."

Ivy gulped, *oh boy, he sure is potent,* she thought and tried to remind herself of all the different reasons why becoming involved with her partner, her brother's best friend, and a man young enough to be her son, was a bad idea.

"I saw you dancing," she abruptly revealed without thought and wanted to immediately slap her own forehead.

"Given you're currently in my arms, swaying to the music, I'd say that was fairly obvious," he smiled at her.

"No," she fumbled, trying to explain herself, "I mean, I

saw you *dancing*. Back at the camp. In the gym."

Apple-green eyes narrowed and she felt him stiffen perceptibly, "Did you just? That was private."

She blushed a little but didn't lower her eyes, "I know. Ryker informed me of that when he caught me in the act."

"Ryker?" he sounded surprised.

"Yeah. He's a little protective of you. In fact, they all are," she pointed out.

"Hmm," was his only response.

"Who taught you?" she asked.

"Who taught me what?" he queried, although she was positive he knew her meaning.

"To dance," she clarified. She was unsure why his answers were so important to her. She just knew she had an intense desire to get to know the youthful earth paladin on a deeper level. She knew he had been trying – all those hours in the car together. But she had feigned disinterest and he hadn't attempted to talk about anything of true importance.

He was silent for so long, she thought he wasn't going to answer but she finally felt his tense muscles relax once more just before his breath fanned across the top of her head;

"No-one taught me; I taught myself."

"What?" That couldn't be right. The skill and the dexterity with which he had moved had not been those of an amateur. "How is that possible? You must have had lessons."

But he shook his head, "You'd be surprised how much you can learn from watching TV and reading books when you have a photographic memory."

"Your parents must have been proud of you, having so many talents," she guessed and was caught off guard when he stopped moving abruptly. Looking up, she saw his eyes were fixed on her face with harsh intensity, "What is it?" she asked.

He shook his head, looking baffled, "You really don't

know who I am, do you?"

He was looking so solemn and serious, she could only shake her head, "What do you mean? Who are you?"

He blew out a harsh breath, "Not here."

Glancing around, she saw they were garnering some interest. Likely because they were still on the dance floor, wrapped in each other's arms and subtly swaying to the now non-existent music. She stepped out of his arms, swiftly quieting her traitorous heart when it whined from the loss of contact. Clearing her throat, she said; "Thank you. For the dance, I mean."

His lips quirked up, making him look entirely too young and edible, "You're welcome. For the dance, I mean."

She couldn't help but smile back and he tilted his head, studying her for a moment, "Do you really want to know more about me?"

"Most definitely," she quickly responded.

"Are you going to reciprocate?"

She frowned at that, "There's not much to tell."

"Oh, I doubt that very much," he murmured, his gaze raking over her from head to toe. "Your room or mine?" he asked and must have read the wary look on her face, "Relax, Ivy. To talk. Just talk."

She hesitated for a moment before finally deciding to forge ahead. She may as well get it over with. "Listen, Lark. About that day –"

"Let's not, okay? Something tells me we're not going to agree about what it meant and I don't want to hear all about your regrets. So –" he continued before she could puzzle out what his meaning was, "your room or mine?"

She studied him for a moment, seeing no hidden agenda. Just his earnest, handsome face, "Mine."

TWENTY-SIX

"You know, I wanted to be a dancer when I grew up – like professionally. Fighting, protecting, being a paladin was never something I wanted to do," he volunteered as he wandered a little aimlessly around Ivy's room.

She scoffed, "Right!"

He smiled at her, knowing the idea was absurd to her but it was true. "Seriously. I also wanted to be a professor, a doctor, a gardener ... anything other than what I was born to be." He paused when he reached the small sitting area of the room and decided to take a seat at the table. His constant prowling was no doubt making Ivy nervous but he'd thought it best to stay on the move. Seeing her sitting on the bed and pulling all that glorious hair loose from the confines of its elastic was playing havoc on his control.

"You're serious," she stated, combing her fingers through her hair. "From what I've seen, you love being a paladin."

"I love being *Max's* paladin," he emphasised. "But I wanted to be everything – anything – my father wasn't. He's a paladin, hence I loathed the thought of being one." He watched the tiny expressions on her face, loving the small play of muscles beneath smooth, mocha skin. The slight vee between her eyebrows was the equivalent of a frown on other people.

"Daddy issues?" she guessed.

Despite the circumstances, he was startled into a genuine laugh, "That's the understatement of the year. My father is Isaac."

Her fingers stilled in her hair, her eyes widened, and her mouth literally dropped open. It was the most expression he had ever seen on her face. Other than when she had orgasmed, of course. And he planned on seeing that particular look of surprised wonder on her face again and again and again. He figured it was pretty bad when he only had to say a first name and people shuddered in revulsion. His father's name and Order was synonymous with fear.

"Isaac? Potentate for the Order of Tor and for Terran? That piece of shit, murdering bastard, arsehole?!" she shouted.

He tipped an imaginary hat in her direction, "That'd be him."

She jumped off the bed, taking her turn to pace around the room. Lark didn't mind her agitated movements. It allowed him to appreciate the full scope of Ivy's hair. Straight, black, and shiny as a waterfall, it fell in a flawless curtain all the way to her butt. He couldn't wait to see her body when it was shielded only by that hair.

"By the Goddess, Lark. I had no idea. I've had a few run-ins with his Order over the years and –"

"You what?" he jumped up. "Are you okay? Did he ever touch you?"

She waved away his concern, "I'm fine. As if I'd let that disgusting, sadistic, pig touch me. I – shit, I'm sorry. I'm talking about your father ..."

His jaw clenched, "No need to apologise. That man is a lot of things. But my father he never was."

Ivy shook her head, causing her hair to swish tantalisingly around her body, "Well, that explains your scars. Oh, hell. I am so sorry. That was so insensitive. I'm –"

He found himself laughing for the second time in minutes. An irate, uncensored, unfiltered Ivy was highly entertaining. "It's fine. Honest."

She just shook her head, staring at him like she had never seen him before, "Isaac? I don't see it at all. You are *nothing* like him. Honestly, if it weren't for the fact that I know you would never lie to me, then I would say I didn't believe you."

He absolutely loved hearing she trusted him to speak truthfully. Maybe the past couple of weeks weren't such a write-off after all and she really had been listening and watching him, just as he had been doing with her, "Telling me I'm nothing like him is probably the best compliment you could give me."

"No doubt," she muttered. "How did you get away from him?"

"The Paladin Trials," he said, simply.

That tiny vee of hers made another appearance briefly before her exotic-shaped eyes rounded slightly, "You flunked them on purpose."

He nodded, "Indeed I did." The relief on her face made him chuckle again, "You thought I was an incompetent child, barely old enough to be recognised as a knight and so inept I couldn't pass a single exam in the Trials."

She just nodded at him, not looking sheepish or even apologetic, "That's exactly what I thought. But then, that's exactly what you wanted me to think ... isn't it?"

He had to hand it to her, she was damn fast. Just another thing to like about her. He leant back in his chair, feeling relaxed and comfortable now, "Yes and no. Yes, I want my father and his associates to think that. Everyone else? I don't really care. I don't base my self-worth on the judgement of others." *Not anymore, anyway,* he added silently, "As for you – no, I didn't want you to think that. I hated that you thought that way. But I wasn't going to disabuse you of the notion. You seemed to need to cling to it."

Ivy abruptly turned her face away from him but not before he saw the slash of colour high on her cheekbones, "What happened then? I don't imagine your father would have been particularly happy about your failure."

"You'd be right. After a rather sound tongue lashing – among other things – he finally kicked me out on my arse. He then made sure to spread the word that his son was a disgrace – no fighting skills, useless with weapons, completely dishonourable, and likely a fag as well. I'm surprised you didn't hear about it. I was the talk of the town for a good long while."

She waved away his last comment, "I don't pay attention to gossip. Not after Beyden's experience with the gossip-whores. Although, I do remember hearing all about Isaac's son failing the potentate and paladin exams. I just never knew it was you."

His estimation of her rose again after hearing her opinion of gossip, "Anyway, I was barely twenty-six at the time and I found myself homeless, permanently Orderless, and disgraced. It was the happiest moment of my life."

He wondered how much more to say and then decided he wanted her to know everything about him sooner or later. He may as well keep talking while she was being receptive, "I was finally free. Free of that man, of his liege, and his miserable excuse of an Order. I was going to leave our society altogether – go live in the human world. Just forget wardens and paladins and chades even existed."

Her perfectly arched eyebrows rose, "You're being

serious," she stated.

"Deadly."

"Then why didn't you?" she asked, curiously.

He ran both hands through his hair, blowing out a breath, "Fate, luck ... Ryker."

Ivy's eyes warmed, "Ryker, huh? For a miserable prick who claimed not to like people, he sure sounds as if he saved more than his fair share of them."

Lark could recount dozens of true stories demonstrating Ry's deep sense of fairness, of compassion, and just plain kindness. But he didn't, knowing the man didn't do it for the fame. Instead, he grinned, "He's all bark and no bite."

She snorted at the absurdity of that and they lapsed into a comfortable silence, both lost in their own thoughts. After a few minutes, he saw Ivy making her way over to him. He was stunned when her voice rang loud and clear with her question;

"Can I see them?"

His body stiffened in automatic denial. He didn't need her to clarify what *them* was. She had already mentioned his scars once and had no doubt received an eye-full when he had been dancing that day. He hadn't lied when he told Max he wasn't ashamed of his scars or embarrassed about them. Though, he *would* be lying if he said he was completely comfortable with someone studying them. Someone he was attracted to no less and who had already expressed concerns regarding his strength.

She must have taken his silence for tacit consent because she offered him a slender hand. Not wanting to break whatever spell they were both under, he accepted it, allowing her to help him to his feet. She circled around behind him and bunched her fingers in his shirt. Her tight grip reminded him of the day he had felt her come apart in his arms and he barely managed to stifle his groan. Now was not the time for lust-filled visions.

She raised the material slowly until it gathered at the nape of his neck, the cool air brushing over the lines and marks on his back, just as he knew her eyes must be. It could have been seconds or even hours later for all he knew, when he finally felt Ivy's soft fingers brush against his back. At first, he remained tense and unsure, not liking the fact he couldn't see her face and gauge her reactions. But by the time Ivy had finished her slow and very thorough exploration of his scars, he had relaxed under her gentle ministrations. She hadn't spoken and neither had he but somehow the silence wasn't awkward or fraught with tension. Instead it was ... peaceful. How he could feel at peace when a sexy woman was tracing the evidence of his miserable childhood, he didn't know.

And then, just when he thought she was done and he couldn't possibly like her even more, he felt the softest, warmest caress over the raised, keloid scar low on his hip. Sucking in a sharp breath, he knew that touch was her lips. She spent the next ten minutes being just as thorough with her mouth as she had been with her fingers. She left no skin unmapped and he knew if kisses really did make things better, his back would be flawless by now.

Finally, she smoothed his shirt back in place and stepped away from him, "I'm sorry," she murmured, voice full of compassion and pain but not pity.

Ensuring his face revealed nothing of the raging combination of like and lust going on inside his body, he turned, "Hardly your fault."

Her dark eyes were luminous, deep pools of emotion he was sure he could drown in, "I'm still sorry."

"Thank you," he said, feeling a connection, deep and sure, rise up between them. Clearing his throat, he broke their shiny new connection. But he wasn't worried now – he knew they could get it back. "Well, we have another big day tomorrow. We should at least try to get a couple of hours sleep."

"You could stay," she suggested, peering up at him with a clear offer in her eyes.

Oh, how he wanted to do just that. But he didn't want to break the fragile friendship they had managed to forge tonight. And he wanted far more from her than just sex. "Not tonight," he said, softly.

Her bottom lip immediately poked out in what was an undeniable pout. She looked so adorable and so put out, he couldn't help saying what was on his mind. Max had said to be patient and he had been. The advice had gotten him this far but it had been a long time coming. Now it was time for him to do it his way.

"Are you going to freak out when I fall in love with you?"

Her bottom lip dropped even further when her mouth fell open, "What?!" Ivy's voice was close to a screech.

Well, I guess that answers that, he thought in amusement. "Just relax," he soothed.

"Relax? You expect me to relax? You just told me you're in love with me," Ivy practically wheezed the last few words out.

"No, I said *when, when* I fall in love with you. Sheesh, I barely know you, Ivy," he shook his head. The look on her face said she thought he was completely insane. Maybe he was but he felt it was only right to give her some advance warning.

"*When* is just like saying you *are*! It's not like saying if," she informed him.

"I guess you have me there," he acknowledged. It was sound logic. "Well ... goodnight, Ivy."

"Goodnight? Goodnight? That's it?"

He stopped at the door, tossing a wink over his shoulder at the pale, trembling woman, "That's it ... for now."

TWENTY-SEVEN

"How did you sleep?" he asked Ivy. They were currently in the Dodge driving to their next stop. They had another good two hours before they arrived and he was determined to pick things up where they left off the evening before. Predictably, Ivy didn't respond. But he didn't let it bother him, not now and never again. As far as he was concerned, he had her right where he wanted her. He had decided he would leave friendship-mode today and head into flirt-mode.

"Now Ivy, you're not going to start the silent treatment again, are you? I thought we were passed this," he tutted at her.

She flashed him an annoyed glance quickly before focusing on the road again. She had informed him she would be driving the moment they met at the car that morning. He had told her she was free to. All she had to do was fish the keys out of his front pocket – perilously close to not-so-little Lark. She had given him a droll look and informed him she would be delighted to – as long as she could use her sickle to do it. A few seconds later she was sashaying to the driver's door holding the keys he had hastily yanked from his pocket himself.

"What can I do to make us friends again?" he asked her, voice full of cheer.

"You can apologise for what you said last night," she snapped at him.

He sighed, making sure to exaggerate the sound, "Ivy, I wish I could. But then I would be lying, Ivy. You don't want me to lie to you, do you Ivy?"

Her saw her hands clench on the wheel, although her expression didn't change, "Stop that."

"Stop what, Ivy?" he asked, the picture of innocence.

"Stop saying my name like that!" she fumed.

"Like what, Ivy? I can't help it if you have a sexy name ... *Ivy.*" He quickly faced the window, not wanting her to see the grin on his face. He was positive he'd heard a genuine growl that time.

"Lark ..." her voice held a warning note.

"Tell me about baby Beyden. Were his eyes always that colour?" he quickly changed the subject, wanting to keep her unbalanced but also wanting her to talk about something that would make her comfortable.

Silence reigned for a couple of minutes before she finally blew out a breath ... and then she talked.

*****

"Well? What do you think?" Lark asked, yawning.

Ivy cast him a glance. He was stretched out in the passenger seat, long legs in front of him and hands behind his head. He looked like a damn model from a fashion magazine. After a restless night spent repeating Lark's insane words over and over in her head, she had expected the drive to be a tense one. And it had been at first – for her at least.

But Lark had pushed it aside with ease and subtlety and she had found herself enjoying their time together once more. Although, there wasn't a minute that went by that she didn't hear his words resounding in her head.

She didn't know what the man had been thinking, telling her that. But she was trying her hardest to believe he'd had some kind of brain fart. It was understandable, he'd had an emotion-filled night, confessing his true lineage to her, showing her his scars. She wasn't sure what had possessed her, touching him and kissing him that way. She also wasn't sure why he had let her see and touch him so intimately. But after hearing the shocking truth that he was the Captain's son of one of the most notorious Orders in history, she'd had a compulsion to tend to him.

To think she had thought him naïve just because of his age. She had no doubt he had seen and lived through more pain and fear than her and Nikolai combined as rangers. How had he managed to stay sane, let alone retain such a sunny disposition?

"Knox is still ten minutes away at least," Lark spoke again, clearly not bothered by her lack of response. "Do we wait or scout the area?"

Refocusing, she acknowledged that the three of them had developed a good routine over the weeks. One that involved all three of them working as a team and none of them ever lone-wolfing it like she had done that first day. But Ivy was starting to feel itchy sitting here in the car with temptation sitting next to her, looking all bored and limber and sexy.

"There are two of us. We can check it out," she offered.

"Thank goodness! I tell you, I'm getting sick and tired of this car – with the exception of the company of course," he smiled, charmingly.

She was too – and ditto for the company. She knew Lark was starting to feel the absence of his liege and Order and decided she'd give Max a call that evening to see how many more chades she wanted them to find. Ivy thought the nineteen plus Knox, making an even twenty, was a darn good number. Before heading out, she had thought they might find a half a dozen who could be saved. But what alarmed her even more was for every chade they had been able to help, they had come across three times more than those they couldn't. Those numbers were huge and Dex had definitely been correct in his estimations of chade numbers increasing. They were also fairly closely located to where Max and the main training lodge was too – another disturbing fact. They hadn't had to travel further than ten hours away in any direction as yet.

Realising she was now sitting in the car alone, she pushed the door open, stretching out her sore back. She had forgone her ranger cloak today but she grabbed her sickle and headed around the front of the car only to find Lark staring at her, "What?"

"You were stretching. It pushed your magnificent chest out. I was leering at you," he replied, happily.

Her steps faltered but she didn't break stride. Although he had been fun and humorous and sweet and kind over the weeks, he hadn't been all that flirtatious. He was apparently stepping up his game. She wanted to be annoyed or even a little scared by the prospect. But instead, she was excited. And more than a little flattered by the attentions of the much younger man who could literally have his pick of women.

"Checking out my tits?" she asked, bluntly. "I thought you were too intelligent for such base, male behaviours."

He snorted, "Honey, there's not a man alive too intelligent for that."

She smiled, enjoying their easy banter. But as her feet stepped onto the grassed area of the paddock, she tensed up, "Do you feel that?" she turned to him.

He was next to her in an instant, frowning as he bent down to lay his hands on the grass-covered ground, "The earth is very unhappy."

Ivy concurred and found it a happy coincidence that they had the earth in common as their element. She swept the area with her gaze, halting when she saw a series of shadows cresting the small hill about two hundred metres in front of them. "There's definitely some here," she spoke softly.

"Some?" Lark stood up, "More than one?"

"Oh, I'd say that's a pretty safe bet," she croaked.

Her tone had him turning around sharply and following her gaze. She felt him still and she knew why. Five. There were no less than five chades here. And all of them looked to be very far gone, perhaps too far gone for any of them to be saved. They crested the hill quickly, their dark shadows swiftly becoming tangible, pale bodies. And then they just stopped.

And waited.

And watched.

"What the fuck?" Lark breathed exactly what Ivy herself was thinking.

"Not good. This is not good," she said. She didn't know what instinct told her these chades were different. Not just unredeemable but something more – something evil. For once in her life she wanted to flee in the opposite direction. The way they were just standing there watching them, it was almost as if they had been waiting for them.

Next to her, Lark was silent and Ivy knew he was talking with his Order. He nodded a couple of times, his frown intensifying but he never once looked away from the threat in front of them and she knew he was capable of springing into action at any given moment. When the five silent, glaring chades suddenly became eight, Ivy gulped, "Lark? What's the plan?"

"Max says they are all completely soulless. Not a single redeemable one in the bunch," he responded.

"No shit! I mean, what are we going to do about them. I know we're good but we're not *that* good. We won't win," she informed him, feeling a little sick because she knew it was true.

"Max says Knox is almost here. He'll help ..." he trailed off as if he already knew what he was saying wouldn't matter. He was silent for a couple of heartbeats, then; "Max thinks she may be able to use her powers through me like she does to heal the chades."

Ivy looked at him, incredulous, "Are you kidding? Last time you all tried something new it almost killed you. And that was with benevolent powers at low wattage. What you're talking about will require much more energy, not to mention a nastier type of power."

Lark clenched his jaw, "Do you have a better idea? Max is our best bet."

She had no doubt if anyone could save their butts, it would be the goddess. But ... "And that will work? You only channel her to heal one chade at a time. There are eight of them," she pointed out, still extremely unsure.

He shrugged, "We're going to amplify the energy."

The eight chades still hadn't moved and Ivy felt a shiver run down her back. It was like they were waiting for something, as if they had a common goal. Historically, chades attacked randomly. They were not co-ordinated. This looked like something else entirely and she saw once again what Dex had been alluding to. The whole reason he sought Max out all those months ago was because he believed the chades were heading in Max's direction with a shared purpose. Seeing the chades in front of her at this moment, she couldn't help but think he was right. They were thinking. They had a purpose. And it absolutely terrified her.

"How are you going to do that?" she questioned Lark, trying to figure out the game plan.

He hesitated then said, "Ryker's going to maintain the link with the Order and Max. That way, she'll have a constant supply of vitality and won't have to split her attention between recharging and channelling her powers through me."

Ivy was liking this plan less and less, "How the hell will that work? If Ryker is maintaining the link with your Order, who's going to be maintaining your link with Max? No way will she be able to do it."

He continued to watch their morbid, silent audience as he answered in a clipped voice, "I'm going to maintain it."

Now she was even more confused, "Only a potentate can do that."

"I know," he turned his head, looking her square in the eye, "I'm a potentate."

TWENTY-EIGHT

As soon as Lark spoke the words, a barrage of questions hit his cerebellum and he winced at the noise level. He'd known this would be the reaction when he told his Order. Although, if he were being honest, he hadn't really intended to tell them – especially Ryker. Max had known of course. It was what she had been referring to that morning on the beach all those weeks ago. She'd seemed very sure that Ryker wouldn't care but that clearly wasn't the case if his colourful language was anything to go by.

'You're a fucking potentate? And you never said anything? What the fuck, Lark!'

Lark swallowed, hearing the anger but also the underlying hurt in his Captain's voice. The vibe coming through the Order link told him the others were feeling the same, *'I'm sorry. But can we talk about this later?'*

He knew he sounded desperate because that is exactly how he felt – bone wrenchingly desperate. The eight chades in front of him and Ivy were no longer standing still but advancing on them with slow, deliberate movements. There was definitely something off with them. More than off, he realised. Evil. They felt evil. The earth beneath him was practically screaming in horror at the betrayal from its guardians.

He felt the moment Max and his Order registered the advancing chades. Shock, disgust, concern. They obviously sensed what he did, that they weren't your average empty chades, because the overriding emotion coming through the link? Fear.

'No time,' Max sounded anxious, *'Ryker? Hold onto the others and keep the vitality coming. Lark? Hold onto yourself. Remember who you are.'*

He was about to ask her what she meant by that when he felt power burst to life inside of him like a supernova. He arched his back, cracked his neck and flexed his biceps. Huffing, he eyed the inferior beings in front of him; they were nothing. They were ants and he was a god playing with a magnifying glass. He was invincible. He had the power to do anything and everything he wanted. He –

'Lark! Lark! Focus, dammit!'

It took a moment to comprehend what the annoying buzz in his head was; a voice. There was something familiar about the voice but he just couldn't put his finger on it. He also had the feeling that there was something he was supposed to be doing. But the colours and the connections everywhere he looked were astounding! Everything had an aura. Everything had a spirit. And everything was connected to something else. He could see colourful threads connecting trees and rocks and disappearing off into the distance. Some were strong and tangible, others looked like he could break them with a whisper. There were so many colours, he couldn't even name them. But there was one that held him spellbound. It was strong and vital and pulsed like a heartbeat. It was green like the earth but sparkled like an emerald. It was coming from somewhere to his left and arching strongly but surely to ...

'Lark! Fucking snap out of it! You're letting the power control you. You need to control the power!'

That annoying buzz sounded in his head again but this time, the sounds of them registered as words and he felt his stomach drop as his brain clicked back in with reality. Looking around him, he saw he and Ivy were completely surrounded by chades. She was at his left side and currently fighting off three of them while he was standing there rhapsodising over his prowess and the pretty colours! He wasted another precious second wondering if this was how Max felt all the time before launching himself into the battle. One swipe of his scythe and the chade in front of him disintegrated into nothing. Holding it up he wondered what the hell it had been imbued with, only to realise it was him which had been imbued – with Max. He was positively saturated in her power.

'Don't bother with your blade. Just look at them,' Max's voice boomed in his head this time.

He did as he was instructed and watched a bright, white light surge from his body and literally annihilate everything in its path. The chades simply vanished as if they had never existed and the poor, innocent earth scorched and blackened. He was about to turn to Ivy when the power left him in a rush and he fell in a boneless heap. Gasping a little, he turned his head ... and felt his heart stop when he saw Ivy's lifeless form on the now barren earth.

"Ivy," he croaked, "Max!" But the connection was gone – all but burnt out. And even as a potentate, he couldn't re-establish the link.

Snapping twigs had him reaching for his scythe as he tried to crawl to Ivy. A heavy but gentle hand stayed the weapon and he looked up into the grey eyes of Knox. "Ivy ..."

he rasped.

Knox nodded, briskly sitting down next to her and placing two fingers against her neck. Lark felt the world crawl to a standstill as he waited for Knox to look back up. When he did, he finally allowed himself to breathe again. The other man was nodding. Feeling weaker than a day-old kitten, he managed to drag himself next to her and was horrified to see three huge gashes on her right forearm. The blackening around the edges indicated she had been clawed by one of the chades. That wasn't good. Their sharpened nails contained a poison that was often deadly.

Knox quickly and proficiently fastened a tourniquet around Ivy's bicep, blocking the blood flow to the rest of her body and hopefully slowing the spread of the toxin. "Peroxide?" he questioned.

"In the car," Lark answered, running shaking fingers over the cool, smoothness of Ivy's cheek.

Knox was back in seconds and pouring the liquid directly over Ivy's wound. Even in her passed-out state, a cry of pain left her lips and her back arched sharply off the ground. Lark gritted his teeth and held her still as Knox upended the entire bottle of peroxide into the open gashes. The wound hissed and bubbled obnoxiously, emitting a sour smell but Lark knew that was a good thing. The peroxide neutralised the poison and as long as it hadn't spread in her system, she should be fine.

Would be fine, he corrected. He wouldn't settle for anything less.

TWENTY-NINE

Ivy woke feeling better than she deserved to under the circumstances. She was a bit light-headed, a little achy, and a lot thirsty. Looking down, she saw the expertly applied bandage around her forearm and gave it an experimental poke. The flesh underneath protested a little but it didn't scream at her. Lark must have somehow managed to treat the claw marks quickly. She couldn't believe she had allowed one of those chades to get that close to her. But then, it hadn't been a normal fight, had it?

She had watched as Lark had started glowing with a faint, pale light and she had been optimistic that his harebrained plan may actually succeed. That optimism had lasted about ten seconds because Lark had then clearly taken a little mental detour. Thinking to give him a swift kick to snap him out of it, she had found herself swiftly surrounded by the pack of chades. Three had come at her immediately and she'd had to fight harder than in recent memory. One side-step an inch too short had resulted in a burning pain across her arm and her sickle had dropped from her nerve-less fingers. At that point, Lark had slashed at the chade with his own blade and it had poofed into nothingness. After that, she didn't really remember much because the burning had turned into a scorching and she had passed out.

A quick glance around the room revealed a hunched over Lark in an uncomfortable-looking, mustard-yellow upholstered chair next to the bed. Clearly, the man had spent the night curled up in it with his too-long limbs hanging over the sides and his neck awkwardly tucked against the back. But the dark circles under his eyes, the messy hair, and the rumpled clothes couldn't detract from his masculine beauty. The man was breathtakingly gorgeous, even after days without sleeping or showering.

The past few days were somewhat of a blur and when she forced herself to focus, she came up with only a handful of disjointed images, sounds, and smells. Her fever must have been fierce for her to have such poor memory but perhaps it was a blessing of sorts. She didn't really need any more images of herself hallucinating, vomiting, and sweating against the sheets.

But what she did know, was that she had been so weak she'd had to rely on Lark for everything. For someone who prided herself on strength and independence, it was her worst nightmare. But somehow, because it was Lark, it was okay. And he had been wonderful throughout it all; wiping her brow, fetching her water, carrying her into the bathroom, holding her at night. Chade poisoning really was a pain in the arse.

She pushed herself up and Lark snapped awake, bolting upright and reaching for his weapon automatically. For some reason, the action turned her on immensely. He truly was a knight, even in his sleep. Seeing no threat, he relaxed and scrubbed rough hands over his face. He then looked at her and smiled, his green eyes lighting with warmth and happiness to find her awake.

"Hey there, beautiful. How're you feeling? You look wonderful," he said.

It should have been ridiculous. She knew she must look like a harpy rolled in warmed-up shit but she knew he was sincere. She knew he truly thought she looked beautiful. Because to him – she would always be beautiful. He had spent the last few days of her illness telling her so, as well as countless other romantic and flirty things. And somewhere along the way, the strangest thing had happened.

Ivy had started to believe him.

With that thought in mind and a fresh lease on life, she rose from the bed clad only in one of Lark's shirts. Walking slowly toward him, she put an extra sway in her steps, stopping only when she was a hairbreadth from making contact with him.

"What are you doing?" he asked, looking confused.

She arched her eyebrows, "Do you really have to ask? I would have thought it was obvious."

"Um, are you hallucinating again? Do you have a fever?" he placed a palm against her forehead and even that turned her on. Maybe chade toxin had an aphrodisiac effect? She'd never noticed before but it could be a decent side benefit.

"I'm not hallucinating. I just want you," she informed him.

His mouth opened and closed for a moment before he sputtered, "Well, you can't have me."

She twirled a strand of hair around her finger, wondering idly if she looked like an idiot or if she was achieving sexy. She knew which one she felt – and it wasn't sexy. She aimed for a seductive purr, "Why not?"

He stood up, walking backwards, "Because you spent the last three days on death's door."

"Exactly. It was horrible and scary – blah, blah, blah.

Let's have some life-reaffirming sex." But the man only continued to look at her with wide eyes as he shook his head, "Come on, you've been throwing yourself at me for weeks. Now you're suddenly frigid?"

He stiffened in insult, "I have *not* been throwing myself at you. And I am most certainly *not* frigid! I have been trying to start a relationship with you; one based on intellect and emotion and affection," he informed her, a little primly.

"And what about sex? Because I could have sworn that day against the car that you were interested in sex too," she pointed out.

"Of course I'm interested in sex!" he barked at her.

"With me?"

He growled, "Of course with you!"

Ivy fought to keep her face blank when she really wanted to grin like the Cheshire Cat. It was so rare to see him looking grumpy and insulted and bad-tempered. Was it evil of her to want to find out how much he could take until his control snapped? Seeing the way he was grinding his teeth, she figured it wouldn't take that long, "What's the problem, then?"

He stiffened his shoulders and planted his feet and she knew he was going to be stubborn, "You've been sick, Ivy. I'm not about to take advantage of a sick woman."

She took a step towards him, "Oh, please. Take advantage of me." Another step, "Come on ... I promise to still respect you in the morning," she cajoled.

He shook his head, "That's not funny."

"No?" she pouted, stepping forward again.

"No," he confirmed.

"Then why are you smiling?" One final step and she was now close enough to feel the heat radiating off his body.

"This is just my default expression," he told her.

He probably meant that as a joke. But this time, the joke

was on him because what he said was true. Reaching up with her pointer finger, she traced the smile right off his lips, "You know, it really is your default look. It should be weird or annoying or something like that. But it's not. It's just ... nice. I like – no, I *love* when you smile at me."

His mulish expression softened and his smile widened, "And I love hearing that. But," he pushed her away from him, "it doesn't change the fact you were poisoned a few days ago. Because of me, I might add. I can't believe I allowed my concentration to lapse like that. Ivy, I am so sorry. So, so sorry."

She sighed in annoyance now. He had been apologising for days. It was one of the things she remembered with clarity. But as far as she was concerned, he had nothing to apologise for. He had been channelling the power of a goddess! What did the man expect? She opened her mouth to tell him so – for the umpteenth time – only to find him beating a hasty exit to the bathroom. She narrowed her eyes; *as if that will stop me.*

She made her way into the bathroom, feeling lucky to be alive and lucky to have such a wonderful man believing she was beautiful. She knew Lark was big on the whole talking shtick but she was more of a believer that actions spoke louder than words. So, she stripped the worn shirt smelling of Lark from her body, letting it fall carelessly to the ground. Reaching for the flimsy shower curtain, she pulled it back and had the pleasure of ogling Lark from the rear without anything in her way.

Despite the horrifying array of scars crisscrossing his back and the top of his thighs he was an absolute thing of beauty. He was lean and rangy but his muscles were clearly evidenced in the way his creamy skin stretched so tautly. His shoulders were broad, his waist trim, and his butt – oh man, his butt! Two globes of round, muscled perfection. She reached out with both hands and grabbed both cheeks, giving them a healthy squeeze before Lark jumped and spun, taking his arse with him.

"What the? Ivy! I – you – you're naked," he goggled.

"Am I? I hadn't noticed," she barely repressed a giggle when Lark swallowed noisily and his eyes began frantically searching for something to come to his rescue. *This is so much fun!* she thought. No wonder the women back at the house tormented their men on a daily basis. This kind of power was heady and could get addictive mighty fast.

Scanning his front just as thoroughly as she did his back, her eyes were drawn to his impressive pecs, subtly chiselled abs, and ... *oh, boy,* his very fine package. Feeling bold and brave and in need of immediate gratification, she knelt down. Keeping her gaze steady on his, she leaned forward and licked the tip of his impressive erection. His whole body jerked like it had been electrocuted but the knight must have nerves of steel for he kept his hands tightly fisted at his sides.

Feeling a moment of insecurity, thinking perhaps she had read him completely wrong and he didn't want her at all, she eyed the lines of strain on his handsome face. His jaw was clenched, his eyebrows pulled down low in a fierce frown, and his eyes were heavy-lidded. But there was a distinct sparkle in them. *Defiance?* she wondered, but as she allowed her tongue to peek out once more, tasting his heady flavour, she finally recognised the flare of darkness in them – challenge. Just like that, she felt her insecurities melt away. He definitely wanted her. But it appeared as if the hunter now wanted to become the hunted. The look in his eyes said it all; *bring it!*

Ivy felt her smile grow as she looked up at him from her position on her knees. She licked her lips and began dragging her hands up over her own body – her stomach, her breasts, her neck – before finally reaching the tie which constrained her hair. Tugging the elastic loose, she shook out her hair until she felt it brush the curve of her arse and began to plaster itself to her skin from the warm water pounding down on them.

"Challenge accepted," she informed her knight.

THIRTY

Uh oh, Lark couldn't even manage a gulp upon hearing Ivy's words. He was thrilled beyond measure that Ivy was taking the initiative and finally showing him how much she wanted him. He had been waiting for even the tiniest hint that she cared for him as much as he cared for her. But having the Asian beauty kneel at his feet and suck down his length like a pro hadn't exactly been what he was anticipating. For example, he figured she might smile at him or something.

He gasped abruptly when Ivy did something magical with her tongue and the tip of his dick. The shock of pleasure had his toes curling and he began reciting Dijkstra's algorithm so he wouldn't embarrass himself. Immediately feeling the loss when Ivy pulled away from him, he opened his eyes to see her peering up at him. Her black hair was plastered to her skin, her lips swollen, and her eyes were dewy. He wanted to throw her against the egg-shell white tiles and screw her brains out.

"What are you saying?" she asked him and he blushed, knowing he must have been babbling out loud.

"I was reciting the algorithm that solves problems for a

directed graph with non-negative edge weights using single-source direct paths."

She didn't even blink, just cocked her head, "Why?"

"So I don't blow like a teenager all over those pretty breasts of yours," he admitted.

She sucked in a harsh breath, gaining her feet in one fluid, sexy motion and promptly placed her lips against his. The kiss wasn't the forceful, sex-kitten kiss he had been expecting. It was gentle and coaxing, a lazy thrust and retreat of her tongue and lips against his own. He found himself seduced by the gentle rhythm just as much as he would have been by the heat and the fire. All the while, her small hands mapped his body, leaving tingles of heat in their wake. Pushing him back against the cool tiles, warm water continued to rain down on them as she stood on her tip toes and ran her tongue around the shell of his ear. He shivered, gripping her slim hips when her teeth decided to tug on the sensitive appendage. She had successfully and correctly identified one of his main erogenous zones.

Being a gentleman, he let her play and explore a little more, feeling his desire increase with each passing touch of her hands and brush of her lips. When she gripped his dick in her hands again, it just happened to coincide with the cooling of the water and he used it as his excuse to pick her up. She gave a startled squeak before wrapping her legs around his waist and he carried her, dripping wet, to the bedroom.

He reached behind him and unwound her legs, lowering her gently to the mattress. He then allowed his eyes to devour her as she languished patiently and uninhibited against the cool, white sheets. That in itself was a massive turn-on – he loved confident women. He took his time looking his fill, his eyes learning and cataloguing every curve, every dip, and every expanse of flushed mocha skin. And the best part about the entire experience? His photographic memory ensured he would never, ever forget even one single detail.

Feeling his dick jerk with impatience, he moved, placing his right knee on the bed, followed by his left as he slowly made his way to his willing woman. Balancing his weight on top of her, he first kissed her senseless, loving her unique taste and the flavour they created together. Moving on, he laved the tips of her breasts until her nipples were wet and tight, before drawing back and blowing on them. Ivy gasped, her back arching instinctively into the cooling effect of his breath. He grinned; seems he had discovered an erogenous zone of his own.

He then spent the next ten minutes learning her body as thoroughly as she had his. He succeeded in wringing two orgasms from her before his control snapped and he needed to be in her body *yesterday.* Pushing her legs wide, he gave himself a couple of hard strokes, delighting in the way her chocolate eyes lit with lust despite her recent climax.

"Hurry up," she demanded.

"Yes ma'am," he breathed, placing the tip of his erection at her wet entrance. Plunging into her sweet body in one smooth stroke, he shuddered, holding his breath and trying to stave off his imminent release. When he had a modicum of control, he pulled back until he almost left the haven of her body before pushing back into her once more. When her hands gripped his back, he felt a moment of unease at the thought of her touching his scars. But then she licked her way up his neck and sucked on his Adam's apple and he forgot all about his back.

"More, dammit. Harder!" the amazing woman beneath him gasped after only a few strokes.

Not one to disappoint, Lark raised himself up onto his knees, grabbing her ankles and pushing them onto his shoulders. He practically bent her in half when he lowered his weight back down onto her and proceeded to piston his hips fast and furious. Each thrust of his hips pushed her further up the bed until he was forced to let go of one of her legs and brace his hand against the bedhead behind her. Otherwise, as gone as he was, he could very well have fucked her clear through the wall.

The combination of Ivy's sinfully hot body and the delicious whimpers coming from her mouth proved to be too much stimulation and he felt his hips falter. Determined to see her through her pleasure first and recalling the sensitivity of her nipples, he leant down and sucked one tip into his mouth – hard. He also lowered his hips a little, ensuring his pelvis rubbed along her clit with every thrust of his hips.

The added stimulation was enough to have her exploding around him, her inner muscles working his length so hard he could barely move. Her moans and half-screams added fuel to his rampant desire and his own pleasure peaked a mere two strokes later. Groaning into her neck, he pumped his hips until he was completely spent, sure he'd never walk again.

Beneath him, Ivy wiggled her hips in a way that him groaning and pumping into her a few more times, despite his satiated state. She hummed her approval. This time, when he felt Ivy's hands stroking over the lines that marred his back, he didn't feel anything but bliss.

THIRTY-ONE

Ivy woke ... in a bed ... with another human being. What. The. Fuck. Clearly after their marathon sex session, she had fallen asleep in bed with Lark. She supposed it shouldn't surprise her – the man was an absolute animal in the sack! But in the past, she had never slept with anyone, not even Alex. She had never allowed her guard to lower that much. And she sure never trusted anyone that much. So what did it mean now, to find her back flush against Lark's front, as he spooned her from behind?

One masculine hand was loosely cupping her breast and there was a hairy leg, settled firmly and warmly between hers. She could feel his breath disrupting the hairs on her head as he breathed deeply and rhythmically, apparently still in the blissful ignorance of sleep. The previous night had been amazing. The sex had been fantastic – the best she'd ever had. She was feeling comfy and cosy and ... *panicky*.

Lark had tried to do the noble thing yesterday and ward her off, insisting she wasn't in the correct state of mind to jump into the sack with him. But had she listened? No. Life-affirming, instant gratification is what she had wanted, she remembered. The only problem, now in the light of a new day, was that she had no idea what the hell she was supposed to do from here.

The hand encompassing her breast gave a small squeeze and she felt Lark move his hips ever so subtly, his morning hardness brushing against the curve of her arse. His fingers on his other hand began weaving lazily in and out through the strands of her hair. He snuffled against her neck, "Hmm, morning."

She felt the words rumble roughly through his chest and fought the shiver they immediately elicited. *Danger! Abort, abort!* she yelled at herself. She was a ranger on a mission to potentially save their whole society. She didn't need to be feeling comfy or cosy or any other pansy emotion. She didn't need to be having sex with her colleague who was one hundred and thirty years younger than her and best friends with her brother. She certainly didn't need to be as attracted to the man's mind as much as she was attracted to his body.

Therein lie danger.

Feeling panic, she sprang from the bed and snatched up her phone, racing to the bathroom. She slammed the door, half of her knowing she was acting like a maniac and the other half wanting to hyperventilate. Searching her contacts, she called the only person she knew would pick up;

"Ivy? You'd better be dying," the sleep-roughened voice threatened, "Do you know what time it is?"

"Get over it!" she snapped, in no mood for Nikolai's good-natured banter.

She heard a pouty hmpf before he asked, "Are you okay?"

"No! I am not okay!" she screamed, "They infected me with their virus!"

"Infected? Virus?" he yelled back, sounding more awake. "What are you talking about? Are you sick?"

"Yesss," she hissed at him, "I'm very sick."

"Chade poison?" he barked out, all business now. She could hear rustling in the background and could picture him throwing on clothes and weapons.

"No, it's not that. Well, it was that. But not anymore. You're not listening to me!" she yelled, knowing she had yet to tell him anything *to* listen to.

"You were poisoned?" he asked.

"Yes," she huffed, impatiently.

"But you're fine now. Not dying?"

She yanked on her hair, feeling her anxiety continue to rise, "Yes, I'm fine now. Death is not imminent."

Nik let out an aggravated breath, "Jeez, Ivy. You scared the crap outta me. What's going on?"

"It's their ... *niceness*. It's contagious. I woke up all happy and safe and warm. I've talked more in the past few weeks than I have in my entire lifetime. And I feel like smiling all the time. Smiling!" she panted.

Her boss had the audacity to laugh at her, "I see. Well, this sounds very bad. I agree with you; it's a virus. Definitely a nasty virus," his words were solemn but his tone was filled with hilarity.

"I'm serious, Nik. Before I left they were calling me family. Family! It's going to be even worse now," she lamented.

"And what's wrong with that?" he questioned, his tone quieting now.

She scoffed, "Come on, we both know I'm not family material."

"Do we? Huh, what about Beyden then? Hasn't he always been your family?"

She gritted her teeth – Nik was being deliberately difficult, "That's different – he's my baby brother."

"And what about your mother? You always told me such

wonderful stories about her," he pushed.

She growled, "You're deliberately twisting the situation. Of course my mother and brother are family – it's not like I have a choice about that."

"No, you don't. But this family has a choice. And they're choosing you. What a wonderful privilege," his voice was soft, rich with rebuke and warmth at the same time.

Ivy felt her panic deflate and shame trickle in. Yes, a family made from choices and love instead of obligation was indeed an incredible type of special.

"Ivy, what's this really about?" her Commander asked her now.

She felt herself hesitate, "I told you –"

"Yes, yes – you're turning soft, nice-infections, and fuzzy viruses – blah blah. You're just letting people in, Ivy, that's all. That carefully constructed wall we all build so we can go and kill our brethren every day – people are finally choosing to see past it. It's a good thing, Ivy. It's about damn time if you ask me. What are you so worried about? Allowing people to see the real you will not take your power away. You're still a hard-arsed, bitch of a ranger. Always will be. Some of us honestly like that about you."

She pictured the red-headed, green-eyed man naked in the adjoining room and felt herself sigh, "I know – that's the problem. He does."

"He?" Nik's voice perked up before turning downright cheeky, "He? Well, isn't this interesting. Do you have a boyfriend, Ivy?"

"No!" she yelled, alarm rising for a whole other reason now. What had she been thinking, calling Nik about something like this?

"Oh, me think you doth protest too much. Tell me about him – no wait, let me guess; he's mature, tall, dark, broad shoulders with rippling abs and a fuck-the-world attitude."

Ivy didn't say anything but knew he could hear the gnashing of her teeth.

He chuckled, "Come on, Ivy. I'm right, aren't I? I bet he's a real bear."

She hated his assumptions, "You're wrong on every count; he's young – thirty-one to be exact, lean with auburn hair, the perfect six-pack, and happy as a lark."

Silence met her ears for a few seconds, before; "Happy as a lark, you say? Or do you mean his name is Lark? Tell me you're not sleeping with that baby-faced paladin!"

She stiffened in insult from his disbelieving tone, "And what if I am?"

"He doesn't suit you, that's all," he answered.

"What do you mean, he doesn't suit me? He suits me just fine! I'll have you know that he's very intelligent and can actually carry a conversation with words that are more than one syllable. He reads books that aren't just pictures. He's open and friendly and caring. And he's a damn good soldier. You should see him cutting down the chades – he moves like some kind of a warrior-dancer-god!"

By the time she finished her defence of Lark, she was yelling and running out of breath. She then also realised two things simultaneously; Nik had deliberately goaded her into revealing her true feelings and Lark was now standing directly behind her, listening to everything.

"I gotta go. But when I see you next, I'm going to kick you in the nuts – hard!" she informed her commander. His deep, baritone laughter could be heard as she hit the *end* button on her phone.

Wondering if she could stay really still and Lark would move on just like a T-rex would, she held her breath. But apparently, he didn't share any DNA with the extinct reptiles because she could feel his breath fanning against the back of her neck and his hands spanning her waist. A definite prod of something hard against her bottom left her in no doubt as to how Lark had received her words.

"Ivy ..." he breathed.

"Yes ..." she responded, breathlessly.

"I'm good with words."

She nodded, "I know."

"But I'm not going to use words now," he informed her.

She swallowed hard, "You're not?"

Soft lips traced the back her neck, "Uh uh ... I'm going to use actions. Ivy ..."

She gulped, audibly.

"Prepare yourself," he warned one second before lifting her up and throwing her over his shoulder.

THIRTY-TWO

Lark sighed, feeling smug, relaxed and just about perfect. He'd been concerned when Ivy had made her mad dash to the bathroom. He didn't want to eavesdrop but had been scared she was talking to someone who would support whatever crazy notions were running through her head. Hearing her admit to her true feelings about him had made him feel like the king of the world. The power of a goddess running through his veins paled in comparison to the feelings her words evoked. After tossing her over his shoulder and throwing her down on the bed, he had proceeded to show her just how far his appreciation went.

Now, two hours later, he was exhausted but sated with a gloriously naked Ivy in his arms. They hadn't spoken but she also hadn't done another runner. He could only hope that meant she wasn't panicking about the 'nice virus' again. He snorted, remembering her words to her commander. The poor woman had gotten so used to being unemotional, a few happy feelings made her believe she was sick. He would help her with that and he knew the others would too.

Presently, Ivy shifted, causing the blankets to slip down. Her high, firm breasts and dusky nipples were completely exposed to his gaze and he felt his mouth water. Too bad her next words had his erection deflating in one second flat.

"You know I had sex with Ryker, don't you?"

He immediately stiffened at the reminder and took his time answering, forcing down the urge to march back to camp and throttle his Captain half to death, "I'm aware," he bit out.

"Does that bother you?" she asked, head tilted on the pillow, long, black hair in utter disarray around her heart-shaped face.

Because of me, he reminded himself. *Her hair is messed up, her cheeks flushed, and her eyes are glassy from pleasure because of me.* He never considered himself to be a possessive person but hearing Ivy talk about ex-lovers had him re-thinking his position. Realising she was still awaiting his response, he answered her honestly;

"Yes, it bothers me. Not because it was Ryker, necessarily ..." although, he was pretty sure he'd be challenging the other man to a duel next time they trained together, "The thought of you with anyone but me is *bothersome.*"

"Really?" Ivy asked, surprise evident in her voice.

Lark cocked his head at her, "Why does that surprise you? After everything we've been through these past weeks, everything I've learned about you. And especially after the amazing night – and morning – we just had. You're perfect in every way to me. Seeing you here like this – relaxed and rosy ..." he broke off, tracing a finger around the pert, dark disc on the tip of her breast, "The thought of anyone else seeing you like this ... well, it makes me see red."

"Even though it was before I met you?" she queried.

"Even though," he admitted through gritted teeth. He

had always thought he was so even-tempered and easy-going. Seems he also had some barbarian in him too. He kind of liked it – not that he would be telling Ivy that.

Ivy was watching him now with a gleam in her eyes he couldn't place. "Max doesn't care that I slept with her guy," she pointed out.

He grunted at that, flopping down onto his back next to her. The post-sex happy glow he was feeling was steadily being sucked away with all this ex-lover talk. "Yeah, well. Max isn't quite right in the head, is she?" he informed his woman, a little grumpily.

And then she did it – something he had never seen her do in all the months he had known her.

She laughed.

The sound was bright and bubbly, a tinkling tone filled with warmth and humour. Right then was the moment he felt himself fall ... and fall hard.

*****

"What is it?" Ivy asked, peering up at the stupefied look on Lark's face, "Are you okay? You look like you've just had a stroke."

"What? No, I mean yes, I'm fine. No stroke."

His chuckle was rough and sounded forced to her ears. But then, what did she know? This whole, relaxing with a lover in post-coital bliss was new to her. "You don't need to be bothered," she volunteered.

"Oh?" he arched an eyebrow at her, still looking a little miffed and she'd be lying if she said his possessiveness and jealousy didn't make her happy.

"You don't need to be bothered because this is a first for me. Nobody else has ever seen me like this," she expanded.

"Huh?" he still looked a little confused and she wondered

if he'd lost some of his IQ when he'd orgasmed so hard earlier.

"Like this ..." she waved a hand at herself and repeated his words back to him, "All relaxed and rosy. I've never been this way with anyone else."

And it was the truth too. She'd had her fair share of sex over the years but it had always been a perfunctory task. Usually something to do as a form of release but sometimes for the sake of having some basic human contact. Alex had been the exception and look how well that had turned out. She had never been interested in anything more intimate. But somehow Lark had managed to change her values in just a few short months. His daily words of romance and of kindness had accomplished what might and force could never have done; break down her fortified walls.

"Talk to me," his voice broke the silence.

"You want to talk?" she asked, surprised.

"Sure. I'm happy to pursue more active endeavours if you prefer. I'm also happy to hold you as we sleep too. But we've already done both. Besides, I've been thinking–"

"Do you ever stop thinking?" she cut in.

He shrugged, "No. Not really. My brain is constantly on the prowl, wheels continuously turning, constantly processing. I'm pretty much a geek. Does that bother you?"

She looked at him, surprised, "No. Why would it?"

"I don't know. Some people find it annoying," he explained.

"Not me. Intelligence is sexy," she admitted before she could censor herself.

"Really? Sexy, huh?" he almost sounded like he was purring as he nuzzled her neck and she felt her body light up with anticipation.

"I thought we were going to talk," she reminded him. She was more than happy to go another round. But she also found herself wanting to know what he had been thinking.

He pulled back, searching her face, "You sure? It's going to be a mood killer."

Her stomach dipped a little but she nodded anyway, "You want to talk about the council," she guessed.

He nodded, "I do. As well as the chades. I have these ideas you see and it helps to have a sounding board."

Her duty as a ranger demanded complete loyalty to the council and any talk against them amounted to treason. She knew better than most what the punishment was for such a crime. But she'd be lying if she didn't admit she had questions – for a long time now. She was also tickled that Lark trusted her and valued her opinion, so she simply nodded and waited for him to speak.

"Okay, well, let's start with the massacre itself and then move on to the timing of it," he began, getting up and pulling on pants. "We all know there has never been a coordinated attack like that ever in all our history, despite the fact that chades have been a part of our world for thousands of years."

She propped some pillows behind her back, intrigued when he started to pace, hands clasped behind his back. He looked like a hot professor gearing up for a lecture. She responded even though he hadn't asked a question, "Right. As long as there have been wardens, there have been chades. But never in the numbers that we've been seeing the past couple hundred years. And certainly not in the numbers we saw before the Great Massacre. Although, what we've seen these last few months ..."

"Exactly, why is that? What happened to make the numbers increase? It's a medical condition – a disease – so what changed a couple of hundred years ago to make the disease more prevalent?"

She thought about that, finding herself genuinely drawn into the conversation, "You think there was some kind of trigger?" she guessed.

He nodded once in the affirmative, "I do. There had to have been. It's the only thing that makes sense. I'm thinking environmental ..."

Now it was her turn to nod as she followed his reasoning, "Right. Because it can't be evolutionary – like a natural progression. It slowed down. After the Great Massacre, the number of chade conversions decreased for a while. They're just starting to increase again now. If it was merely evolutionary, we would have seen a steady increase in the numbers over the years – or at least a constant number."

She looked up to find Lark grinning at her, "You're right," he said, "Intelligence is sexy."

She ducked her head, feeling a warm flush heat her cheeks. His approval meant a lot to her, "How does this help us?" she asked.

He grunted, "I don't know. But I think if we figure out the trigger, we can figure out the motive behind the attack."

She sat up straight again, "You think there was a specific purpose for the massacre?"

"Of course. Don't you? Why else?"

"Food," she automatically stated, but Lark was already shaking his head.

"That made sense when we thought chades were driven purely by instinct – or evil. But we know better now, thanks to Dex and Knox and all the others."

She couldn't dispute that, "Then if not for vitality, why then?"

Lark shoved his hands in his pockets, pacing again now. With every turn, she caught glimpses of his scarred back and she remembered feeling them beneath her nails when she clung to him during sex. The rough texture added a little something extra to the experience – though she wasn't insensitive enough to say so out loud.

"To destroy evidence, to kill the most powerful wardens, to diminish paladin numbers," Lark ticked off his reasons.

"Wait ... destroy what evidence? And what makes you think the powerful wardens were targeted?" she asked, trying to keep up.

He stood in front of her, "Don't you think it's interesting that not a single member of the council was killed during the massacre? I know a lot of other powerful, well-respected wardens fell victim to the chades – Verity and Flint included," he said, naming Diana's and Ryker's first lieges. "I think we should consider who within the council was present during the massacre. I think we should also look into who recalled all the most important Orders back here right before the attack," he continued.

"Ryker's Order, Dex's Order, Diana's Order ... three of the most reputable, respected and strong Orders at the time. And there was at least a dozen more. The council pulled dozens of wardens away from their usual tasks – even the ones who had permanent postings. I know for a fact that Ryker had never been to Australia before, for example. And Dex's Order – sure, Darius is great with the history books but so were a lot of other paladins and wardens, including the majority of the council members. Any number of local wardens could have helped with mere research like they proclaimed. So why was his Order reassigned here?"

"Because there was a chade epidemic and they needed the extra numbers to help fight as well as to help get answers. They needed the numbers and the soldiers," she was playing devil's advocate, but her brain was ticking.

"No, no, no. That doesn't work," his energy was positively frenetic now as he warmed up to the topic. "If that was the case, why didn't they call in more rangers? There were hundreds of rangers around the world that could have been called back. But they weren't. Only the truly powerful wardens."

Ivy felt her mouth drop open, "Holy shit. You're right. I never thought of that."

"Apparently nobody else has either," he said. "You see? It was never about stopping the chades. It was about herding specific wardens into the one area. And that area? The training centre and council headquarters which were all coincidentally burned to the ground." He sat on the edge of the bed, his face filled with excitement, "What was stored in those buildings?"

She frowned, knowing the answer was important but not quite there yet, "Records?" she hedged.

"The Chronicles!" Lark said. "Written documentation of everything in our society from the beginning of time."

"By the Great Mother ..." she whispered, feeling the rightness of all that he'd said in her gut, "What was in the Warden Chronicles that would cause someone to instigate an attack, slaughtering hundreds of Mother Nature's keepers, just to ensure they were destroyed?"

"Now that, my dear Ivy, is the real question. And one I don't have the answer to – yet."

She expelled a breath, rubbing at the now faint claw marks on her arm. They no longer bothered her and the wound was healing quickly. She knew not even a scar would remain by the time Max got her hands on her back at camp. Lark had already informed her of such.

"Are you okay?" he covered her hand with his own.

She smiled weakly at him, "My head is spinning," she admitted. "So ... what now?"

He stood up and began gathering up the rest of his clothes, "Now? I think it's time we headed home, don't you?"

She sucked in a deep breath and nodded. Home sounded pretty damn good to her.

THIRTY-THREE

He was so lost in his thoughts, he didn't see the wall of human flesh until he almost ran into it, "Aargh!" he screamed, clutching his runaway heart, "What the hell do you think you're all doing?"

Cali, Diana, Axel, Darius, and Dex were blocking the doorway, arms crossed, faces looking serious. He felt his belly clutch, "What is it? What's happened?"

"Nothing's happened. Everything's cool," Axel immediately reassured him.

Lark was glad to hear it but something was clearly bothering them and he didn't allow himself to relax, "What's going on, then?"

Cali cleared her throat, "It's an intervention."

"Pardon?" he asked, sure he was hearing incorrectly.

"An intervention," Cali repeated. "Like the one you guys held for me."

Lark eyed the five of them now with a mixture of annoyance and amusement. He allowed the amusement to win – for now, "And why exactly would I need a Dex-sex intervention? I promise we haven't been together like that since I found out about the baby." That made them all laugh, even the ever-serious Darius.

"It's not about you and Dex and your sordid affair," Cali informed him.

"Then what's this all about?" he was positive he already knew but he wanted to make them say it.

"It's about Ivy," Diana said.

Just as he suspected and that's why he was equal parts annoyed and amused. They had been home for exactly fifteen hours and thirteen of those had been spent debriefing and catching everybody up on what had transpired over the last four weeks. He was beyond pleased to hear the redeemed chades were doing well and their friends were happy and safe monitoring and serving them. He had been more than a little shocked to learn Knox was Kane, Kai, and Kellan's father. The man hadn't once mentioned it the entire time they'd been away. Thinking about it now, he couldn't believe he had missed the signs. The triplets certainly resembled their father, particularly their grey eyes.

They had also discussed the episode with the 'evil' chades, although he had glossed right over the part about him being born a potentate. It didn't escape his notice that Ryker hadn't brought it up either and he knew the other man was just biding his time. The upcoming confrontation bothered him a little but there was nothing he could do about it, so he chose not to dwell on it. He and Ivy had rehashed their theories about the council, the chades, and the massacre. Many of their points had not been well-received at first but as they began to toss the ideas around, everyone agreed it all made a terrible kind of sense. Lark had other theories – big ones – but he was keeping them to himself for now. It wasn't something he could afford to bring up and then be wrong about.

After thirteen hours of talking and thirty minutes of hugging he had finally managed to escape to his room with Ivy for a shower – and shower sex. He had made no attempt to hide his affections for the ranger but he also hadn't been obvious either. He knew she wasn't ready for that yet. However, given they had both emerged from the spiral staircase ten minutes ago with wet hair and satisfied smiles, he knew the gang would be wanting answers.

"What about her?" he asked them in response to their comment.

"You're in love with her," Cali pointed out.

He nodded once, "I am." Even if he hadn't told her that yet, he knew it was obvious to the people who knew him the best.

"But she's not in love with you," Axel added.

Lark scowled at his friend. How dare he make assumptions about Ivy's feelings! So what if she didn't love him? He sincerely hoped she would one day but he would never pressure her or expect more from her than she was capable of giving. What they shared now was more than enough for him. He told them as much and they all clearly heard his anger in his waspish tone.

"I'm sorry, man. I just don't want to see you get hurt. I know what it's like to be in a one-sided relationship," Axel's voice echoed with past hurt.

Lark felt his irritation deflate. He knew they were just concerned for him. He had been the same when he realised Cali was sleeping with Dex – an ex-chade. And as loud and as brash as Axel could be at times, he really was a genuine, caring guy who'd been crushed by a past relationship. He sighed, "I appreciate the concern – I truly do. But you don't need to worry about my feelings. Or Ivy's."

"You sound very sure of her," Cali stated.

"I am," he promised.

She fidgeted a little, "Well, it's just, she's not exactly the most demonstrative person. How can you be sure?"

"Not demonstrative?" he questioned in surprise, his mind immediately going to the bedroom last night when Ivy had ridden him like a cowgirl and proceeded to sleep ranged over his chest for the remainder of the evening. He couldn't help the raunchy grin that tilted his lips as he looked at his friends.

"Okay, ick. I can tell your mind has reverted to the gutter," Cali shook her head at him.

He laughed, "Trust me, Ivy shows her affection more than enough. Just because she's not as touchy feely as the rest of you, or into kinky public sex acts –"

"Hey! It was one time and you were supposed to be in bed!" Darius interjected, blushing and making them all laugh.

Diana picked up his hand, "It's not that we're not happy for you, Lark. We just want to make sure you're not alone in your feelings."

"I'm not," he assured them, completely confident in Ivy's feelings for him. They were hard-won by him and so darn reluctant on her part, he knew there was no way she would be with him if she didn't feel something special for him down to her very bones.

"Okay, Lark. We believe you," Diana smiled brilliantly at him.

"But would it kill her to hold your hand or something?" Cali demanded.

He shook his head at her, she was like a dog with a bone and her protective instincts had gone up ten-fold since she became pregnant, "I'll tell you what, we'll hold hands and skip along the beach at sunset, holding a bunch of white daisies and singing a love song. How about that?"

She pouted at him a little and Dex wrapped an arm

around her, his dark eyes twinkling, "That ought to do it. I mean, that's how we prove our love, isn't it?"

Cali huffed, "Fine, fine. You win. I give up."

Lark walked over to her, kissing her on the cheek and giving her far rounder tummy an affectionate pat, "Thank you."

"You're welcome," she responded, quietly.

"Am I interrupting?"

Ivy's voice had them all whirling to the doorway and Lark grinned at his lover. She looked decidedly uncomfortable, as if she were encroaching on him and his circle of friends. But she didn't back away or excuse herself. That more than anything told Lark she was determined to give their relationship a chance.

"We were just discussing public displays of affection," he informed her. "Cali believes hand-holding is the only way to show someone they are liked."

"Not the only way," the woman in question said, "just an easy way."

"Is that so?" Ivy queried, her face remaining impassive and her tone dry as per usual.

Cali finally had the good grace to squirm, "I'm just sayin', a little hand-holding wouldn't kill you," she mumbled.

The corner of Ivy's mouth kicked up minutely and Lark felt the impact of that tiny smile in the skipping of his heart. Such a small sign of amusement and yet to him it was as warm and as beautiful as the sun. He knew his woman now, knew her nuances and he recognised the mischievous glint in her eye. Sure, to most her feelings, thoughts, and affections weren't obvious. But with his photographic memory and his high IQ, he was overly skilled in reading the smallest of facial expressions and body language. Ivy's small reactions were like glaring beacons of light to him. He didn't need or want her to suddenly become a giggly, bouncy, loved-up female with small hearts in her eyes and a spring in her step. She was absolutely perfect just as she was.

The small flash of amusement left Ivy's face as she walked over to Cali, grabbing her hand and holding it without a word. Everyone was staring dumbstruck; "What?" Ivy demanded, "I thought you wanted to hold hands?"

A full ten seconds of silence met Ivy's attempt at humour before they all erupted into unrestrained laughter. Cali pursed her lips before joining in the laughter and giving Ivy a quick hug, "You're all right."

THIRTY-FOUR

Lark thrashed, trying to break free of the icy fingers of terror that was his nightmare.

"Lark! Lark!" he heard her voice and was finally able to draw in a shaky breath of the frigid air which surrounded him in the soulless pit he was in. Drawing in another ragged breath, he decided that breathing was good – very good. But he still couldn't see a way out of the blackness.

"Lark, can you hear me? Come on, my sexy boy-toy, come back to me."

Boy toy? he thought. The notion was such a stark contrast to the desolate environment he was trapped in that he was able to fight his way back to consciousness. He opened his eyes and sat bolt upright, seeing Ivy watching him with concern. Lifting a shaking hand to his face, he wiped at the cold sweat which had accumulated there.

"Bad dream?" Ivy inquired, mildly.

He barked out a rough laugh, "How'd you guess?"

"I'm observant," was her droll response.

The very clear joke warmed him as nothing else could and

he smiled genuinely at her this time, "Thanks for waking me up."

She shrugged, "No biggie."

"Trust me, it is to me," he assured her. "These dreams ... they're changing. Or staying the same, rather. Repeating the same thing over and over ..." He knew he was mumbling and likely not making any sense but he was trying to figure out what about Max's ongoing nightmares that bothered him – more than usual, that was.

Ivy tucked the sheet around her naked body more firmly and crossed her legs, "What's staying the same?"

"Max's dreams, they used to change every night. I mean, there's always common elements; the blackness, the cold, the helplessness. But they've been shifting. A few weeks ago, when I woke up I felt a sense of familiarity – like déjà vu. Now I know why. It's because the dreams are repeating themselves. She's dreaming about a particular chade ..." he trailed off, trying to align his scattered thoughts.

He knew Max felt the pain of the chades, that she dreamt of them and took the weight of all the pain and the hopelessness and the fear of those lost wardens into herself. But lately, he could swear what she was feeling was coming from just one chade – not them as a collective. And the chade was bad news. It was like all the other chades were Storm Troopers and this one was Darth Vader. There wasn't just a sense of nothingness or despair about this guy. There was maliciousness, evil – intent. And there was something about a finger ...

He shook his head hard as the nightmare fell through his fingers like water. "Dammit!" he muttered, wishing his mind would hold onto it long enough to fit the puzzle pieces together.

"Dreams are fickle," Ivy offered, stroking his arm.

He really wanted to lean into the touch but he knew she

was doing it subconsciously and he didn't want to alert her to the fact. Instead, he drifted for a while in the comfy quiet of the room. "Wait a minute," he swung his head toward her, "Did you call me your boy-toy?"

Ivy pursed her lips, "No."

He grinned at her in the darkness, "You did. I heard you even in the midst of my nightmare. You called me your boy-toy."

"So what if I did?" she asked now, "You are a boy and I do toy with you ..."

He dived on her, making her gasp when the decidedly *un-boyish* evidence of his desire pressed against her hip, "Hmm," he nuzzled her neck, "I think I like being your boy-toy."

She gripped his arse, bring him closer, "That's a good thing because I like it too. In fact, I love it," she admitted.

He felt his love for her bloom and he couldn't resist leaning down to kiss her, slow and deep. After a minute, he pulled back and simply stared at the graceful angles of her face.

"What's with the look?" she asked him, breaking the spell they were under.

"What look?"

She touched his face, "That look right now. It's the same look you got when I thought you were stroking out."

He laughed, "Only a woman who thought niceness was contagious would confuse the look of love with a haemorrhagic brain bleed."

She snorted, only to choke when his words registered, "Love?"

He had intended to wait to tell her but oh well, "Yes, Ivy. Love. I love you."

She shook her head, aggressively, "You can't."

"I do."

"Well, stop it."

"No."

"I won't say it back," she warned.

He shrugged, settling his weight more fully upon her, "That's fine. Your response is irrelevant."

"It's irrelevant?!"

Wow, he hadn't known her voice could go that high, "Sure. It won't change anything. I don't care if you don't feel the same way. I'm in love you. That's all there is to it."

She pushed at his shoulders, "You're insane."

He laughed, "Why? Because I love you?"

She shoved at his shoulders again, this time bringing her knee up dangerously close to his goodies. He allowed her to push him back and she immediately sat up. "Well, now you've ruined it. We can't go around doing this anymore," she waved a hand between them, indicating their naked state.

He lounged on his side, completely unconcerned but thoroughly entertained, "We can't? Because I was kind of thinking being in love might add a little more spice to the sex."

"I'm serious, Lark," her voice held a note of anger. "Things are going to change now. You're going to expect me to change. Maybe leave the rangers, come play house with you? Keep recharging Dex, maybe be his personal paladin?"

He didn't so much as flinch at her harsh tone, "Why would I want you to do any of that? I fell in love with you just as you are, Ivy. I wouldn't even know what to do with the Ivy you just described. I want you – just as you are right now."

"Will you stop saying that?" she growled at him.

"I don't know why you're so upset. I did warn you," he reminded her, probably not helping the situation.

"Lark ..."

"Ivy ..." he mimicked.

She huffed at him but then he saw her shoulders hunch,

"I have nothing to offer you," she whispered the words.

That had him sitting up, "That's not true. Besides, I'm not asking for anything. Those three words are given freely with nothing expected in return. They are a gift, Ivy – not a responsibility or a burden. Just a gift. Hasn't anyone ever given you a gift before?"

"Not that kind of gift," she muttered.

He picked up her hand and kissed each finger, "Well, this one has a no returns policy. Sorry, not sorry," he sang.

He felt rather than saw the small smile on her lips as she laid her cheek against his. Coaxing her back down, he drew her in tight. "Talk to me," he urged.

She poked a finger into his ribs, "All I do is talk to you. I swear, you make me feel positively chatty."

Lark smiled, feeling happy and satisfied, "I like listening to your voice. Tell me something I don't know. Um ..." he thought about it for a second and then asked, "Why did you so readily agree to work for Max? How did you get your brand?"

*****

Ivy felt herself stiffen once more and she hesitated, prevaricating; "She showed me something."

"Showed you?" he asked, voice lazy.

She nodded, "In my head. After that debacle at Caspian's, Beyden was forced to tell me about Max. I didn't believe him at first despite what I had seen her do. I mean, come on – a Custodian? So I confronted Max, figured she was manipulating my brother somehow."

A laugh rumbled in his chest beneath her ear, "Really? I would have loved to have seen that. What did she show you?"

Her first reaction to the unwanted question was to tell him to mind his own business. But because it was Lark and because she was trying to react like a normal person rather than one always in combat, she answered steadily, "I don't want to say. It's not that I don't trust you or anything, it's just –"

"Hey, hey ..." he interrupted, rolling her beneath him once again and propping himself up on his forearms, "It's fine. No pressure. You don't have to tell me. I was just curious and making conversation. You're allowed to have things that are just for you," he assured her.

She nodded but she still felt guilty. He had given her so much; fun, laughter ... love. And what had she given him in return? Maybe some world-altering orgasms but that was about it. She knew why she was holding back on the whole Max thing. It was because of what Max had shown her. Ivy was worried that if she thought about it too hard or spoke about it out loud that she would somehow jinx herself and the possible future Max had shown her would not come to pass.

When Ivy had demanded answers after the fiasco at Caspian's house, Max had explained who and what she was patiently. Ivy had scoffed and been her typical rude self. Max hadn't blinked an eye, just asked her if she would be willing to work for her as a spy. At first, Ivy thought she was joking – no way would the woman be stupid enough to admit to sedition in front of a ranger. But Max's turquoise eyes had remained steady and guileless on hers and Ivy had been quick to disabuse her of her notion;

"I know you're new and all but offers like that will get you killed."

Max didn't even blink, "No they won't. You are going to work with me. In fact, we're going to become good friends – sisters even."

"Is that right?" she scoffed.

Max nodded, sending her thick, wild hair soaring,

"Indeed. Do you want to see?"

Ivy shook her head, utterly confused, "See what?"

"Possibilities. Possibilities you can help make happen."

Thinking the woman was getting crazier by the second, Ivy had foolishly agreed. And it had been foolish, she admitted. For what Max had shown her was all her secret hopes and wants and dreams. They had seemed so real, so tangible, that she'd felt like she could reach out and touch them and she had known that Max was the real-deal. But what was it that Max had shown her?

A room full of chades who were once again men. Men who were wardens and once more warriors and guardians for nature. The room had been filled with light and laughter. There had been no sickles in sight and no thieving of vitality. Just for that one possibility alone, Ivy would have jumped at the chance to serve Max. But right at the end of the vision, Ivy had felt something else; a rough hand holding her own.

She had been too afraid to look up to see if the warm hand had a face but the feeling that came from the hand engulfing hers had been enough to have her going down on one knee and swearing fealty to the custodian on the spot. A gentle smile from Max and thirty seconds later, Ivy had been sporting a circle of black symbols on her upper arm.

"Ivy?"

The deep voice startled her from her reverie and she saw Lark watching her with concern.

"Where were you?" he asked, tucking an errant hair behind her ear.

Unable to help herself, she leant into the touch, "I was in the future," she answered, honestly.

His eyebrows raised, "Oh? And what did you see?"

Pushing him to his back, she straddled his trim waist, "How about I show you?"

He groaned, his hips bucking up and his hardness

already seeking entrance into her body. She didn't disappoint him and she didn't make him wait. The trip down memory lane coupled with Lark's words of love, had her feeling a little desperate. Gripping his shaft in one hand she held it steady as she slid down effortlessly. She gasped, her head falling back on her shoulders as he filled her to capacity. Her internal muscles clenched of their own accord and this time it was his turn to gasp.

She felt a surge of womanly triumph at the sound and she planted her hands on his pecs, leaning forward. Her hair created a dark curtain of intimacy as she touched her lips to his. The kiss started out slow and sensual but quickly turned fast and hungry as raw desire swept throughout her body. Pushing up again, she ran her hands over his perfectly proportioned and deliciously limber body as she began to pump her hips.

He let her set the pace for all of five minutes before her deliberate movements proved too much for his control. He gripped her hips and began to thrust into with enough force to have her grabbing his wrists just so she could remain in place. As she had come to expect, his cock somehow managed to hit every sweet spot she never knew she had and she felt her skin flush hot with her impending release. Aware of every nuance of her moods, her man chose that moment to reach between them and run a thumb over her sensitive mound.

"Yes!" she gasped out, her body losing all finesse and coordination as her orgasm rushed through her. His harsh curse quickly sounded in the dim confines of the room and she felt his body clench tight with his own release.

Moaning, she allowed him to roll her to her side and cuddled into his front. Soft lips touched the top of her head and she closed her eyes tightly. She didn't need Lark's photographic memory to retain the sights and sensations of the night. She knew the pleasure and the words were forever

seared into her brain.
    And her heart.

THIRTY-FIVE

Lark was still riding high the next morning. Despite her words to the contrary, Ivy's lovemaking had taken a decidedly intimate turn. All concerns of evil mastermind chades and bad dreams had vanished amidst the hours of slow, sweet pleasure. He didn't need the words – those would come with time. For now, he was content with Ivy's actions.

"Lark, a word?"

And just like that, Lark felt his happy mood evaporate. He turned to face his Captain and sure enough, the man's face was as serious as his tone. Figuring he knew what this little ambush was about, Lark decided to go on the defensive, "Ryker, I'm sorry. I know I lied to you and I know how much you hate that. I promise I won't do it again. It's just –" If he wasn't mistaken, Lark could swear he was on the verge of hyperventilating. The thought of disappointing the man who had given him everything, cut him to the quick.

"Whoa. Slow down, there. Take a couple of breaths," Ryker placed a warm palm on the back of his neck and squeezed reassuringly. "Good, now ..." he said after Lark did his bidding, "want to tell me what you're apologising for?"

Lark glanced up, seeing concern on Ry's face, "For not telling you I was a potentate. I know I broke all manner of laws; the IDC must be notified of every potentate. I know there's only allowed to be one potentate in every Order. I know how sparse potentates are now and the council needs every single one. But I honestly hadn't even thought about it in years. After I managed to convince my father I wasn't born with the gift, I just forgot about it. I mean, it wasn't like I was ever going to be in an Order. And then Max came along and I just –"

"Lark! Will you shut up for a minute?!" Ryker yelled to be heard over Lark's continuous chatter, "I don't care," he then said, blandly.

That sure shut him up and Lark found himself blinking a few times in confusion, "You don't care?" he repeated.

Ryker shook his head, "Nope. Couldn't give two shits, to be honest. I just don't understand why you kept it a secret. What did you think would happen if you told me?"

Lark shrugged, feeling a little embarrassed about his over-reaction now, "Before Max? I guess it was a non-issue. But after Max? I was terrified you would tell the council and they would make me leave the Order. One potentate per Order. That's the rules."

Ryker scowled, "And how long has it been since I've given a fuck about the rules?"

Lark felt his lips twitch and his shoulders relaxed for the first time in minutes, "A long time, I guess."

Ry grunted, "That's right. I'm in love with my liege – completely against the rules. I'm in an Order that was never sanctioned by the council – completely against the rules. Multiple members of my Order are in intimate relationships – completely against the rules. I have a former chade living in one of my bedrooms who also happened to knock up one of my paladins – really fucking completely against the rules."

Lark laughed as Ry's list went on and on, "I see your point."

"Good," Ry cleared his throat and shifted a little uncomfortably, "Just so you know – you can come to me about anything. I may not be a genius but I'm a good listener and I'm always here for you ... and stuff."

Lark felt his smile spread slowly until he was sure it consumed his entire face; an uncomfortable Ryker in touch with his feelings sure was a thing to behold. Instead of teasing the man, as he was inclined to do, he clapped him on the back, "Thanks, man. I know that."

Ryker cleared his throat and nodded once, "Good. That's settled then. Unless you want a death match to prove who should be Captain of the Order?" he asked, grinning as well now.

Lark recognised the evil glint in Ry's brown eyes and knew he would end up slammed to a mat if he took the man up on the offer, "Um, that would be a no ... Sir," he added.

"We'll consider the matter closed then. I actually came to speak to you about something else ..." he trailed off and his face returned to its earlier seriousness.

Lark felt dread pooling in his stomach, "What is it?"

Ryker looked him straight in the eye as he answered, "Wardens and paladins are being recalled from their posts from all around the world. They're being given orders to assemble here – at the local headquarters."

"The council?" Lark questioned.

"Yeah," Ry nodded.

Lark frowned, his mind quickly processing the ramifications of such a move, "Why?"

"Ostensibly? To meet Max – so all wardens can present themselves to her, as an opportunity for them to show their respect."

"You don't believe that," it was a statement.

Ryker clenched his jaw, "No, I don't."

Neither do I, he thought, remembering his theories about the council recalling Orders right before the Great Massacre. "Who is in charge of calling them in?" he asked next.

"Mordecai."

The name surprised him. It really wasn't the name he had been expecting to hear. He had thought maybe Ravyn, Ares, or Cinder would be behind such a bold move. They were the ones who had been so outspoken in their dislike and distrust of Max. Blu, Garrett, and Autumn had been her biggest supporters. And Mordecai had been the wild-card who could go either way. It seemed perhaps the man had now chosen a side. Although, it didn't quite sit well with him.

Lark had observed the Death Warden many times now because he had a disconcerting habit of staring at Max. The others thought he was cold and creepy – unless you asked the girls, who thought he was hot. But Lark could swear he saw something else in the man's green eyes. Something he wasn't quite ready to believe. Not until he had a chance to investigate and think a little more, in any case.

"Maybe someone should have a chat with him. I'd be happy to," he offered. In fact, he was going to insist upon it. Luckily, his Captain nodded;

"That's what I was thinking. And I was hoping you'd volunteer. I think your observation skills would come in handy. I want your take on the guy."

It was good that Ry already had him in mind for such a task, but Lark wanted the opportunity to talk to the warden one on one. Before he could formulate a good argument however, Ryker spoke again;

"That's not all I wanted to talk to you about. There's something else."

"Oh? What is it?" Lark asked, easily.

"It's Isaac."

He immediately stiffened upon hearing his father's name and he was sure he went pale. Despite the years away from the man and his own newfound perfect situation, the thought of his father still terrified him. He swallowed hard, steadying his voice, "What about him?"

Ryker's gaze was direct and steady, "His Order is one of the ones being recalled. He's here."

THIRTY-SIX

She found him in the gym beating the crap out of a punching bag. He was sweating and panting heavily as he hopped around the bag, throwing punch after punch and making the bag swing wildly. It looked like he was working off some major aggression and she wondered what had happened between waking her up with soft kisses against her shoulder, to now.

She had never seen him like this. She had seen his tightly reigned control. She had seen his melancholy when he had danced. She had seen his fierceness when he fought the chades. She had even seen him when he was annoyed and frustrated. But she had never observed him in a mood so *raw*. She hadn't thought he was capable of it but she should know better than to think she had him all figured out by now. The guy was about as deep as they came – it was one of the things she liked most about him. Unsure if she should approach him or just leave him alone, she decided on the middle ground and sat herself down on the bench to wait him out.

His vicious energy lasted longer than she would have thought and it was a full fifteen minutes later when he finally stopped punishing the bag. She thought he would turn around and say something to her, knowing he must have noticed her presence by now. The man noticed everything, especially when it came to her. It always made her feel special. But instead, he just leant his head against the bag, hugging it to him as he sucked in harsh breaths. She felt herself get even more concerned now and began making her way over to him.

"Lark ..." she said softly, wanting to alert him to her approach. She saw him stiffen but he gave no other indication he had heard her and she felt her gut clench; something was very wrong. She may not be able to say the 'L' word like he did but she was as emotionally invested as she was capable of being. Seeing him obviously hurting, hurt her and she placed a tentative hand on his back.

He flinched at the contact, hissing; "Don't!"

She immediately removed her hand, startled at the anger in his voice. Had she done something wrong? Was this little rage-against-the-innocent-punching-bag routine, about her? Maybe he had changed his mind about how he felt about her. After the 'intervention' his fellow knights had held, she knew he had thought the whole thing to be humorous and endearing. But what if he had reconsidered – even after his declaration last night? Well, if she was going to get dumped, she wished he'd get on with it;

"Whatever it is, just spit it out."

He chuckled but the noise sounded bitter as he pushed away from the bag and faced her, "What?" he asked, acerbly, "I'm not allowed to have a bad mood?"

She thought about it for a moment because it was just so strange to her. Sure, he was allowed to have a bad mood. Everyone had bad moods. She just hadn't thought it was possible. He was always just so ... *Lark*. Another rough chuckle had her looking up once again and she was relieved beyond measure to see a wry smile on his handsome face this time as he shook his head;

"You look so confused," he pointed out, beginning to unwind the wraps on his hands.

"I guess I am. I've never seen you like this. I'm not sure what I'm supposed to do," she admitted.

"What do you want to do?" he asked, throwing the long length of bindings to the floor.

She shifted from foot to foot, feeling vulnerable because what she really wanted to do was hug him. But if this little fit of temper was about her, there was no way she wanted to admit that. But then she remembered his words of love from the night before and knew the courage such an admission took, especially considering he hadn't heard the words in return. She decided to be honest; "I want to hug you."

He continued to eye her for a few seconds before speaking, "That would be just about perfect."

"Yeah?" she took a step forward.

"Yeah," he nodded.

But she still hesitated, "A second ago, you acted as though you didn't want me to touch you."

He winced, "That wasn't about you ... it was about where you touched me. My back. I was lost in some memories ..."

Not needing to hear any more, she reached up and drew him down into her arms. He came readily, pulling her in close and aligning their bodies perfectly. She felt him sigh hugely before he finally relaxed into the embrace, burying his face against her neck. "It's not about me," she stated.

"Huh?" his voice was muffled against her skin.

"Whatever has you so upset. It's not me," she explained.

He finally pulled back, tugging playfully on her ponytail, before stepping away. He ran a hand through his sweaty mop of reddish-brown hair before placing both hands on his hips, "Of course it's not you. You're perfect. I'm sorry if I made you feel any different ..."

She hushed him with a finger to his lips, "Don't apologise to me for my own insecurities. Just tell me what's wrong ... please." She knew it wasn't just bad memories – he lived with those every day.

She saw him clench his jaw before he spoke, "It's my father."

She stiffened, "What about him?"

"He's here," he informed her.

Ivy cursed and automatically reached for her sickle, swearing ripely when she realised she didn't have it. When Lark tried to step around her, she pushed him back, frowning over her shoulder when he chuckled at her.

"Relax, Wonder Woman. He's not literally right here, right now."

Despite being the butt of his jest, she was happy to see the teasing glint back in his emerald eyes. She relaxed her stance minutely, "Tell me."

"Orders are being recalled from all over the world with instructions to congregate here so they can meet Max. The Order of Tor is one of them. For all I know, he's already at the Lodge."

"And that makes you mad," she guessed. It sure made her mad. She wanted to hunt the sick fucker down and remove his head from his shoulders right this instant.

"Mad? No, not mad," Lark responded, surprising her.

"But what about ..." she waved her hand at the punching bag.

He shook his head, "That's not anger. My anger runs cold – not hot. What you saw was fear," he snorted, "More than four years away from the man and just the sound of his name makes the spit dry up in my mouth. The man terrifies me," he revealed, colour infusing his cheeks.

She wouldn't allow him to feel even a second of shame over that fact. He had every right to feel afraid of the monster that had tormented him as a child. She was afraid of him too, if she was being honest. Isaac made her sick and scared and filled with loathing. Placing her hands on her man's cheeks, she drew him down so she could press a series of soft kisses to his lips. He held still under her ministrations, letting her soothe him – the act soothing herself in the process. Finally, she teased his lips with her tongue, feeling his mouth open and then she was tangling her tongue with his in a deep, searing kiss. She allowed the moment to spin out until warmth turned to heat, before tearing her mouth from his;

"I won't let him touch you again," she promised, fiercely. Instead of saying he could take care of himself or he didn't need a woman to fight his battles for him, he only smiled brilliantly at her;

"Thank you. I won't let him touch me again, either."

"Well ... good, then." Considering the matter settled, she moved on, "You said Orders – plural. Do you know how many?"

He shook his head, "No. But I intend to find out soon. I've asked Mordecai to come here to answer some questions. Surprisingly, he's agreed. He'll be here tomorrow. I do know that Stefan is here too – Cali's former liege. And I understand a bunch of Dex's old paladins are making their way back."

She contemplated the new information for a moment, "All these people, all connected intimately to your family ... you think it's deliberate?"

Lark angled his head in the direction of the changeroom before heading toward it, "I have no doubt. The question is why."

"An army?" Ivy suggested, feeling ice form in her gut. Lark shrugged and yanked his saturated tee shirt over his head once inside the changing area. She had to force her thoughts to stay on the very serious matter at hand rather than the creamy expanse of muscled skin in front of her eyes.

"If it's an army, who's recruiting? And who are they planning to strike at?" Lark asked.

Ivy figured the questions were rhetorical but she answered nonetheless, "At Max. Although, I can't understand why someone would initiate such an attack considering Max hasn't made any bold moves. It just doesn't make sense."

"It doesn't. But I'll figure it out, mark my words."

She knew he would. No-one could outsmart her guy. And wasn't it a special kind of luxury that she had someone to call her own? *Life is weird,* she thought, realising Lark was still pacing now and still talking;

"And if that's not enough, I still can't shake the feeling about this chade Max – and I – keep dreaming about."

"Is this about your nightmare last night?" She hated the nightly dreams which haunted him but she couldn't fault his duty or dedication to his liege.

"Yeah. It's the damn Darth Vader chade," he huffed in aggravation.

She blinked at him, "The what?"

"It's what I've been calling this super evil chade Max keeps dreaming about. He's not like the others. He's different – more important somehow. I just know it."

"You're saying Max is dreaming about one chade in particular?" she was trying to understand what had him so agitated.

He stopped pacing to stand in front of her, nodding his head fervently, "Yes. Over and over ... he haunts her."

"And he's not the same as other chades. In what way?" she pressed, hoping to help ease him by being a sounding board. It had worked pretty well in the past.

"Well, he has the same look – white skin, black hair, skinny, black eyes. But ..." he broke off, literally shuddering.

"But?" Ivy encouraged.

"But his eyes seem to have an awareness in them – an evil awareness." He held up his hands, "I know how dramatic that sounds but there's no other way to describe it. He's like those chades from when you got hurt – only worse. The blackness in his eyes isn't devoid of all emotion like other chades. It's filled with malevolence, hate, calculation. Plus, he's wearing a ring. I mean, how weird is that? Chades don't wear jewellery."

Ivy felt herself freeze; *a ring?* She'd heard a story once about a chade with a ring ...

"Ivy! What is it? Ivy?!" she felt hard hands grab her upper arms and give her a small shake.

Refocusing her gaze, she saw that Lark's face was filled with worry and wondered how long she'd spaced for. Wanting to reassure him quickly but also explain, she patted his chest, "I'm okay, I'm sorry. It was just the mention of a ring. I – I've heard about a chade with a ring ..."

"What?" he grabbed her arms again, "Where? Tell me!" he demanded.

She shook her head, "I don't have all the details. But I know someone who does," she confirmed.

"Nikolai?" he guessed correctly, his ability to read her now well and truly honed, "We have to tell Max."

He began dragging her out of the changeroom and she had to physically dig her heels into the tile. She didn't think he even realised he was still shirtless; "Wait, Lark. Just wait! Let's not get alarmist – it could be nothing. Let me talk to Nikolai and see where it leads, okay?"

He stopped and drew in a deep breath, "Shit. Sorry. You're right, I just –"

"It's fine. I feel the same urgency as you, trust me. I'll call

Nik immediately and ..." she trailed off as Lark moved back into the room and stripped his track pants off, leaving him blessedly naked. She saw him smirk at her and she cleared her throat, "Well, maybe not immediately ..."

"Hmm," he murmured, reaching behind him to turn on the closest of the three showers. "It seems I'm *very* sweaty. I probably need someone to wash my back for me."

She was already peeling off her clothes and tossing them to the tiled floor before he even finished his sentence. Thoughts of evil fathers and chades flitting to the back of her mind for now, "I'm sure I can accommodate you."

He reached for her as steam began to fill the room, "You're so good to me."

No, Ivy thought as she pressed herself against his hard frame, *you're so good to me.*

THIRTY-SEVEN

'Mordecai and his paladins are here,' Beyden announced via the bond. He was on patrol at the front of the property.

Lark felt adrenaline surge through his system at the announcement. He'd spent another restless night, trying to come to terms with his theories. Instead of tossing and turning and disrupting Ivy – who was now officially staying in his room with the eye-rolling blessing of Ryker and the grudging acceptance of Beyden – he had spent another night out under the stars. Zombie had abandoned Max again in favour of keeping him company and Lark had used the mutt as his chosen sounding board. By the end of his explanation, the poor pup had looked just as confused and concerned as Lark felt. But Lark was also sure that he was right. Hence why his adrenal glands were currently working overtime.

"I still think we should have asked Blu or Garrett to come. They would have been more forthcoming with answers," Darius pointed out from his seat beside him.

But Lark only shook his head, "No. It has to be Mordecai."

"Because he's the one in charge of gathering all the wardens?" Diana asked, eyeing him suspiciously. The woman was very canny.

"Something like that."

"What aren't you telling us?" Her lover questioned now – he was awfully canny too.

"It's just a theory," he tried to appease them. "I promise I'll let you know as soon as it's proven true or false."

"Which one are you hoping for?" Darius asked.

"Huh?"

"Your expression – it's troubled," Darius pointed out. "I can't tell if you want your idea to be right or wrong."

"Neither do I," he murmured.

Ryker walked in at that moment and herded everyone into the formal living area. Lark cringed as he looked around and saw all the bodies in the room. He had not won the discussion with Ryker about speaking to Mordecai on his own. However, he considered it a small victory when he had managed to convince Max to stay with Zombie in the bedroom until they deemed it secure for her to come down.

A few seconds later, Beyden entered the room, formally introducing Mordecai and his four paladins. Ryker stepped forward to give a traditional greeting in return and people took their respective seats. Lark saw Mordecai's frosty green gaze seek out every corner of the room and he knew in his gut he was searching for Max.

"Thank you for coming here, Councilman," Darius began. He was the most diplomatic of the bunch and would get everything started. Lark would step in when he felt the time was opportune.

Mordecai inclined his head, "You said you had questions."

"We do. We are concerned with the growing rumours circulating regarding Max's motives and purpose. As you can imagine, we are worried for her safety," Darius offered.

"I'm aware of them. But as I'm sure you're all very aware, the council can't control rumours," his voice was even and his face revealed nothing. Even his paladins were still and expressionless. These guys put Ivy to shame.

"Even when they are clearly slander? Max passed your little test. She proved she was indeed a Custodian. She also proved that chades could be saved, that they suffer an affliction," Lark stated, testing the waters.

"That she did. The council is trying to change. Unfortunately, change doesn't happen overnight." For the first time, the warden sounded a little disappointed in that fact and Lark thought he knew why; the man had been forced to wait years for change already.

"No, it doesn't," Lark agreed. "In fact, change can take years, can't it?" he asked, pointedly.

Mordecai's eyes never left his own, giving nothing away. The man was good. He had learned to perfectly mask his face from all tells. No wonder he was known as 'The Shark'. He was as cold as one and very likely, just as deadly.

"Was there anything else?" the man asked, looking past Lark as if he were dismissing him ... or not wanting to go down his line of questioning.

Ryker gestured to Lark, ignoring the warden's clear desire to change the interviewer, "Yes. Lark has more questions."

Lark cleared his throat, "You weren't here for the Great Massacre."

Mordecai didn't blink, "No. I was in India. There had been a devastating earthquake in the Himalayas. I was there easing the emotional burdens of the survivors as much as I could."

"But you were aware of the increasing chade numbers and also the recalling of so many Orders to the area," Lark stated.

"I was."

"Were you the person responsible for ordering the return of so many wardens and paladins like you are now?" he tried very hard to keep his voice casual and polite.

"Not that I see the relevance ... but no," he answered, curtly.

Lark pressed on, knowing puzzle pieces were falling into place – at least for him; "It must have been devastating to learn of the loss of so many wardens and paladins, knowing you couldn't do anything to help – being so far away and all."

Mordecai's jaw clenched now and one of his paladins shifted ever so slightly. Lark knew he was hitting a nerve, "Is that why you wanted to do something more proactive to try and help? To try and stop it from happening again?"

"The world wouldn't survive another loss of her caretakers," Mordecai stated, looking him dead in the eye. And Lark knew without a shadow of a doubt that he was right. He opened his mouth to ask his next question but stopped, unable to form the words he needed. In fact, he felt like he was unable to breathe. This was too big for him, too important. What the hell had he been thinking?

*****

Ivy saw the second her man began to panic. She wasn't sure what it was about but it physically hurt her to see him stumble and doubt himself. His continued silence was drawing the attention of his Order and before she even thought about it, she crossed to him and grabbed his hand in hers in her first public display of affection. Hell, Cali was so big on hand holding, Ivy figured she'd score a few points from his friends too. She was just about to ask Lark if he was okay when the feel of the hand holding hers registered. She gasped, looking down, the feeling of déjà vu sweeping her under as quickly as a tidal wave. Unlike in the vision Max had shown her, this time Ivy's eyes followed the arm that was attached to the hand. Then she followed the shoulder and traced her eyes up the neck, only to finally arrive at the face of the man who owned the hand.

Lark. It was Lark.

"It's you," she breathed.

Lark's forehead creased, "What's me?"

"The hand," she explained. "You're the hand!"

He looked down at their clasped palms and entwined fingers, "I'm the hand?"

"Yes!" she yelled as if it should be obvious, "You're the person attached to the hand. I so wanted it to be you but I didn't really know, you know? Sure, I could have tested the theory at any time but I was afraid to hope. And then, what if I was wrong? I wouldn't have been able to bear it because I'm already in love with you. But I was supposed to be in love with the hand too. So I –"

"Whoa, hold up," Lark tilted her chin up, forcing her gaze away from his hand, "You're in love with me?"

"Of course I am! I love the person attached to the hand and you're him." He was usually so bright, she had no idea why he wasn't following her now. She was being very clear.

"I have absolutely no idea what you're talking about and I don't care. I just love you," he gripped her other hand bringing them both to his chest.

"Me too. I mean, you. I love you. I don't love me. I –" His lips cut off her inarticulate, insane ramblings and she melted against him, completely swept away in the moment of clarity. She should have reached for his hand a long time ago but she had been terrified. Both that his wouldn't be the right hand and also that it would. But none of that mattered now. All that mattered was the man holding her tightly as he devoured her mouth. She was in love for the first time and she didn't matter who knew. Which was probably just as well considering they were in a room full of people, including her brother.

A persistent throat clearing had them finally breaking apart, "Not that I'm not happy for you both. But we're kind of in the middle of something ..." Ryker gestured to their guests and Ivy felt herself flush under the scrutiny of the Death Warden.

Mordecai was one of her immediate superiors and she more often than not reported directly to him. She was positive he had never seen her with such blatant emotion and disregard for their laws. She had always been the ideal, cold, rule-following ranger. She pulled away from her boy-toy but she didn't go far. And she didn't release his hand.

"My apologies. Lark, you were saying ...?" she prompted him, nodding in encouragement. She knew he had something important to say and she knew it had to be now.

He took a breath and faced the imposing warden once more, "What did you do? What did you do that was so proactive?"

The man was silent for so long, Ivy was convinced he wasn't going to answer but then he spoke. And his words sent off a flurry of curious and confused murmurs throughout the room; "I prayed to the Great Mother."

Lark nodded, looking pale but resolute, "I'm sure we've all done that. But this time was different, wasn't it? This time, Mother Nature answered."

A series of *huh*s and *what the fuck*s came from Max's Order but Lark never once looked away from Mordecai.

"She did," Mordecai confirmed.

"But that's not all she did, is it?" Lark demanded, softly ... silkily.

Ivy felt the danger and the implied threat of that silky

voice down to her marrow and noted the goosebumps that rose unwittingly to the surface of her skin. *Damn,* she shivered, *he really was Isaac's son.* As for Mordecai, she had to give him credit; his face remained neutral and his green eyes retained their trademark coldness. Given he was surrounded by seven extremely protective paladins with very itchy blade hands, he sure was calm under pressure.

His eyes flicked around the room before returning to Lark as he answered, "No. She didn't just answer the prayers and grant the wish of one lowly warden. She demanded a sacrifice," he explained, voice cool and flat. "Balance. The scales must be balanced. A gift given requires a sacrifice returned."

"What kind of gift?"

"What kind of sacrifice?" Darius and Ryker asked simultaneously.

Ivy saw the death warden's jaw clench as he remained stubbornly silent. Unfortunately for him, Lark was in total badass mode and she realised that giant brain of his had figured out the mystery that was Mordecai and Mother Nature well before this impromptu meeting. She found the combination of simmering violence and intelligence a heady and arousing mix ... and was going to demonstrate her appreciation to the earth paladin as soon as humanly possible.

"Max," Lark stated, "Max is the gift. And Max is the sacrifice. She's your daughter."

*****

"You're my father?" The whole room turned as one as three words whispered brokenly into the room. Ryker rushed over to her but she quickly side-stepped him and she spoke again, her voice forceful this time, "Is it true? Are you my father?"

"No," Mordecai whispered but he looked completely devastated to Lark and he knew that everyone had been able to see the lie.

"Lying piece of shit," Axel stepped forward, palming his blade and all four paladins behind Mordecai did the same.

Mordecai motioned them back, "I'm not lying. I'm not her father," Mordecai yelled, controlled façade finally slipping. "I'm not her father any more than you are. It takes more than a bit of DNA to make someone a parent – to make someone family. You know that better than most," he said directly to Lark before raising his eyes and looking at each member of their Order in turn, "You all know what it takes to make a family. I'm not it, nor was I ever supposed to be."

"So, she was just what? A sacrificial lamb?" Darius's voice held barely suppressed rage and Lark saw the situation deteriorating quickly. This was exactly why he had wanted to talk to Mordecai on his own. He had been hoping for cooler heads to prevail. And deep down, he had been hoping he was wrong so he didn't have to see the look on Max's face that was there right now.

Ryker advanced on Mordecai, "Do you have any idea what she went through?! She was on the streets! She was a child on the streets with no memory, no protection, and no name. And you've known about her all along? For fuck's sake! She named herself after a stray fucking dog!"

With that, Max let out a tiny noise of distress and fled the room.

"Max ..." Mordecai's voice cracked and he took a single step in her direction only to be brought up short by a wall of paladins. Mordecai's paladins snarled and took up arms next to their liege and Lark did something he had vowed he never would; he created a psychic bridge and yelled at his Order, using his potentate abilities.

'Stop it! All of you! Ryker, go after Max. She needs you.

The rest of you, back the fuck off! Fighting the Valhalla Order isn't going to help Max and I promise you, once she has time to process, it's not something she is going to thank you for.'

His Order had no choice but to listen to him because they couldn't ignore or break the link. The only people stronger than him in their Order now were Ryker and Max and they were too preoccupied to care. Ryker had thankfully heeded his advice and darted out after her. Lark felt the same desperation as the rest of them to tend to their liege but Ryker would be the best person to handle his love right now. And they needed to handle Mordecai.

He knew the others would just as happily kill the man along with his paladins. But he couldn't allow that to happen. He had a feeling they were going to need the Death Warden in the coming weeks. And he was positive the man was going to need them. Because despite the fact Mordecai was once again looking cool and collected, he could no longer fool Lark. Lark had seen the look of utter devastation on his face when Max had learned the truth. The man cared. His little speech had been worth exactly shit-all.

"How about we call it a day, hmm?" he suggested casually. "Mordecai, thank you for coming. Ivy will see you out," he spoke formally, hoping to infuse some common sense into the room. Ivy nodded at him and he knew he could count on her to think and act rationally.

To his surprise, Mordecai balked, "I can help."

Several rude snorts and suggestions about just what he could do with his offer of help came from behind him and Lark spanked them all through the link again as if they were wayward children; *'Quit it! Remember who you are and who you're representing.'*

"What makes you think we need your help?" Lark asked quietly but politely.

"I just need a chance," Mordecai responded, not answering the question.

Lark looked to his friends and family and one by one they relented, stepping back and sheathing their weapons. Getting a look filled with pride and love from Ivy gave him that added boost he needed to spank the Death Warden too;

"Seems to me you were already given one – the chance to be a father. You may already have blown it. *But,* on the off chance that you haven't … try coming back tomorrow when things have settled down a little."

It was the best he could do. He only hoped it was enough.

THIRTY-EIGHT

"Ivy tells me you want to know about a chade who wore a ring," Nikolai stated.

Silence met her commander's statement and he raised his eyebrows at her. She shook her head at him. After all, what could she say? The last twenty-four hours had been a doozy. Lark's confrontation with Mordecai had resulted in the biggest secret reveal since *Star Wars* and the whole household was still reeling with the information. Unfortunately, the urgency for information about the chades remained and despite what had to be a very fragile psyche, Max had donned her goddess hat and summoned Nikolai to the house first thing this morning after Ivy had explained what little she knew about a ring-wearing chade.

It was pretty much nothing, only that Nikolai had spoken of a unique chade who had kept a reminder of his previous life by wearing a ring. It was strange because chades had no awareness of vanity or possession or pride. Nik had only mentioned it a handful of times and hadn't gone into much detail. It had always made him somewhat uncomfortable –

295

nervous even – so she had never pushed for details. The idea of a jewellery-wearing chade had been intriguing to a degree but she wasn't really the curious type. To her mind, most curious people were just nosey and needed to mind their own business.

They were all now congregated in the large living area off the kitchen. And by all, Ivy counted no less than sixteen occupants in the room, including Max and her seven paladins, Dex, herself and Nikolai. But the real surprise was the addition of Mordecai and his four paladins. She had been surprised to see he had taken Lark up on his suggestion to return today, given he looked so unbelievably uncomfortable. Even his blank, stoic face couldn't hide his discomfort. And she would know; she had perfected that exact same poker face many years ago. His four paladins were alert behind him and looked to be as thrilled with the situation as their liege was. But, he had professed to want to help – to be given a chance – so here he was, Ivy supposed. Even if Max was pointedly ignoring him and the rest of her Order was glaring daggers in his direction. It didn't escape Ivy's notice that Max hadn't ordered him away either.

"That's right. Thanks for coming, Nikolai. I appreciate it," Max finally responded, her smile a little shaky.

Ivy watched Nik smile slowly in Max's direction – it was his 'pillaging' smile, she knew. The one he used to bait, hook, and then reel in unsuspecting women. The man was dangerously good looking, a complete rogue, and a tireless flirt. When she had first arrived, Axel had reminded her so much of Nik that they could have been twins – in the personality department anyway. They both even had that glint of bitterness buried in their shining eyes that hinted at complicated and unresolved pasts. Although the flirting was a natural part of Nik's personality, it also served to hide deeper issues. Issues she was honoured enough to be privy to because she was his best friend.

"Stop it," Ryker demanded, causing Nikolai's eyes to widen.

"Stop what?" Nik asked innocently, as if it hadn't been hundreds of years since he'd had an innocent bone in his body.

"You know what," Ryker glared at him, dragging Max closer to his chest and earning an eye-roll from his woman for his efforts.

The possessive behaviour amused Ivy and was kind of sweet in a way but she sure as hell hoped Lark wasn't going to start with that kind of barbaric behaviour – not in public anyway. It would most definitely piss her off, even though she revelled in his jealousy over her past lovers. She caught his eye and noticed he was grinning at her as if he could hear her thoughts. *How does he do that?* she wondered, a little grumpily.

He chuckled a little, earning curious stares from his fellow knights. They looked from him to her and back again and she cursed herself for getting caught mooning at her boyfriend. Talk about embarrassing. She firmed her jaw and pointedly ignored the humorous looks aimed in her direction, most especially the wiggling eyebrows of her commander. She huffed; the man was such a dick.

"The chade with a ring ...?" Darius prompted.

Nikolai cleared his throat and straightened his back, his demeanour turning serious but also still a little coy as he asked, "Why do you want to know?"

"None of your fucking business," Ryker growled, clearly more than a little annoyed with the man.

"Well, considering you demanded my presence at the butt-crack of dawn to ask me about long-forgotten confidential information, I'd say it's most definitely my business," Nik rebutted, his temper on the rise.

Ivy shared a look with Dex – the only other occupant who knew Nik on a personal level. Years ago, Dex and Nikolai had been drinking buddies, well before Dex had taken his sabbatical as a chade. He wasn't as close to her commander as she was but she knew Nik had considered the famous Charlemagne a friend. Seeing the rolling eyes and shaking head of the former chade, he must have known Nik well enough to realise when he was gearing up for a fight. A long, stubborn, completely irrelevant, time-waster of a fight, Ivy predicted.

"A superior has asked you a question. Max is a Custodian," Ryker informed Nikolai coldly. "If nothing else, chain of command should be something you understand."

Nik leaned back in his chair, "Oh, I understand chain of command very well. I also understand confidentiality orders and sealed records. This particular chade falls under both those jurisdictions."

"Nothing trumps Max," Ryker growled.

"Really? Since when? You're not planning a little coup, are you? There are so many nasty little rumours flying around, after all," Nik shook his head.

Ryker looked ready to throttle Nikolai and Ivy sighed, knowing Nik could dance around like this all day. She also knew Ryker could not – he'd very soon punch her commanding officer and good friend in the face. Chaos would then ensue and Nik would no doubt find the entire debacle extremely hilarious.

Ivy knew Nik had every intention of sharing his information with them. He was just fucking with the surly Captain because the opportunity presented itself. Besides, Ivy knew he believed in Max and also trusted her and her intentions – even if she hadn't known the full extent of his confidence until a few moments ago when he had removed his jacket.

"Instead of whipping out your dicks and comparing length, Nikolai why don't you just roll up your sleeve?" she suggested, cutting the tension. She couldn't believe the number of man-children in the room.

"Aww, Ivy," Nik pouted, "You always spoil my fun."

She shook her head at that, "I always save you from yourself is what you mean."

He winked at her, blowing a kiss and she smiled one of her rare public smiles at him. The man was incorrigible.

"What does she mean by rolling up your sleeve?" Lark asked, obviously trying to follow her lead and steer them back on track.

Nik shrugged, his expression turning a little wary but not enough to suppress the constant twinkle of mischief in his eyes, "She probably wants to check out the guns. Since you all Shanghaied her, she doesn't get her daily fix anymore. Poor deprived woman."

He was looking directly at Lark, no doubt waiting for a scathing response or a flash of jealousy or something. She hadn't been able to talk with her good friend about the new circumstances of her relationship with the earth paladin since he had goaded her over the phone days ago. But he had obviously come to the correct conclusion that she and Lark were now in a relationship. Too bad Lark wasn't a hot head like some of his fellow knights and couldn't be drawn so easily into such a transparent trap.

Lark leered at Nik, his eyes turning sultry, "Well now, don't tease. I haven't had the privilege of ogling your guns yet. Lemme see."

Nik grinned in appreciation, "You're funny," he informed Lark, before turning to her, "He's funny. If I knew you had it in you to fall for a funny guy, I would have tried harder."

"No you wouldn't have," she knew. There had never been anything remotely sexual between them. "Now, will you stop faffing around?"

He considered her for a moment, testing her seriousness and recognising her impatience, "Fine," he huffed. "I'm on your side, you know. I've given you all the benefit of the doubt before. I don't think it's too much to ask for you to enlighten me as to why this is so important to everyone. Besides, there's another council member in this room – one I follow orders from directly. I can't just roll over and reveal state secrets, as it were," he pointed out.

Mordecai stirred, "Tell them anything they want to know."

Ivy saw Nikolai's eyebrows wing up in surprise even as he dipped his head in acknowledgement, "Would you like to take the lead then?" he asked, respectfully.

All eyes turned to Mordecai, who remained cool as a cucumber; "I have no idea what everyone is referring to, nor why it is so important. I have never heard of a chade who wore a ring."

He looked and sounded sincere, Ivy thought. And he was one of the members of the council whom she actually respected and trusted. She only hoped that trust wasn't misplaced and he truly was in the dark about this and many other things. Otherwise, it would be a hard blow to the little custodian, even if she had only just learned the truth about who Mordecai was.

"And just how do we know you're on our side anyway?" Ryker demanded, glaring at Nik. He clearly didn't want to back down from their little pissing match. Nikolai must have really irritated him.

Nik flattened his lips, a sure indication of stubbornness. She walked over and smacked him up the back of the head, "Grow up and spill. You're wasting time."

"Hey! I'm your boss, you know. Where's the respect?" he whined.

Ivy said nothing, just continued to stare at him with her arms crossed. But Ryker finally seemed to deflate a little, grumbling;

"Mine don't have any respect either."

The room suddenly filled with snorts, coughs and eye-rolls and she saw Nikolai and Ryker make eye contact and share a look of long-suffering. Great, the two idiots were bonding over their perceived hardships. Arms still crossed, she prompted, "Nik ..."

He huffed one last time but proceeded to roll up the sleeve on his left bicep. A perfect circle of seven small symbols was mapped on the muscular appendage. The mark was new. He didn't have it the last time they had seen each other, although she'd had hers. He had taken a great interest in the brand, out of concern for her, she knew. She wondered how long he'd had his.

"This little gem popped up about two months ago," he revealed, answering her silent query. "I assume it means something to everyone?" he asked.

"It means you're loyal to me," Max smiled at him, eyes shining with happiness now.

"It does? I am?" he appeared to think about it for a moment, before shrugging negligently, "I guess I am. Gotta believe in something, right? And a goddess seems like a good bet. I should mention though, only one other member of my Unit has the same mark, other than Ivy."

"Dylan?" Ivy guessed but Nikolai shook his head;

"Cayson," he supplied.

"Really?" Ivy was shocked. She had been sure Cayson was working as a spy for the council. "I thought he was spying on us," she revealed.

"He was," Mordecai said. "For me. Cayson is Aiden's brother," he gestured to the Captain of his Order.

"No shit? Well, what do ya know?" Nik murmured,

casually. But Ivy recognised the annoyance and anger simmering beneath the surface. She had no doubt he would be taking his subordinate to task in the near future for keeping secrets.

"Okay, now we've discovered that Nikolai isn't an all-around dick and is on Team Max, can we please focus on the original purpose of this meeting?" Cali asked. Once a morning person, she was now rather grumpy first-thing because she could no longer stomach her morning cup of coffee.

"Certainly," Nik agreed, easily, as if he hadn't been the one stalling. He rolled his sleeve back into place, covering the physical manifestation of his faith in Max. "I am most certainly familiar with a chade who wore a ring – on his right pointer finger to be exact. Only, he wasn't always a chade, was he? He was a warden first – a damn good one – and he wore the ring almost religiously because it had been a gift from his father. It had his Heraldry on it, not an uncommon gift in those days," Nikolai began his tale.

Ivy was so tuned into Lark now that she felt every move he made and she noticed how his gaze was pinned on Mordecai hovering in the doorway. Lark's green gaze was intense but his head was cocked ever so slightly to the side. It was a sure sign that he had noticed something off with the man and he was trying to puzzle it out before storing it away. She followed her man's line of sight and focused on the Death Warden as well. His posture was now rigid instead of relaxed. Had he recognised something Nik had said already? She flicked her eyes back to Lark and he gave her the barest of nods, indicating he had noticed too. Nik had begun speaking again and she focused her attention in his direction once more.

"It was over a hundred years ago. Although the chades were a persistent and troubling menace, they hadn't yet reached the huge numbers we saw before the Great Massacre – or the numbers of today. Still, there were a great many rangers and wardens alike whose sole task was to determine why wardens were choosing to desecrate their elements."

"That's not what –"

Nikolai held up a placating hand, "I know, Max. That's not what was happening. Chades don't choose to turn their backs on nature – it's an illness. But we didn't know that back then. Well, I guess there were some who thought of it in that way – I know Blu did and Verity broached the subject many times too, Diana," he said, looking at the death paladin and speaking of her former liege.

"I never heard him talk about it. The majority of time I was in his Order, we were tasked with following human criminal activity – balancing the loss, reconciling justice, providing new life in the wake of tragedy. That's how I became a consultant for the FBI and other law enforcement agencies," she explained. "But I do know talk of the chades made him sad though," she added, contemplatively, "I was always curious why."

Nik was nodding as she spoke, "He was quite the advocate for the poor beasts – in the beginning at least. I guess with him being a Life Warden and highly empathic, he wouldn't have been able to block out the emotions and the plight of the chades."

Ivy saw everyone turn to look at Max upon hearing Nik's last words. They all knew she was highly sensitive and empathic and was continually battered by the chades' feelings and emotions – or lack thereof. Ivy saw her shift uncomfortably in her seat, never comfortable being the centre of attention, before she spoke;

"Please continue, Nikolai."

Her Commander tilted his head in her direction, "He was

from a renowned family and also a loving one. They wouldn't give up on him – were desperate to find a cure. As such, they volunteered him for the research projects that were being conducted at the time to determine a cause, treatment, and the hope of a cure."

"What kind of research projects?" Dex questioned, jaw set.

Nik gazed back at him dispassionately, "The kind of research projects recorded in the Warden Chronicles. These things were always documented."

"The same Warden Chronicles that were burned to a crisp when the chades attacked?" Lark asked.

Nik nodded, "The very same."

"Convenient," Max snorted, looking more pissed by the second.

"I've always thought so," Nik agreed.

"Have you just?" Ryker arched a dark eyebrow, scepticism clear in his tone.

Nikolai merely shrugged, not rising to the bait this time. No doubt, he felt the same as Ivy did on this subject; they didn't need to justify their actions to anyone. They were soldiers just like sworn paladins and had a duty and a purpose to uphold. They might not always agree with their superiors and not like the tasks they were given but it was their job. Someone had to do it.

Abruptly, Dex pushed away from the wall he was leaning against and advanced on Nik. Ivy tensed, ready to defend her friend and superior, but remained where she was when Nik simply lifted a finger in her direction, "Can we please stop calling it 'research' and start calling it what it was? Experimentation. Torture."

"Same thing really. It gets the same results in the end," Nikolai sounded bored, cold even.

Ivy knew he was anything but. Just like her, he felt for the chades and wanted nothing more than to ease their suffering and end their plight. Looking around the room, she saw the same disgusted and livid looks on nearly every face – other than Max, Mordecai and his Order. Max could no doubt see and feel Nikolai's true intentions and emotions. And Mordecai and his men had been around long enough to know the way of the world. They couldn't afford to be dainty with their methods if they wanted results.

Ryker abruptly faced Mordecai, "Do you have anything to say about this?"

Mordecai's paladins stirred at the accusatory tone but the warden's green eyes remained steady, "Like what?"

"Gee, I don't know. That you were aware of the torture of your own people? Maybe that you sanctioned it?" Ryker's voice was laden with sarcasm.

"How else were we to get answers? We're talking more than a hundred years ago. Not exactly the time for medical or scientific advancement. Methods were rudimentary, techniques were raw and experimental. The wardens and rangers involved in the research were the leading minds in society. Besides, it was determined very early on that chades don't feel pain," he added, as if it justified his actions.

"Don't feel pain?" Max's voice was incredulous as she spoke to the man directly for the very time that day, "All they feel is pain!"

Mordecai merely shrugged and Max turned away in disgust as if she couldn't bear to look at the man who had helped give her life. If Ivy hadn't been watching so closely, she never would have seen the anguish in those cold, green eyes when his daughter turned away from him. Ivy rarely felt sympathy for people in situations of their own making. Everyone had to live with the consequences of their own choices. But she knew there was more to the Death Warden than met the eye.

She had caught a glimpse of his left bicep the day prior when he had made his exit. Ivy had only seen a hint of black but she had recognised it for what it was. Mordecai was loyal, she was sure of it. So, why he seemed determined to keep painting himself as the bad guy, she didn't know. Men were just idiots sometimes.

"I think we should get back on track," Diana voiced, breaking the thick tension in the room. "Nikolai, do you have any idea if the research yielded any results?" she prompted.

"Oh, they yielded results all right. Just not the ones everyone was hoping for," Nik shook his head. "The tests didn't cure him. In fact, they seemed to make him worse."

"Worse? How can anything be worse than a chade?" Beyden asked, looking worried. Ivy didn't blame him – she didn't want to imagine anything worse than a chade either.

"As we all know, men lose their humanity when they regress from warden to chade. They don't feel anything anymore, they lose their conscience. They are like emotional blackholes – no joy, no fear, not even hate. They hunt down and feed off wardens based on pure instinct – not because they are evil," Nikolai recounted.

"Right," Max nodded along with everybody else, "but I take it this chade wasn't like the others?"

"In the beginning? He was just the same as all the others I'd seen. I know I said they don't feel anything and I'm still not convinced all of them do. But some of them – there's a bitterness there, a disappointment, hopelessness. I guess those are the ones with their souls intact. The ones you've been searching for," he added, glancing between Lark and Ivy before continuing;

"But this one? He didn't show any of those subtle signs and in the end? Yeah, he was different. Very different. He was angry for one – totally pissed off all the time. He was malevolent and malicious – vengeful even."

Max was frowning in thought, "Malevolent? How so?" she asked.

Nik ran a hand down his face, "He liked to hurt people. And not just by sucking the vitality out of wardens either. He would hurt them just to watch them bleed, just to see pain on the faces of his victims. You've all seen prey animals take down their meals, right? They do it for survival and are quick, merciful killers. That's what most of the chades are like. But not him, he played with his victims. You don't ever see a lion digging around in antelope entrails for the joy of it, do you? This guy loved entrails," he shuddered, "And he used to laugh."

Dex straightened again, "Laugh? He could speak?"

"Not speak in so many words," Nik seemed to hedge, "but laugh for sure. The sound was like nails on a chalkboard, only worse. It would send shivers down my spine and leave me feeling queasy. It was creepy as fuck."

"You said he couldn't speak 'in so many words'. What did you mean by that?" Lark asked, picking up on Nik's small capitulation.

Nik seemed to hesitate, looking at Max and getting a firm nod to continue. He sighed, "Sometimes ... I think he was communicating with the other chades who were in the same facility."

Ivy saw the colour leech out of Max's face and Ryker's arm immediately went around her. A quick change in pressure in the air told Ivy that Max's Order was rallying around her and sending her energy, automatically adjusting to their liege's needs. Looking at Lark, she saw his eyes were focused on Max as well as if she were the only person in the room. Ivy waited for jealousy to hit but it never did. There was no resentment, no envy that her man was bonded intimately to another and loved another deeply. There was just pride over him being a strong, valued member of his

Order and fulfilling his duty. She had been worried that perhaps she wouldn't be able to handle the dedication she knew all paladins had to their lieges. But it didn't appear to be an issue they were going to face.

"Communicating how?" Max asked, presently, her colour looking normal once more.

"I have no idea. But it wasn't verbal. It was almost as if he could get inside their heads. They would go from docile to crazed in seconds."

"So, it wasn't just communication. He could also affect others, make them angry like him," Max's voice was a low mutter, almost as if she was speaking to herself but everyone heard her loud and clear in the tense quiet of the room.

"That's how it looked to me. And that's what I put in my reports," Nik assured her. "There was a series of instances where the chades got loose – even in our protected encampments where chades can't manifest themselves as their elements – they somehow broke free. This chade wasn't one of them but it looked to me like they were all heading in his direction."

"They were working as a unit?" Axel questioned.

Nik nodded, "They were. I'd never seen anything like it. It absolutely terrified me. All the chades were beheaded on the spot. Research pretty much ground to a halt after that and we were ordered to kill on sight from that day forward. No more tests, no more research. The only ones who were to be imprisoned were those who had not yet turned fully or those wardens with violent tendencies, mental health issues and the like."

"What about the chade with the ring? Was he beheaded on the spot too?" Max asked, and the whole room seemed to hold its breath waiting for the answer.

Nikolai looked at Max head-on, "No. He was still secure in his cage. But he was deemed too dangerous to live. He was slated for execution the next day."

"And was he killed?" Max followed up.

"His father requested he be given the final rights to carry out the execution. He argued it was his duty and his burden," Nikolai's hand shook a little on his lap as he glanced toward Mordecai in the doorway. The warden of death looked positively green but his eyes were hard as they glared at the Commander of the Rangers as if daring him to continue. Never one to back down from a dare, Nik forged ahead;

"And given the chade's father was a member of the International Domain Council, he was granted such final rights. The chade with the ring was given into the custody of his father at daybreak the following day."

"You didn't see him killed, did you?" Lark spoke rapidly, answering his own question; "Of course you didn't. Because he's still alive. He's the one who amassed those chades and coordinated the attack that resulted in the Great Massacre. He's the one unifying the chades now. It's the only thing that makes sense. And who knows how powerful he must be now, all these years later ... Mordecai, do you know –" he broke off abruptly when he saw the empty doorway.

"Fuck!" Ryker yelled, jumping to his feet and palming his scythes, "That son of a bitch! It's him. It's been him all along. He's the father of that chade – the one he let go."

"I'll kill him," Darius growled, chest heaving with his anger.

"Get in line little brother," Dex was pure menace, his eyes now black once more as they stared holes through the blank space where Mordecai and his paladins had been just minutes before.

The ground gave a shake, causing Ivy to wince. Emotions were running high and she was worried about what could happen if they didn't get a hold of themselves; Max's paladins were mighty fierce and protective bastards. She looked at

Max, expecting to see pain and rage on her face but all she saw was a puzzled little frown. Her eyes were locked on Nikolai's and he shook his head as if they were silently communicating.

Max blew out a breath before whistling sharply; "Everyone calm down. Don't bother hunting Mordecai down. He's not the one you want."

"What? Then who the hell is?" Ryker demanded.

"Garrett," Nikolai stated. "The chade was Garrett's son."

EPILOGUE

Mordecai's rage knew no bounds as he drove recklessly fast away from the home by the sea ... and away from his daughter.

"Mordecai ..." Aiden's voice was soft but sounded like a gunshot in the tense silence of the car.

"Don't," was Mordecai's clipped response.

"Mordecai, you –"

"I said, don't!" he yelled, his powers slipping free and weaving insidiously into the minds and bodies of the other four occupants of the car.

As a Death Warden, he was unable to cause death or even sickness as his title implied. But he could see scars – both physical and emotional. His duty was to heal people of their burdens; grief, loss, depression, pain. He took it all into himself, just internalised the whole miserable shebang, to ensure humanity remained just that – human. But the flip side of seeing those scars? He could also tear them wide open, just like he was doing right now.

The harsh breaths and shuddering bodies of his four

paladins were loud enough to be heard over the desperate beating of his heart and he forced himself to dial back his powers. Closing his eyes for a brief second, he inhaled deeply and commanded the sticky, dark energy back into his pores. Aiden, Bastien, Tobias, and Madigan began breathing normally almost instantly. He felt no censure from them, nor any condemnation. Their understanding only served to fuel his ominous mood further. He would have much preferred their rebuke.

'Sorry,' he uttered, telepathically through the Order link.

The four men had been with him since he was twenty years old – sixteen hundred years and counting. They were more than colleagues, more even than family. Their lives truly were symbiotic and he didn't know what he would do without them. But if any of them tried to talk him off the ledge one more time, he wouldn't be held responsible for his actions. The coldness he was known for was now flowing like black-ice through his veins as he thought about his destination.

Other than his paladin brotherhood, he had told one person about his deal with Mother Nature. He had entrusted the world's greatest secret to just one other; his trusted friend and confidant of over a millennium. Life Warden and head of the International Domain Council; Garrett. His fingers clenched on the steering wheel, causing the leather to creak in protest as he pictured those fingers wrapped around his best friend's neck.

"Nowhere to hide," he muttered, "I'm coming for you, *friend.*"

A NOTE FROM MONTANA

Hi everyone! So, I know a lot of you are probably cursing my name right now; *'Really, Montana? You ended the book there? You can't end it there!'* Well ... I did ;) But I wanted to take a moment to personally let you know what is coming up next for Max and the gang.

Book five, *Custodian*, will be the end of Max's story arc. Where she came from and why, who are the baddies? All will be answered in *Custodian*. It will be a bit of a special edition because there will be no new romantic couple. Instead, each and every character that you love will have a few chapters from their perspective – even those who are yet to have their own book.

But don't worry, *The Elemental Paladins* won't end there. After all, someone has to tidy up the mess left at the end of book five ;) And who better than our gentle giant, beast paladin? That's right, Beyden will be book six. And what about that incorrigible flirt, Axel? Our fire paladin will be book seven. After that? Who knows ...

Until we meet again on the pages,

Montana xxx

ALSO BY MONTANA ASH:

WARDEN
ELEMENTAL PALADINS: BOOK ONE

PALADIN
ELEMENTAL PALADINS: BOOK TWO

CHADE
ELEMENTAL PALADINS: BOOK THREE

COMING UP NEXT:

CUSTODIAN
ELEMENTAL PALADINS: BOOK FIVE

MEET MONTANA!

Montana is an Aussie, self-confessed book junkie. Although she loves reading absolutely everything, her not-so-guilty pleasure is paranormal romance. Alpha men – just a little bit damaged – and feisty women – strong yet vulnerable – are a favourite combination of hers. Throw in some steamy sex scenes, a touch of humour, and a little violence and she is in heaven! She is a scientist by day, a writer by night, and a reader always!

FOLLOW MONTANA!

Email: montanaash.author@yahoo.com

Website: http://www.montanaash.com/

Facebook: https://www.facebook.com/montana.ash.author/

Twitter: @ReadMontanaAsh

Lightning Source UK Ltd.
Milton Keynes UK
UKOW04f2336140917
309215UK00002B/374/P

9 781925 666502